I0633846

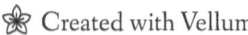 Created with Vellum

For...

...does anyone even read these things!?

PROLOGUE

WELCOME TO NEW ORLEANS, where werewolves and vampires roam.

The werewolf? *Moi.*

The vampire? My best friend. But this story isn't about her. She's had her moment of glory, her day in the sun—ironic, considering she's a vampire—and her claim to fame. Fame being the operative word.

No, this story is about me.

The sidekick.

I never thought I'd play the lead role in my own story, but thanks to a life-changing adventure across the pond, here I am. For those who don't know, it's been a year since some psychopathic bunghole went all Jack the Ripper on me and turned me into a werewolf. A feat once thought impossible. Werewolves are born and not made, after all.

Pfft, wrong.

I'm the first person in the history of lycanthropy to be born human and then changed. Huzzah! Life accomplishment complete. Not.

Believe me, there's nothing charming about being a werewolf.

The shedding, the drool, the howling... none of it fun.

Some people talk about how awesome it would be to run freely under a full moon. But come on! Have you ever gone running before? It. Sucks. Whether you're on four legs or two.

Then there's the fact that I'm allergic to dogs, which absolutely includes wolves. Every time I shift, I descend into a sneezing fit worthy of the dwarf himself.

And we mustn't forget the whole "mate" thing. Humans are lucky. They find someone, fall in love, marry, pop out a few children, then get divorced. Rinse and repeat as many times as they like. But werewolves? We have mates. As romantic as that sounds, believe me, it's not. According to my mother, a mate is someone biologically designed to help you produce the strongest offspring. There's no love or emotion to it. Just a little switch inside us werewolves that gets flipped at the most inopportune moment.

I met my mate before I was turned. And for a year, I've been avoiding him. Until now. Before today, I wasn't ready to settle down and have pups. I may *never* be ready... But if that woman touching his biceps doesn't back the F-train off, I might have to go all prehistoric on her ass and show her why it's unwise to go sniffing around a werewolf's mate.

Things are about to get pretty darn hairy up in here.

TWO POINT FIVE SECONDS.

That was how long Sam's date had to get her grabby little hands off my man before I ripped them clean off.

Oh, sorry, was that a little violent?

Thanks to the unwanted beast now residing in my body, that tended to happen more often these days. It was hard enough being a vampire's best friend, now I was a werewolf to boot. I kept experiencing all these new urges and desires, like exhibit A: bitch-slapping the tall drink of water with long, flowing locks and wandering hands. Hands that were currently curled around Sam's flexed biceps.

I saw red.

The wolf in my head growled, and I barely managed to swallow the unwelcome sound before it escaped my throat. I'd learned early on that growling tended to upset the normies—a.k.a. humans. Truth be told, it upset me too. This wasn't me. I wasn't some slavering animal. Far from it, in fact. In all my relationships, I was the sensible and boring one. The *Mother Hen*—as my best friend, Anna, called me. I was the cool to her hotheadedness. The prude to her imprudence. The careful to her carelessness. Just like Rizzo sang in *Grease, I don't drink or swear. I don't rat my hair...*

But apparently, I do growl, howl, and shed all over the furniture.

Sigh.

This thing inside of me had a mind of its own. One it *loved* to lord over me. Like right now. In my mind's eye, it flashed its fangs and pawed at the darkness, restless and anxious to claim its territory.

Which I *so* wasn't okay with.

Sam wasn't some possession I could claim. Not that the wolf agreed. It wanted me to march onto the dance floor and snatch Ms. Grabby Hands by the hair and toss her out into the cold. I, however, had more manners than that. I hoped.

"Yikes. You look like you're about to murder someone."

I started at the sound of Anna's voice. My vision came back in focus just as she plopped down on the nearest chair and stared at me. Cradled lovingly in her hands was a plate of precariously tall cake that, when whole, made a three-tier monstrosity in the shape of a bat. I lifted a brow, then met her gaze. She couldn't eat cake, and neither could ninety percent of her guests, considering they all checked the *undead* category on the local census. Vampires and solid food didn't mix, much to Anna's dismay. But that hadn't stopped her from ordering a wedding cake. Anna had always possessed a certain fondness for confectionery baked goods, a love not even death could cure. Had I a guess, I would wager she'd used her few non-vampire guests to swing the cake, all so she could sniff a slice.

It was a weakness I understood well. Except, mine was chocolate—my one *true* love in this world. Imagine my heartache when I was told that werewolves, much like dogs, couldn't eat it. Cue my inner drama queen, throwing her arms up in the air and screaming at the skies when I'd learned that little tidbit of information. Afterward, much like the proverbial toddler, I'd immediately gorged myself on a box of my favorite chocolate treats only to find myself praying to the porcelain gods for the next day and a half.

I could handle just about anything, but take away a woman's chocolate and you take away her reason for living. I refused to abide by this. One day, I'd find a solution, even if it killed me.

Anna scootched around in her chair and perused the dance floor. The instant her gaze fell on Sam and his lady friend, she frowned. Before the ceremony, Anna had warned me Sam had brought a date, so I'd been given a little time to prepare myself, but even I could admit it hadn't worked. Seeing them together was akin to someone stabbing me in the gut, over and over and over, just for laughs.

"Who is that woman?" I asked, distantly aware of my fingers drumming against the table.

"No idea. She's his plus one, so there's that."

My lip curled of its own volition. If I were in wolf form, I'd be flashing my fangs right about now. The worst part of all this was it was all my fault. I first met Sam almost two years ago, back when I was human. He'd immediately known that we were mates. He'd even been open and honest about it. And I—well, I stomped on his heart. Multiple times.

Now, I got to sit here and stew in the epic disaster that was my love life.

Clearing my throat, I refocused my thoughts. "What else?"

"She ordered the salmon," Anna said.

Okay, so not a vampire—which I already knew. The one perk of being a werewolf was the heightened senses. My nose could pick up on the slightest scents. Overwhelming but often helpful. And thanks to that little skill, I could smell a fanger a mile away. Anna had a particular aroma about her now, one I'd never noticed as a human. It wasn't unpleasant, but she didn't smell like sunshine and roses either.

Anna pursed her mouth, a telling tic of hers that told me I wouldn't like what she had to say.

"I also know this isn't their first date."

My chest tightened. I'd suspected as much because who in their right mind would bring someone they'd just met to a wedding. But that didn't make it any easier to hear.

Anna turned back to me and lowered her plate to the table. "How do you plan on winning him back?"

Right. Because I'd made that bold proclamation before walking her down the aisle. Trust Anna to remember that small detail.

Sighing, I reached across the table and snatched her plate, dragging it closer. The smell of vanilla, sugar, and a hint of Bailey's tickled my nose. I reveled in the scent. There weren't many problems sugar and booze couldn't solve.

I grabbed a nearby fork and sliced off a chunk of cake. Anna's face took on a wistful expression as I popped the piece into my mouth and started chewing. When she'd first been turned, she'd chosen to eat vicariously through me, fetching me her favorite snacks such as Cheetos and popcorn. Guess some things never changed.

"Honestly, I don't know if I can," I said after swallowing. "It's been a year." A year since I ran away, a year since I'd been turned into a werewolf, a year of ignoring Sam and Anna. Was it any wonder he'd moved on and found himself someone new? "That's a long time. I can't expect him to just ditch his new...," I choked out the word, "girlfriend. I wouldn't even know where to begin."

"Do you want to be with him?" Anna asked, leaning forward. "Like, for real? Because when we last discussed this, you weren't convinced."

I nodded. I remembered that conversation. Remembered us in England, sitting in the snow beneath a tree, discussing how Sam only wanted me due to his biological urge to procreate.

Werewolves were funny beasts. Unlike vampires, we didn't mate for love. Our mates were chosen solely for the purpose of producing the strongest offspring. This natural instinct that drove us toward the best possible partner. When I'd learned of that fun little tidbit, I'd jumped ship and bailed on Sam—*after* sleeping with him. Hell, I'd left the country just to escape him.

Then, by some sick twist of fate, I'd been turned into a werewolf, and now, suddenly, things were so much clearer. Now, I understood the call. Now, I understood how badly I'd screwed the pooch— metaphorically speaking.

In short, I was a terrible, *terrible* person, and I would count myself lucky if Sam so much as spoke to me again.

Disheartened, my attention darted to Sam, and I jumped when I realized he was staring right back at me. He and his date were dancing, their arms wrapped around each other, but Sam's gaze never wavered.

I shivered and refocused my attention on Anna. "Yes, I want to be with him." No doubt about it. In fact, it was the only thing me and the wolf agreed on.

"Good!" A smile crossed Anna's lips. "Because I would bet every last dollar in my incredibly flush bank account that he still wants to be with you."

I gave a dry laugh. "Yeah, right. He wants me. *That's* why he's here with another woman."

"Please. She's just a distraction. We don't even know her name. Shows you how unimportant she is if he hasn't even introduced her."

"He hasn't introduced her because that would be awkward. You're my best friend."

"Nah. It's because, at the end of the day, she doesn't matter."

Even I winced at that. I didn't like the idea of him using this woman just *because*. But it also killed me to imagine Sam feeling *feelings* for someone else.

Man, this mate business *sucked*. Why couldn't it be any easier?

"Was it like this for you and Vlad?" I asked.

A soft smile curved Anna's mouth. "No. The concept of being with him terrified me at first, but I never ran away."

Oh, ouch. I felt that barb. Not that it wasn't deserved. When things got rough, I'd run away from everyone and everything. Tucked tail and jumped ship all the way to Mississippi. Becoming a werewolf had obliterated my life, and I'd needed help. At the time, the only person I'd been willing to ask was Reggie, my sperm donor. I'd only learned of his existence about a year and a half ago, but that had made it easier to knock on his door. And seeing as how he was the alpha of the Mississippi Pack, he'd helped me gain control of the monster within.

"What do I do, Anna?" I stole another bite of cake. "How do I fix this?"

"Well, may I suggest starting with an apology?"

I scoffed. "Really? That's your advice?"

"Better than not saying you're sorry," she said, shrugging. "It's probably something he needs to hear."

I refrained from rolling my eyes. Not because her suggestion was silly, but because *obviously,* I was going to apologize. I needed to know what to do after that. "And then what?"

"And then, my love..." She perched her chin on her hand and smiled. "You pour your heart out. You tell him what you're feeling and what you want from him. Then you wait and find out if he wants the same."

"That simple, huh?"

She quietly chuckled. "No. Not that simple. Emotions are never simple. They're raw and painful and often make you feel like you're standing naked in the snow. But I think you owe him a little vulnerability. He deserves to know where he stands with you, even if that means ending things entirely. If you can't care for him the way he needs, set him free. Don't string him along."

I slowly nodded.

Anna leaned back in her chair and folded her hands in her lap. "But if I can make one more suggestion?"

I lifted a brow.

"Do it elsewhere. It's my wedding, and I'm just not in the mood for any drama."

I snickered under my breath. Yeah, I could understand that. I really did need to talk to Sam before the night ended, but I could certainly take that conversation elsewhere. Anna was like my sister. The last thing I wanted was to possibly ruin her wedding by getting in a fight with Sam or his date.

"And speaking of my wedding..." Anna winked, then stood, her gaze now locked onto something across the hall.

I turned to find her new husband, Vlad, striding toward her, a single rose in hand. The love these two shared made me ache inside. Their path hadn't been an easy one, but they'd come out stronger in the end.

I wanted that. A partner. Someone I could rely

on and love with my whole heart. It was what had sent me running in the first place. When I'd first learned that werewolves were driven to procreate, it'd terrified me to think that I might never find love. That Sam was only interested in me because of what I could give him—children.

But watching Anna fight for her true love had given me hope. And hope was a powerful thing. Maybe there was more for me with Sam. I certainly felt something deeper for him. Unfortunately, I had no idea what he felt for me.

With a happy laugh, Anna skipped toward Vlad. Once within reach, he bowed at the waist and offered her the rose. I wasn't the only woman to swoon at the sight of him doting on his new wife. These were romance goals right here. The man certainly knew how to play the game.

Anna took the rose, then walked into his open arms and kissed him. The room erupted with cheers. Together, Vlad and Anna swept out onto the dance floor and began swaying to the music, now lost in each other's eyes.

Damn. They really knew how to make a girl want something deeply.

"They're quite the beautiful couple," a familiar voice said.

My mouth curved into a grin, and I turned. "Hi, Mom."

"Hey, baby." She took Anna's abandoned seat and lowered her wine glass onto the table. Concern dimmed her eyes as she studied me. "How are you doing?"

Right to the hard question. "I'm okay. It's... tough being back. Seeing all that I missed. But I'm adjusting."

She nodded, a sympathetic smile softening her features. "Anna missed you, but she never begrudged you for leaving. I just thought you should know that."

I bit back a wince. Anna might not have held a grudge, but I had. It was the sole reason behind my leaving. Our whole lives, we'd been best friends— inseparable, most would say. But then she'd been turned into a vampire. And soon after, me into a werewolf. I wish I could say I handled my transition with grace and poise, but the truth was far messier. I'd blamed Anna, accused her of dragging me into her problems and nearly getting me killed. I'd unfairly placed all my blame on her. Emotions were strange like that. They colored your reactions.

After some time away, I'd realized that none of what'd happened had actually been Anna's fault. More like, wrong place, wrong time. But by then, I'd already been gone for so long that I hadn't felt comfortable reaching out to her. Then I'd learned of her wedding and knew I couldn't put our reunion off any longer. I'd already missed out on all the fun that came with being her maid of honor. I didn't want to miss out on the rest of her life.

Thankfully, she'd shown far more mercy than I had and immediately forgave me. Because that was Anna. Me? I tended to hold onto things longer. Took me longer to process them. Hence, the running away.

"So, tell me how you're *actually* doing now," my mother prodded.

I couldn't help but smile. Such a mom thing to ask. "Really, I'm okay. A lot of adjustments, but Reggie has actually been really helpful. He taught me how to shift and integrated me into his pack."

Her face whitened. "You're a part of *his* pack?"

"Mom." I squeezed her hand. "Don't worry, okay? He's actually been great to me."

"Yeah, now that you're a werewolf," she griped. "This is the man that abandoned us when you were born human. But now that you're like him, *now* he has time for you?"

I didn't have an answer to that because she was right. Reggie had done exactly that. He'd wooed my mother, knocked her up, then bailed the second he realized I'd been born human. It wasn't until I was practically mauled to death by a werewolf that my latent genes activated. *Then* he'd decided I was worth his attention.

At first, I hated him. But as I came to understand the wolf inside, I also grew to understand Reggie. I would *never* think of him as anything but my sperm donor. He did, however, work well as the pack alpha. That was where our relationship ended though.

My true father was and always would be the man who had stood by my mother's side and helped raise me. The man who was currently stealing Anna away from Vlad for a quick dance.

"Why couldn't you join the New Orleans Pack?" my mom asked.

I shot Sam another secretive glance. Thankfully, this time he was distracted. I wasn't sure I could handle another of his piercing stares right now. "Because of Sam."

Understanding smoothed my mother's frown lines, and she nodded. "Are you going to talk to him?"

"Eventually. I have to. I can't live like this."

"You know you have my full support, baby. No matter what you decide to do. I just wish life had been kinder. This isn't the path I wanted for you."

"Me too, Mom. But I'm alive, right? That's something to be thankful for."

"Absolutely. I thank God every day for that."

I winced and shot a furtive glance around the room, but no one seemed to hear my mother dropping the G-word. Vampires tended not to like hearing it.

"Anna says I need to talk to Sam, lay it all out. What do you think?"

"You know me, baby. I'm all for the truth. Even if it's scary and causes pain. Wouldn't that be simpler than lying to yourself or someone you love?"

I ignored the hypocrisy of my mother's statement, considering she'd lied to me my entire life about my true parentage, and instead focused on the scary L-word she'd just uttered. Love? I wasn't even sure if I loved Sam. I had feelings for him, sure. But love? I only knew that my wolf wanted him. That *I* wanted him. For now, that would have to be enough.

"Go to him," my mother continued. "Take him outside where you two can talk in peace. That is, if you can get him away from his date."

That would be the hard part. I couldn't imagine she'd be fine with him leaving to talk with another woman. Maybe it'd be best to wait until he was alone. But so far, I hadn't seen the two of them apart.

I shot Anna a glance and watched as Vlad reclaimed her as his dance partner and dipped her in his arms. She giggled, then lifted her head and kissed him, her hands threading through his hair.

Yeah, I wanted that.

So, maybe I needed to make fate work *for* me instead of against me. Maybe I needed to ask for a little help separating the two, then dragging Sam's ass outside.

"Thanks, Mom," I murmured.

"I should go steal your father back before he charms every woman in this place."

I laughed. My father absolutely was a charmer. He'd already moved on to a new dance partner, spinning her in tight circles before handing her back to her original partner. The man was so laid back and always knew how to have a good time—a talent I sadly hadn't learned from him.

Rising to my feet, I snuck onto the dance floor, grabbed Anna's hand, then pulled her away from Vlad. His eyes widened, but he quickly smiled when he caught sight of me.

"Sorry, Battikins. Need to borrow your wife for a moment."

His expression went all gooey at the word wife, and I rolled my eyes.

"Just bring her back to me," he said, his accented voice deepening with emotion.

Laughing, I looped my arm around Anna's elbow and led her away.

We may have been separated for the last year, but she would *always* be my partner in crime. And it was time to stir up a little trouble.

2

"DARE I ask what we're doing?" Anna quietly questioned.

An impish grin claimed my lips. I loved how even though she hadn't a clue, she'd still come with me. Because she and Vlad weren't the only soulmates here tonight. Our sisterly bond would span the ages, even past my death.

"I need help separating Sam and his date," I murmured. "So we can talk alone."

"Ah, so you need me to distract What's-Her-Face." She rubbed her hands together and chuckled.

"Well, you are the Queen of Shenanigans."

"I got you, Boo." She laughed, then shook her

head. "I'm almost offended by how easy this'll be. Gimme something more challenging next time."

Easy? She already had a plan? And why didn't that surprise me?

Before I could question further—you know, ensuring she didn't intend to bite someone or something—Anna blew me a kiss, then swaggered to the front of the hall, her dress swishing against the floor. She snatched something from a nearby table, then pointed at the DJ, who turned down the music and reached for the microphone.

"Alright, ladies! Gather 'round. According to the bride, it's time to catch the bouquet!"

Squeals of excitement rang through the room, and like a herd of elephants, women from every direction stampeded toward Anna, their hands already held out in anticipation. I grimaced at the sight of the fawning women. Some traditions you just didn't mess with. I was grateful I wouldn't be participating. The thought of catching the bouquet right now terrified me. I had enough going on in my life without tossing a silly superstition into the mix.

I shot Sam a covert glance and spotted his date weaving through the throng to join in the excitement. *Yes... Yes... join the dark side.* And no,

Emperor Palpatine's voice was *not* echoing through my head. Not at all.

As for me, I inched along the back of the room, careful to keep from being spotted. Sam stood among the men but thankfully off to the side. His expression appeared almost wary, as though he feared the thought of his date catching the bouquet. I almost laughed. Maybe I should have asked Anna to throw it directly at her. Just to torture him. But that strayed too close to tempting fate. I didn't want to catch the bouquet, but I sure as heck didn't want *her* to catch it either.

I was a complicated person.

Tiptoeing toward Sam, I stole another glance at Anna. She had every woman—except me—eating out of the palm of her hand, teasing them as she faked a few throws, then giggled. She briefly caught my gaze, winked, then finally heaved the bundle into the air. My breath hitched, but thankfully, she'd aimed the cursed thing in the opposite direction of me. The horde of women all gasped before dashing after the bundled flowers. Arms extended, they screamed and cooed, their fingers grabbing at the air, all while mine snatched Sam's hand and wrenched him toward the exit.

He didn't resist.

In fact, his hand tightened around mine as he chased me outside.

Giddiness warmed my stomach, and I found myself laughing as we escaped the hall and bolted out into the chilly January night. Why Anna had chosen a winter wedding, I had no idea. But since I hadn't been here to help with the planning, it seemed best not to question her motives.

With Sam's hand still in mine, I pulled him around the building corner, then stopped next to a pair of benches resting in the middle of a small grassy field. There wasn't much else out here other than a parking lot, but we didn't need anything more than that.

I released his hand, then turned to face him. The escape plan had worked. Now, I had to move on to the next part.

Talking.

Lord help me because surely no one else would.

I drew a deep breath and *finally* met Sam's gaze. My word. Somehow in the year we'd been apart, I'd convinced myself he couldn't possibly be as handsome as I remembered. Clearly, my brain had been playing tricks on me because he was *far* more attractive than I recalled.

Anna had always compared Sam to a

lumberjack. But to me, he looked more like Superman. His dark hair, sharp jawline, stacked muscles, and immense size all *screamed* superhero. And he had the personality to match. Caring, determined, fearless.

I still remembered the night an evil vampire had abducted Anna. Sam and Anna had only just met, but his concern for her wellbeing had touched me. He'd spent the entire day tracking her through the city by scent alone. His dedication and devotion to a perfect stranger told me so much about him. Especially considering how he and Anna were two entirely different types of paranormal creatures. But he hadn't cared that she was a vampire. He'd only cared that she was my friend and therefore needed saving.

Cue the *swoon*, right? The man was perfect.

The Clark Kent to my Lois Lane.

"Lucy."

Great googly moogly. That voice. I'd forgotten how deep it was and how it affected me. How the sound of it seemed to reverberate through my entire body.

I shivered and wrapped my arms around myself, trying to hide how my little hairs were standing on end.

When he lifted a brow, I cleared my throat and forced myself to breathe. Apparently, I was mentally unprepared for this moment. I'd been so focused on separating him and his date that I hadn't given a lick of thought about what I would say when we were alone. And now, staring into his piercing amber eyes, I couldn't find the words. How did people spill their guts so easily? Just confess everything while the other person stared at them? Geez, it felt like my throat was closing up.

"Is there something you want?" he asked. "Or did you just plan on staring at me all night?"

Was that an option? The man was the epitome of gorgeous, and I appreciated damn fine art. So, yeah, I definitely wouldn't mind staring a little while longer.

"I, uh..." I blew out a heavy breath, still unsure of what to say. Why was this so hard? Maybe because I had no idea how he felt about me. For all I knew, he hated me. Or worse, gave me no thought whatsoever. Maybe this was nothing more than an ex pestering him at a friend's wedding.

Thanks, anxiety. I really needed that kick to the ovaries right now.

Anna hadn't been wrong when she'd said emotions were hard and messy. It terrified me to consider speaking my feelings aloud. What if he laughed at me? I had to believe he was a better man than the image my worst nightmare conjured, but I couldn't shut that little voice off in my head.

"You, what?" he pressed.

Start simple. "I thought we could talk. You know, catch up. See how you've been."

Coward. Coward. Coward!

I winced at the sound of my own voice echoing in my head.

Sam's expression fell flat. "Hmm."

Really? That was it? A grunt?

I almost laughed. I'd forgotten how reticent Sam could be. If he wasn't particularly close to you, or if you annoyed him, he tended to speak in grunts and growls. It drove Anna insane when he did that. At the time, it'd been fun watching her try to drag a conversation out of him. Now, it was torture.

"H-How have you been?"

Sam crossed his arms, his suit jacket straining against his rippling biceps. My eyes practically bugged out of my head. If possible, he seemed even bigger than before. But surely, that was just my imagination.

He didn't immediately respond. Instead, he unleashed what I called his "alpha gaze." The one all alpha werewolves seemed to have. I'd first noticed it when my sperm donor welcomed me into his pack. The younger, weaker members always cowered beneath the stare, but not me. In fact, seeing it on Sam's face only emboldened me. Reminded me that he wasn't the only badass werewolf on the block.

I mimicked his stance. His gaze briefly dropped to my cleavage before darting back to my face. But I'd noticed it. And he knew I had.

"You really want to do this?" he asked.

I arched a defiant brow. "Do what? I only suggested we talk. Catch up a bit."

He shook his head, his hair a bit longer than the last time I'd seen him, then strode to the nearest bench and sat, his legs spread wide. I laughed at the sight of his manspread, then took a seat on the other bench. The cold wood immediately chilled my tush.

"You expect me to believe you dragged me away from my date just to have a little *chat*?"

"Maybe."

"Enough games, Lucy," Sam growled.

My gaze immediately fell to my lap, where my folded hands rested.

Anna's words rang through my head, reminding me to apologize. I could do that, especially considering I *was* sorry. It wouldn't cost me anything to offer him that.

With a deep breath, I squared my shoulders and once again, met his gaze. This was the moment of truth. I couldn't hide from it. Nor did I want to. I wanted the air cleared between us. I wanted a chance to be with him because I *wanted* him.

I also accepted that he might *not* want those things. And yes, it terrified me, but I was willing to take the chance. Because like my mother had said, "*Isn't it better to know?*"

"I am so sorry," I finally said. "For everything."

Sam's brows shot upward. He seemed almost surprised, as though he hadn't actually expected an apology out of me.

"I never should have left like that," I continued. "I wish I had handled the situation differently. Better—"

"Better," he repeated, his eyes narrowing.

My head bobbed. "If I could change things—"

"Lucy, I don't care that you left."

I winced and closed my eyes. Yeah, that stung.

"No. I didn't mean it like that." He sighed and leaned back against the bench, pinching the bridge of his nose. "Of course I cared that you left. What I mean is, it wasn't the leaving that upset me. It was that you left without talking to anyone. To *me*. You just took off without so much as a word. We had no idea if you were okay or what was happening to you. For crying out loud, I had to learn about your attack from Anna. You kept everything from me."

I stared dumbfoundedly at Sam. This had to be the most I'd ever heard him say in one breath. Guess he really did have some feelings on the matter. And then his words sank in, and I flinched.

"I want to know why," he said, his voice deepening with emotion. "After everything..." He drew in a steadying breath. "Why?"

Geez Louise, that was a loaded question. I knew the answer, but I'd never spoken it out loud. Considering I'd only just rolled into New Orleans tonight, an hour before the start of Anna's wedding, I hadn't been given a chance to explain until now.

"I was scared," I finally whispered, admitting my weakness.

"Scared." Sam's brows slammed down into a severe frown. "Of what? Me? You *know* I would never hurt you."

I shook my head. "No, not you. I could never be scared of you."

I wrapped my arms around myself, suddenly wishing I'd had the good sense to grab my jacket before ducking outside. We might live in Louisiana, but the winter nights were still chilly for us.

"Scared of what I'd become." When Sam started to speak, I held up a hand. "Let me get through this, please."

He nodded.

"You were born a werewolf. For you, it's a way of life. You were raised knowing what you are and what your life held in store for you. But for me..." I choked on my words, my throat tightening once more. "Sam, when Anna, Vlad, and I returned from England, I wasn't in a good headspace. I was so *angry*. So hurt. I was grieving the loss of my human life. *My* life. In the span of a single night, everything I thought I knew about myself had changed. I was suddenly having these thoughts, these feelings, and I-I had no one to talk to."

"You *had* me," he snapped.

Damn it. I was screwing this up six ways from Sunday.

"I'm not trying to hurt you," I said. "I'm trying to explain what was going on in my head at the time."

He gestured for me to continue, but his impatience was evident in the tapping of his foot.

I rubbed my face and sighed. "When I left for England, I knew two things. One"—I held up a finger —"we'd just slept together. And two"—a second finger popped up—"werewolf matings were purely about making little wolf cub babies."

Alarm shot across Sam's face. "We do *not* have wolf cub babies."

"A joke," I mumbled. "Sorry. Not the right moment. What I'm trying to say was I didn't understand the first thing about how this whole mate thing worked. Then I was attacked. And..." I tipped my head skyward and blew out a fogged breath. "God, Sam, I can't even begin to describe to you what I went through that night."

"And you'll never need to," he said, his voice softening. "Anna shared the details when she told me what happened, but I'll never push you to talk about it unless you want to."

Great. So he knew all about it. The worst moment of my life. A time when I was at my absolute weakest. He knew I'd nearly died. That my body had been mauled by some unknown werewolf working for the Queen of Vampires.

"Lucy, there's no shame in what happened to you."

I gritted my teeth and ignored that comment. People who'd never been through a trauma tended to say stupid stuff like that. But now wasn't the time to correct him.

"My body might have quickly healed," I continued. "But my mind didn't. I blamed Anna for everything. I was angry. *So* angry. And utterly terrified. When we landed in New Orleans, the only rational thought I had was to get as far away from her and all this as possible. So I ran. I didn't even stop to think about it. I just ran and didn't stop until I found my birth father."

The day before Anna was carted off to England, I'd learned about my sperm donor's existence. I'd also learned he was the Mississippi Pack alpha, but at the time, that'd meant nothing to me. The man had abandoned me and my mother the instant he realized I was born human.

According to my mother, Reggie's actions were common in the werewolf community. We possessed a biological urge to mate with the best suited partner, to produce the strongest offspring. But that didn't guarantee that the offspring would be born a werewolf. So once Reggie learned of my "defect," he'd taken off for parts unknown, and my mother had kept his existence a secret. Until I'd brought Sam home to meet her. The instant she laid eyes on him, she knew what he was and what I'd become involved in.

"Last we spoke, you wanted nothing to do with him," Sam said. "So why seek him out?"

"I had no idea how to handle it all," I said. "The attack, my change, all of it. I didn't know what to do."

"You go to the people you love," Sam said. "To the people who love you. You trust that they can help you."

"Except I blamed those people," I whispered. "I just felt like I needed a fresh start. I needed to get away from Anna and Vlad and away from their vampiric lives. And away from—"

"Me."

I froze, my heart breaking at the sound of utter despair in his voice.

"You wanted away from me."

"Sam, I..."

He rose to his feet and pushed a hand through his hair. The look of utter torment on his face nearly broke me.

"Sam." I rose on shaky legs and neared him, one hand outstretched. When my fingers connected with his forearm, he spun around and stared at me.

"What do you want from me, Lucy? What did you hope to gain from this little chat?"

"I'd hoped to explain things. Everything I just said... that was how I felt back then. I don't feel that way anymore. Can't you understand that? I needed time away, to learn to adjust to this new reality, to work on my issues."

"Yes, but in the meantime, you abandoned everyone."

Anger flared brightly within me. "I had a right to leave."

His face shuttered. Perhaps that'd been the wrong thing to say. Perhaps I could have worded it better.

"That's not what I meant," I said, sighing. "Sam, come on. Being a werewolf is second nature to you. But to me, it's more of a..."

"Curse?" he said, finishing my sentence.

"Well, yes! Can you blame me for feeling that way?"

A tic formed at his jawline. His silence was answer enough.

"Listen to me." My fingers curled around his forearm. "I came back. Doesn't that count for anything?"

His silence persisted, and my damn nerves were twisting me all up inside. When his mouth finally parted, I nearly fainted from anticipation.

"Lucy—"

"Sam! There you are!"

I practically jumped at the sudden intrusion. I spun on my heel, expecting to see Sam's girlfriend bearing down on us. Instead, it was another woman stalking toward us, heels clicking against the pavement as she approached.

Frowning, I shot Sam another glance. Was this another girlfriend? Anna had mentioned that he'd been seeing *people*. But surely not all at the same time, right? *Right?*

"Christina." Sam straightened to his full height. "What are you doing here?"

"We've been looking all over for you."

We've?

When Christina's narrowed gaze flicked to me, Sam cleared his throat. "Lucy, this is Christina, one of my pack members. Christina, this is Lucy. A former..." He cleared his throat.

Former. Gah. My heart just shattered into a million pieces. I mean, technically, I *was* a former. But that didn't make it any easier to hear. I gritted out a smile and nodded a small hello.

Christina fiddled with the hem of her jacket and concern darkened her eyes. She closed the distance between her and Sam and laid a hand on his arm. The wolf inside nearly came apart at the sight of her touching him, and a faint growl trickled out before I could contain it.

Both Christina and Sam shot me surprised glances, so I masked what just happened with a forceful clearing of my throat. *Nothing to see here, people.*

Christina shook her head, then turned back to Sam. "Your father's requested you. There's been an attack."

3

"An attack," Sam repeated.

If I hadn't been watching him so closely, I might not have noticed the slight change in his posture. In the blink of an eye, he went from personal to business mode. All emotion vanished from his face, and his body tensed as though preparing for bad news. Quite eerie to witness the change, to see his "alpha personality" switch on. Would that happen to me too? No one had mentioned it, but perhaps it was a werewolf thing. I often thought of myself as having a dual personality now. Maybe it was part of that.

"I'm afraid I haven't been given much detail yet," Christina commented. She wrapped her arms around herself as though to ward off a chill. "I only know that your father activated the pack emergency protocol approximately an hour ago. An alert went out to all our phones, ordering us to report in. But no one had heard from you."

Sam grumbled something under his breath, then patted his pants. "My phone isn't on me. I think I left it in my car. Who was attacked?"

"One of our pack members."

Sam startled. "A pack member? That's..."

"Unheard of. I know."

"I'm sorry," I interrupted. "But why is that unheard of?"

Sam barely glanced my way before answering. "The New Orleans Pack—*my* pack—is strong and one of the largest in the country. To attack one of our members is not only an act of war but suicide as well. *No one* would risk going to war against my father."

"Your father?" I whispered.

He finally faced me, but I didn't like the hint of accusation I saw deep in his eyes. "My father is the alpha of the New Orleans Pack."

I blinked. Sam's father was the local alpha? The big honcho? Why hadn't I known this?

Shock silenced me, and I dropped my gaze, staring at the pointed toes of the lilac-colored flats I'd worn for

Anna's wedding. The uncomfortable truth was that I knew very little about Sam. When we'd first met, I'd only cared that he was a werewolf, and I was a human. Beyond that, I hadn't bothered to learn much more about him. I'd been so focused on *ignoring* the whole "mate" thing that I'd never taken the time to get to know him. And I had no one to blame for that but myself.

It also made me wonder what else I didn't know about him.

I quickly ran through what little I *did* know, but it didn't consist of much. He was a werewolf who belonged to the local pack, and he was my mate. Now I could add his alpha father. That was the extent of my knowledge.

Shame burned my cheeks, seeing as how *he* knew *everything* about me.

He'd met my parents when he'd accompanied me home to Perish, seen the schools I'd attended, where I'd grown up, and the many places Anna and I had gotten into trouble. I'd shown him my favorite coffee shop, Anna's and my former apartment, everything. He knew about all the events that had led me and Anna to New Orleans in the first place, and how she'd been turned into a vampire, how I'd helped her adjust to her new life. Hell, he'd even been part of her rescue party when she'd been abducted.

But me?

I knew zilch about him.

I was literally the worst.

Well, that all stopped now. I'd returned to New Orleans with the intent of wooing him, and I refused to let something as simple as this stand in my way. Claiming him as mine meant learning every little thing about him and involving myself in his life.

It also meant treating him a hell of a lot better.

I was sadly quite aware of my history of ignoring and running from him.

He deserved better.

"Okay, so you're the pack heir," I murmured, reacquainting myself with this new image of him.

"Guess that means we finally have something in common," Sam commented dryly.

I cocked my head and raised a brow.

"Reginald is the Mississippi alpha," Sam said. "And you are his only werewolf child. So, since you belong to his pack, that makes you his heir."

Wait. What? This raised so many questions. Like, "How did you know Reginald is my father? I never told you his name. And how did you know I'm a member of the Mississippi Pack? Have you been tracking me?"

Sam rolled his eyes. "Hardly. You're the first human-born turned into a werewolf. *Everyone* is talking about you. A guy can't go a day without hearing your name right now. I've known where you were for a while now. And since it's every werewolf's responsibility to know all the pack alphas, I know who Reginald Hayes is."

My narrowed gaze flicked between Sam and Christina. She seemed riveted by our conversation. I wanted to ask her to leave—this was none of her business, after all. But it wasn't my place.

"Your father *is* Reginald Hayes, right?" Sam confirmed when I didn't immediately respond.

The sound of his voice startled me back to the conversation. I pushed Christina's presence from my mind and nodded. "Uh, yeah. Reggie."

"Then that makes you his only lycanthropic child. And the heir to the Mississippi Pack."

A nervous laugh trilled past my lips. It sounded like a cross between a wheeze and a sharp giggle. "Nuh-uh. I'm no one's heir. I'm just a pack member. Nothing special."

"Hmm." Sam studied me. "Guess we'll see."

I shot Christina another glance. She watched me

with a sympathetic expression. I shook my head again but couldn't think of anything else to say. I'd recently learned there was a standard hierarchy among werewolves, and Sam was correct. The eldest child born to an alpha was the heir. But me? I wasn't even a real werewolf, not like Sam, who'd been born one. Surely Reggie wouldn't have claimed me as his heir. Only a fool would give that much power to someone like me. Besides, wouldn't he have told me when he brought me into the pack? I couldn't imagine him keeping a secret like that from me.

Then again, we *were* talking about the man who'd abandoned an infant the instant he realized she was human.

Yeah, maybe he *would* keep something like that a secret. It wasn't like I really *knew* anything about him.

"Sam," Christina whispered, her voice shattering my thoughts. "Your father—"

"Right." Sam smoothed his hands down his suit jacket, then turned to face her. "Tell me who was attacked."

"I don't know exactly. I only know it was someone from the Jenkins family."

Sam winced, and a flicker of pain darkened his face. Guess he knew them.

"Give me five minutes to pop back inside and offer the bride and groom my congratulations. Then we'll go. I'm sure my father is livid that I haven't responded to his calls."

Christina forced a small smile. "There might have been some talk of beating you senseless."

I gasped, my hand instantly darting to Sam's arm.

His attention dropped to my fingers. If I wasn't mistaken, he wore a tiny smile, almost as though he enjoyed my reaction. I, on the other hand, didn't understand it. I just knew that if his father so much as touched a hair on Sam's head, I would lose it.

"He doesn't mean it, Lucy. My father would never harm me," Sam commented. His other hand fell on top of mine, his fingers giving a gentle squeeze before he pried loose my grip.

"Right." I gave a breathy chuckle. Sam could take care of himself, but apparently this beast inside me had a protective streak. I'd need to keep that in mind. "I guess you'll be going then." Ugh, I hated how my voice changed, how disappointed I sounded. If I'd known the wolf would turn me into a classic, clingy girlfriend, I might have kept my distance.

Ha.

Yeah, right.

"Guess so," he rumbled.

I took a step closer and laid my hand on his arm. "Can I see you again? Before I head back to Jackson?"

Sam considered my question with a deep, probing stare. It didn't bode well that he hadn't immediately agreed.

But before he could respond, a phone chimed.

Christina patted her jacket, then fished her cell out of her pocket. Neither Sam nor I moved, considering he didn't have his phone, and mine was tucked in my purse inside the reception hall. Christina's phone lit up, and she sucked in a sharp breath.

"What's wrong?" Sam demanded, his gaze still holding mine.

"The victim is Brenda Jenkins," Christina responded, her voice hoarse.

"Brenda?" Sam broke our connection, then grabbed Christina's phone and peered at the screen as though it could give him all the answers. "But she's human."

Fear ratcheted my pulse, and my hand flew to my mouth, my fingers touching my bottom lip. "She's human?"

Christina nodded, chewing on her thumbnail.

"And she was attacked by a werewolf? You know that for sure?" I demanded.

"That's what the first message said."

My breath quickened, and my blood turned to ice. As though sensing my impending panic attack, Sam's hand clutched mine. His touch grounded me and staved off the fog creeping in on my vision.

"Breathe," he said, his voice anchoring me to the here and now.

"Maybe you should come with us," Christina murmured. She touched my wrist, as though offering me silent comfort. "You, uh, have experience with this since you're the first human to be changed into a werewolf."

"I-I don't know how much help I can provide," I stuttered, my thoughts going hazy as memories invaded my mind. "I remember the attack, the feel of that creature's claws..." I shuddered and sucked in a bracing breath. "But I was unconscious for the rest."

Sam's hand gave a painful squeeze, but I relished in it, using the pain to banish the unwelcome memories.

He considered me, then nodded. "Any information you could provide would be helpful."

After a moment's hesitation, I agreed. While I

didn't love the idea of baring my soul, Sam was right. Even if emotional support was all I could provide.

"Okay. Christina, head to my car. Lucy and I will go inside and say our goodbyes."

I gave a jerky nod.

Christina offered me a final pitying look, then vanished into the darkness. I had to assume she knew which car was Sam's. I sure didn't.

His hand tugged me forward until we stood a hair's breadth apart. I could *feel* his warmth and wanted to curl into it like a lazy cat.

"Are you okay?" he asked.

"Sure."

He frowned. "It's just us here, Lucy."

"I'm fine, Sam."

He stared at me for a moment, then with a sigh, released me and stalked back toward the reception hall.

For some reason, I had the feeling I'd failed a test. Great.

Scolding myself, I chased after Sam. Stepping into the reception hall was like stepping into a whole other world. Anna never did anything small, and the hall had been decorated precisely to her instructions. Streamers, balloons, the epic three-tiered, bat-shaped cake, a buffet fit to feed an entire city, a DJ with strobe lights, you name it. But all of it was at odds with the developing situation. Knowing there was a woman out there, going through what I'd gone through, suffering like I'd suffered... it packed a punch that left me breathless.

I jogged after Sam as best I could in my fitted dress, only to find him already shaking hands with Vlad. Sam extended a hand to Anna, but she quietly scoffed, then dragged him in for a hug. Anna wasn't short by any means, but Sam was monstrous. So much so that her head barely reached his shoulders.

He stepped back, allowing me a moment to say goodbye.

"I'm going with him."

Surprise widened Anna's eyes. "You are? Really? But..."

I leaned in and kissed her cheek, careful not to smudge her makeup. Considering she didn't have a reflection, I didn't want to do anything that would ruin her appearance.

"Lucy—"

"I need to be with him," I murmured to her, hoping the music drowned out our voices.

Vampires have crazy good hearing, but so did werewolves. And while I'd apologized to Sam, I wasn't ready for him to understand the extent of my confused emotions yet. I needed to sort that out for myself before confessing anything to him. And to do that, I needed to spend more time with him. At least, that was the logic my brain kept feeding me. Honestly, I wasn't sure how much to trust the damn thing, considering it'd been invaded by a wolf.

"What's going on?" Anna asked.

"I'm not sure. Someone's been attacked. And Sam's father called the pack home to deal with it. But Anna... it was a human attacked by a werewolf."

Horror blanched her face—a neat trick for a pale vampire.

"Be safe," she whispered, leaning in for another hug. "You're coming back, though, right? No taking off this time?"

My heart twinged. "I'm never leaving your side again. Well, except for right now."

She gave me a weak smile. "As long as you come back, and not in a year."

"I'll call you tomorrow if that makes you feel better."

Relief smoothed her immortal face.

"When do you leave for your honeymoon?"

"Day after tomorrow. So you better call me, or I'm gonna have to hunt your ass down."

I chuckled. "You got it. I'll drop by for a visit before you guys leave."

"Good."

Stepping back, I reached up and patted Vlad's shoulder. He gave me a brief smile, careful not to expose his fangs, then took Anna's hand and led her back onto the dance floor. "YMCA" blared out of the speaker system, and let me say, I've never seen anything quite so strange as a bunch of vamps getting their groove on to the Village People.

Chuckling, I turned to see Sam speaking with his date. What brief amusement I'd found in watching the vamps dance died. It was like someone had dumped freezing cold water over my head. His date didn't even seem upset that he'd ditched her for the past twenty minutes.

Cripes, if they kissed...

The wolf growled. Thankfully, this time I was able to swallow the sound before embarrassing myself. But for the first time, I agreed with the beast. No way in hell would I stand here and watch him kiss another woman. I was a glutton for punishment, but that just seemed torturous.

Thankfully, they parted with little more than a nod.

I released a harsh breath and told myself to *pull*

it together. I couldn't let Sam see me like this, all riled up with jealousy. When he started to step back, I turned away and faced the dance floor, watching Vlad and Anna shimmy their hips and mime out the letters Y-M-C-A. At the very least, I could pretend I hadn't been watching Sam like some lovesick puppy.

"Ready?" His deep voice made me shiver.

I turned with a forced smile. "Yup. You?"

"Yes. Let's go."

I expected him to sweep dramatically out of the hall, but instead, he cocked his head and stared at me. "You know, Lucy, I said I would never push you to talk about what happened to you in England. And I meant that. But if you ever *did* want to talk about it, I'm here. And if that doesn't work for you, we can find someone who will. A professional."

I winced and dropped my gaze.

His index finger crooked under my chin and lifted my head. When our gazes met, he caressed my cheek, then pulled his hand away. "Stop hiding. You have nothing to be ashamed about. What happened wasn't your fault. The fact that you're standing here only proves how strong you are." He brushed a stray hair off my cheek and smiled. "You're a survivor, Lucy. And if I can promise you one thing, it's that I'll never let anyone hurt you ever again. I'll kill anyone who tries."

His vehement words left me speechless. No one had ever said anything like that to me before, and I found myself shivering as I followed him out into the night.

Welp, this was awkward.

Seemed like Sam wanted to drive in silence, even after that bold proclamation he'd made. *I'll kill anyone who tries*. Damn, it made my heart beat faster just thinking about it. But what did it *mean*? Was it merely an alpha werewolf thing? I'd heard they could get pretty protective. Or was it a sign that he still cared for me?

I wish I could ask, but Sam truly did seem more interested in silence. He sat in the driver's seat, his fingers gripping the steering wheel for dear life. Maybe he regretted his words? Or maybe he just preferred to drive in silence. I had no idea. Yet another thing I didn't know about him.

Well, one thing he might not know about me was I hated silence. Especially super-dee-duper awkward ones like this.

I reached toward the radio and cranked the volume dial. But instead of music, the sound of piercing static filled the car. I cursed and cranked the dial down until silence reigned once more.

"Cripes," I muttered. "Don't you listen to music?"

He grunted a non-verbal response that almost sounded like a laugh. "I hate the radio."

"You hate the radio," I repeated. Was he kidding me right now? No one hated the radio. It played music. It literally was the only part of the car created for entertainment purposes. No one *hated* the radio. "So, you're insane then? Good to know."

Another half-chuckle, half-grunt.

Sam leaned to the side and popped open the glove box. His phone sat inside. He briefly took his eyes off the road to study me, then he handed me his cell. "Turn on Bluetooth."

Ignoring that he hadn't said *please*, I tapped his phone and did as he said. Within seconds, his car and phone were synced, and the soft sound of music trickled through the car. This time, when I turned the volume up, I took my time, my head cocked to the side.

"You listen to classical music?" I asked.

"Contemporary classical." He tapped the blinker and changed lanes. "Music these days is little more than people singing about their body parts and sex."

I bristled playfully, pretending to take offense to his statement. It wasn't that he didn't like the radio, he didn't like *modern music*. Who didn't love music? My god, it was like I didn't know him at all. Which I didn't, but that wasn't the point.

"Listen to it," Sam continued, his fingers moving to the soft beat. "Yiruma's work is beautiful. It's art."

"Sure, but so is Beyoncé."

Sam threw me a withering look. "Beyoncé, seriously? That's who you're going to use as a comparison?"

"Okay, Adele! She's amazing."

Sam sighed. "Should have guessed you'd like pop music."

"Hey!" I bit back a smile. "I like other artists too."

"Really? Like who? And it better not be someone like Miley Cyrus."

"I'm surprised you even know her name, Classical Boy."

Sam chuckled, and it was this deep, breathy

sound that did all sorts of wonderful things to my lady bits. Somehow, I had the feeling that he could breathe on me, and it would turn me on. But maybe that was a good thing. Better than being stuck in a passionless relationship.

"Okay—what about Phil Collins or Bryan Adams?"

A low groan punctuated the piano music. "Those are your choices?"

"Wow, you're a music snob!"

We hopped on the Danziger Bridge. I wasn't entirely sure where we were headed, but I trusted Sam. So rather than pester him for the deets, I sat back in my seat and instead listened to his music. I had to admit, it *was* really pretty, even if there weren't any lyrics. I could see myself playing it at night before bed, to help me relax before falling asleep. But it didn't pump me up, not like Queen B did.

Thankfully, our differing choices in music wasn't a deal breaker. I could handle a little instrumental, so long as he could handle a little 90s pop—my guilty pleasure. Spice Girls would always have a hold on my heart.

"So... how'd your girlfriend react to you having to take off?"

Sam's head whipped around. "My who now?"

"Your girlfriend? You know, the woman you brought to Anna's wedding?"

Blinking, Sam's gaze kept darting between me and the road. After a few silent moments, he burst out laughing and pinched the bridge of his nose. "Oh wow. How long have you been waiting to ask me that one?"

Embarrassment burned my cheeks, but I didn't answer. He didn't need to know how deeply my obsession ran. Not yet, anyway.

"Cameron isn't my girlfriend," Sam finally said.

"So, who is she then?"

"She's literally just a friend." He reached for the radio and turned down the volume until I could barely pick up on the notes. "She and I have an arrangement of sorts."

Oh crap. Like a sex-buddy arrangement? My stomach twisted with the thought.

"We go with each other to events like these to avoid people pressuring us into finding dates. She has no desire to date, and neither do I."

My stomach wrenched for a completely different reason. "Oh." Did him not wanting to date extend to me as well? We were mates, so didn't that negate the whole dating aspect? Except, I knew werewolves didn't mate like vampires. So maybe not? Maybe he just wanted to pump out a few kids and move on with his life. Which I *so* wasn't looking for.

Blinking back tears, I turned and stared out the window. I hadn't grown up in New Orleans, but I knew a little bit about the geography, thanks to Anna's and my frequent visits prior to her meeting Vlad. And I knew that the Venetian Isles were nearby, carved into the shores of Chef Menteur Pass. If I had to guess, that was where Sam was taking me. I didn't know much about the area, except that it stood separate from the rest of the city and was recently upgraded to a suburban-style community. While the area consisted primarily of marshlands, there was also a good portion of greenery for werewolves to run around, especially southeast of Lake Borgne.

Finally, we turned onto a residential street, and Sam parked outside a large two-story house with a boat parked out front, along with *a lot* of vehicles. Seemed wise to assume Sam's pack had arrived.

"Come on," he said as he killed the engine. "My father is probably inside."

Sam's father. Right. The alpha of the New Orleans Pack. That wasn't intimidating, not at all.

"Does, uh, does he know about me?"

"Know about you?" Sam quirked an eyebrow, his face silhouetted in the pale moonlight. "Like, that you're coming?"

"That." Along with *other* things I was too afraid to ask right now. "And that I'm apparently the heir of the Mississippi Pack?" My voice wavered. For some reason, the thought of being the heir terrified me. To the point where I wanted to pack every bag I had and run again. But I'd promised Anna I'd never do that again. And I liked to think I was a woman of my word.

Sam touched the back of my hand, offering me a silent show of support. "Everyone knows you're their heir. Well, except you apparently. But don't worry, so long as you asked for permission to enter my father's territory, then all will be well."

I blinked. "Um, permission?"

Sam froze. "Did you not do that?"

"I didn't know I had to! New Orleans is my home. Why would I need to ask permission to come home?"

Sighing, Sam pinched the bridge of his nose. "Because it's proper procedure to first ask permission before entering another alpha werewolf's territory. Has Reginald not taught you the rules?"

A frustrated growl slipped past my lips. "Apparently not."

"It's alright." Sam reached out and patted my hand. "I'll take care of it."

Relief loosened my muscles. I didn't know everything there was to know about werewolves yet, but I did know they were territorial AF and I really wasn't in the mood to get into a pissing contest with Sam's dad tonight.

"You don't have anything to worry about," Sam continued.

I met his gaze. "Because you'll protect me?"

His mouth crooked with amusement. Then he reached out and touched a stray lock of my hair. "You don't need protection here. Not from my pack."

"Is there anything I need to know? Like how do I address him? Do I call him alpha?"

"Just call him Adrien. That's his name after all."

Adrien. Got it. I could do that. "And your mother?"

"Elena."

Adrien and Elena. I kept reminding myself that Sam had met my parents, so it was only fair that I meet his.

"Then there are my sisters," he continued. "From

oldest to youngest is Aimee, Sophie, Isabelle, Monique, and Claire."

I choked on a breath. "You have *five* sisters?"

"What can I say? My parents wanted a big family. And I was their only son."

Oh my god, he was the oldest, too, considering he was the heir. So he had five *baby* sisters. The realization hit me like a ton of bricks. No *wonder* he was so protective. It might not have anything to do with me at all and everything to do with his upbringing. I didn't like that one bit.

"Are you close with your family?"

"Of course," he said, as though that were a no-brainer. "You'll love my sisters."

Here was hoping. Because I was an only child. And Anna's brother was an absolute shit that I'd spent most of my life smacking around and telling to smarten up. Beyond that, I knew zilch about sibling bonds. Reggie had fathered other children, but he'd abandoned them too. The man only cared about siring werewolves, a prodigy he'd never been granted. Fate or karma?

"Are they all going to be inside right now?"

"Probably. It's a pack emergency. Come on, you're not scared of five little girls, are you?"

Before I could answer, Sam ducked his head and

climbed out of the vehicle. When I didn't immediately follow, he glanced through the front windshield with his eyebrows raised as if to say, *well?*

Every bone in my body screamed at me not to go in there. It felt like a proverbial viper's nest. *Five* sisters and his parents. Not to mention his pack members. I wanted to know Sam, more than I currently did, but this was too much all at once. And I certainly hadn't imagined meeting his family under these circumstances. But I'd agreed to come. So now I had to face the consequences of that. Meaning, it was time to meet the fam.

Groaning, I slid out of the car and forced myself to stand straight. My palms were already slick with sweat, and my stomach twisted with dread.

"How young are your sisters?" I asked as I shut the passenger door. "Give me a range here."

"Well, Claire is the youngest, and she's about to turn ten. And Aimee is the oldest, she's twenty-seven."

Sweet baby Zeus. His sisters ranged from pre-teen to adult.

I was *so, so* screwed.

"Good lord, you'd think I was leading you to your death with a face like that."

I stuck my tongue out at Sam, but then made an

effort to school my expression. I had a feeling his family wouldn't particularly appreciate the look of abject terror on my face.

"Come on, Lucy," Sam said, offering me his hand.

I rounded the front of the car and clasped his hand, using the warmth of his touch to ground me. Surely it wouldn't be as bad as whatever image I'd conjured in my head. His family would likely be too busy dealing with the attack to notice Sam had brought a stranger home.

As he led me up the porch, I caught a whisper of the noise inside. More people than I could pick out, even with my heightened senses. I knew the New Orleans Pack was larger than the Mississippi Pack, by at least double. I also knew this house couldn't hold the *entire* pack all at once. But that didn't help my nerves.

Sam pushed open the front door and led me inside, where I was immediately greeted by the smell of cinnamon cookies and coffee.

"Oh, perfect, Sophie must be here," Sam commented, more to himself than me, I suspected.

Sophie was... the second oldest sister, if I remembered correctly. And if his eldest sister was twenty-seven, it seemed safe to assume Sophie was in her early to mid-twenties.

"She's the baker," Sam continued. "Every time she comes home, she and my mom spend hours in the kitchen, cooking up all sorts of goodies."

A nostalgic smile pulled at my lips. My mom had always loved baking. Me? I burned pre-made cookies —it was a talent. Anna had always laughed and said between the two of us, we'd surely starve. It wasn't that I sucked at following instructions, and more like, every appliance in the world was out to get me. I must have done something in a previous life to anger the machines. Because I would set the temperature, wait for the oven to preheat, slide the cookies in, and bake for the exact time stated, only to pull out these little black husks that tasted about as good as you'd expect.

After a while, I'd given up. Why continue wasting my time and money when I could just go to the grocery store and buy all the cookies I wanted? At least then, the money went to something I could actually eat.

"Sam!" someone squealed.

A young girl came barreling out of nowhere, then threw herself into his arms. Based on her size and estimated age—because I *so* wasn't a kid person and didn't really keep track of that kind of stuff—I'd guess this had to be Claire, the almost ten-year-old. Long, dark hair spilled down her back in glimmering waves that made me blink. Sam's hair was wavy and luxurious too. Must be a family trait. But when Claire turned to face me, it was her piercing amber eyes that rendered me silent. They practically glowed in the dim entry light. Sam's were that color too, but his didn't possess the startling brilliance of Claire's. Damn, the genetics were strong with these two.

"Hey, squirt," Sam said, heaving her easily into the air. With muscles like his, that didn't surprise me. "Been causing trouble?"

"Always," she said, giggling, as though this were an inside joke they shared.

"Good. Remember, always—"

"Keep them on their toes," Claire finished.

"I should have known that *you* were the wretch teaching her that nonsense!" another voice joined the fray.

My head turned to find what had to be Sam's mother stalking toward them, waving a wooden spoon in the air. Much like her son and daughter, Elena had gorgeously long black locks, except hers were peppered with streaks of gray that lent her a wise old oak appearance. She couldn't be *that* old, with Sam closing in on thirty, but having children put a strain on women's bodies, or so I'd been told. A little gray was to be expected.

Her light amber eyes darted to me, and she stopped, her eyes slowly widening. "Oh, I didn't realize you were bringing home a friend." When her gaze strayed back to Sam, her mouth pursed disapprovingly.

"It's fine, Mom," Sam said. "She's one of us."

"She is?" Another close inspection. Then she blinked and her face cleared. "I'm sorry. Usually I can sense other werewolves, but you..."

I cleared my throat, not really in the mood to divulge my personal history. Like the fact that I wasn't born a werewolf. Reggie had said my scent was different from other werewolves, but he hadn't explained how. I made a mental note to ask Sam about that later.

"I'm so sorry," I said, "about your pack member."

Elena's brows furrowed. "And what pack are you with?"

"Mississippi," I said. "But I knew Sam personally as a friend before I—" I bit my tongue to keep from saying anything else. Honestly, my life story wasn't any of their business. But she was Sam's mom. So, maybe I should have just laid myself bare? Ugh. I hated this.

"Oh." Elena's hand touched her lips, and sympathy softened her features. "Oh. You're *her*. Aren't you?"

Before I could respond, Elena swept forward and practically engulfed me in a mother's hug. The kind that always made a child cry. And damn it if my eyes weren't welling with tears. How was it mothers could do that? Make someone feel so vulnerable with simply a hug?

"Well, welcome to our home!" Elena said as she drew back, her hands cupping my shoulders. "I hadn't realized you were friends with Sam. Guess my son's been keeping secrets from me."

I shot him a quick glance to find a little color brightening those scruffy cheeks. "Not now, Mom."

She waved her spoon in the air one more time, then took Claire from his arms and set the girl on the floor. "You, go play and try not to get under foot. There's important business to discuss tonight."

"But, Mom—"

"Don't *but mom* me. Do as I say."

Even I felt the sharpness of an alpha's tone there. Guess Sam's mom had some bite to her as well.

Which made sense, given that she was the pack alpha's wife.

Claire huffed, then stomped up the stairs, all the while mumbling about how she was never included in pack business.

"And you won't be until you're older!" Elena called up after her.

I had to bite back a grin. Something about Claire reminded me of Anna. And if that were true, it meant that little girl was going to be a handful.

"Come in," Elena beckoned. She patted Sam's cheek affectionately. "Your father has herded the pack members into the dining room. They're gathering as we speak. It won't be long now before he starts the meeting."

Sam snagged his mom's hand before she could leave. "How's Brenda?"

Pain and compassion twisted his mom's expression. Eventually, she sighed and shrugged. "We haven't a clue. We haven't dealt with this sort of thing before."

"I..." I bit my lip, wondering what to say. Yes, I was the only human to have ever been successfully changed into a werewolf, but that hardly made me an expert in the topic. And from the sounds of it, if Brenda survived, I wouldn't be the only member of this very exclusive club anymore. Not that I wished this fate on her. "Can I see her?"

Something flickered in Elena's eyes. "Perhaps after the meeting. I'm sure Adrien will want to ask her family first. Do you think you can help in any way?"

"No," I admitted. "Not at all. I didn't do anything special."

"You survived, dear," Elena said. "And that makes you all kinds of special."

Those damn tears welled again, but I cleared my throat and turned away before either mother or son could see it. Elena gripped my hand, gave it a squeeze, then returned to the kitchen.

"I'm not sure how my pack will react to your presence. Usually the meetings are members only," Sam said. "But given the circumstances, they might be grateful to see you, to assure the Jenkins family that there's a chance she'll survive."

I nodded.

"Are you ready for this?"

To meet the majority of the New Orleans Pack? Or to meet Sam's dad? Honestly, I had no idea. But I was here, and I was done running away from my life and my fate. So with a steadying breath, I nodded and followed Sam into the dining room.

THE DINING ROOM was more like a banquet hall from the size of it. Like holy crap. My mouth gaped as I studied the room, taking in the dozens of people crammed into it, all standing practically shoulder to shoulder. In the middle sat a long hardwood table with at least twelve seats, which made sense considering the size of Sam's family. The table had been adorned with an elegant centerpiece, and each chair had a place setting. But no one sat. Instead, they all stood in a giant pack, talking over each other, each demanding answers that no one seemed to have.

It was, in a word, overwhelming.

Reggie had introduced me to the Mississippi

Pack, but the events had always been small. He organized his pack into "inner" and "outer" members. Those closest to the alpha belonged to the inner circle. It was their responsibility to pass along information to the outer circle members, who tended to be actual family members of someone in the inner circle. So when he held pack meetings, there were a dozen people tops. This here was madness. At least thirty people stuffed into this room. The energy and heat and scent and *everything* was too much.

I backed out, my hand clutching at my chest. I'd never felt air ripple like that, as though their combined power was literally sucking the oxygen out of the room.

"Lucy?" Elena murmured.

I blinked and found myself standing in the kitchen, my hand still clutched to my chest. "Sorry. That was..."

She smiled understandingly. "I know. It takes a bit to adjust. You were changed about a year ago, right?"

I nodded.

"When Sam's father and I first heard of you, we discussed your situation a few times, but Sam never mentioned you two knew each other."

I ducked my head and shuffled my feet. "I, uh, hurt Sam."

When I didn't say anything more, Elena placed a comforting hand on my shoulder. This woman was the epitome of a mother. I had a feeling her children loved her dearly. Hell, probably everyone who met her. She had such a caring soul.

"He probably didn't want to talk about me back then," I finished.

Silence stretched between us until Elena took a breath and patted my shoulder. "Well, you're here now. Perhaps that's the first step to repairing whatever was broken between you."

I nodded. That was the goal, anyway.

"You should get back in there," she said. "Sam probably wants to introduce you."

Right. And then all those eyes would be on me. Asking me questions. Demanding answers. Things I wasn't sure I would be able to answer. But, like Elena said, this was the first step.

I pressed my hands to my stomach and stepped back into the dining room. Sam caught my gaze when I entered and lifted a brow as though to ask if I was all right. I nodded. I could do this.

"Father," he said, drawing Adrien's attention

mid-sentence, and gesturing toward me. "May I introduce someone?"

Just like that, the pack fell silent. And one by one, each member turned to face me. Their stares were unnerving and downright terrifying. For a moment, I flashed back to England, when I'd stared into the eyes of the beast and known death was coming. Werewolves were ultimately predators. A truth I was still learning to cope with daily. Even when looking in the mirror. To face being turned into the same creature as the one who'd nearly killed me had taken a lot of time and effort. Hell, I wasn't sure I'd ever come to grips with it. But I was trying. That had to count for something, right?

"This is Lucy Williams. Heir of the Mississippi Pack."

My gaze darted to Sam's father. A deep frown darkened his expression. "You're one of Reginald's daughters?"

One of... as though everyone knew just how big of a slut my sperm donor was. I bit back a wince and nodded. They didn't need to know that I hardly considered myself Reggie's daughter.

Sam's father, Adrien, straightened and focused on me. He seemed to be studying me, and it felt as though he could see straight through to my soul.

"Oh, I know exactly who you are. You're *that* daughter, the one who was turned into a werewolf."

Chatter immediately broke out through the room. Great, clearly everyone knew of my attack. I averted my gaze while everyone snuck glances at me and discussed the situation with their closest neighbor.

"I thought she could help us understand what might happen to Brenda," Sam commented.

Adrien nodded. "You realize how extraordinary you are, right? To have survived such a thing?"

I drew a deep breath and straightened my shoulders before addressing Adrien directly. "I've spent the last year in Mississippi learning about werewolves. During that time, my alpha, my"—I choked on the next word—"father tried to figure out how I survived. He thinks the attack activated my latent werewolf genes." I ignored the tremble in my voice and pushed onward. "Maybe... maybe the same thing will happen to your pack member?"

Voices rose in unison, people all struggling to be heard over the combined noise.

"Quiet," Adrien barked.

His pack instantly fell silent, and Adrien circled the long dining room table as though eager to get a closer look at me. "Tell me about your attack."

A deep growl vibrated through the room. "Father."

Adrien blinked, shocked perhaps by his son's response. He glanced over his shoulder, and whatever he saw in Sam's face must have convinced him to take a different approach.

When he turned back to me, a slight smile crooked his lips. "I apologize. That was rather insensitive of me. But please, I'd be grateful to hear as much as you're willing to share. Perhaps we can find some answers."

"There's not much to tell, I'm afraid," I said. "It all happened so fast. One moment I was staring the creature down—sorry, the werewolf—and the next..." I trembled as the memory surfaced. I closed my eyes as though that would keep me from reliving it. "Unimaginable pain."

A warm hand pressed down on my shoulder, and I opened my eyes to find Sam standing beside me, his presence offering me whatever strength I needed to borrow.

I offered him a weak smile, then turned back to the room. "I doubt the details of the attack are important. And unfortunately, I was unconscious for the rest. My best friend found me. I later learned that they thought I was dead since she couldn't hear my heart beating. And for a vampire, that's..."

Adrien nodded.

"But I guess it started again and when I came back, I was a werewolf. My injuries healed, and I returned home and found Reggie."

"You can't recall anything else? No ritualistic ceremony? No tonics or herbs used? Nothing?"

"No, nothing like that," I confessed. "The beast just... ripped me apart. The intention was to kill me."

"How can you know that?" someone from the pack asked. I didn't catch who.

"Because the Queen of Vampires sent him to kill me and my friends."

Shock rippled through the room. Even Adrien seemed stunned by my admission.

"So, you're the one," Adrien finally said, shooting his son a strange glance I didn't quite understand. "You're the girl my son wanted to follow to England to help break her friend out of the queen's dungeon."

Sam straightened his shoulders. His father had forbidden him from tagging along, declaring that his heir would not involve himself in vampire matters.

"Which means you two are ma—"

"Dad," Sam whispered before giving a slight shake of his head. "Not here."

My gaze jumped between the two of them. Sam hadn't told his mother about me, but he'd apparently told his father everything. Even that we were mates.

Adrien inclined his head, then stroked his chin. "So, the queen orchestrated the attack. A queen who wouldn't have known about your lineage, I assume?"

I shook my head. "I'd only learned about it right before leaving for England."

"Then it sounds as though Reginald might be onto something with his theory. We've always wondered why some children are born human. Even two of my children are human," he admitted. He pointed at a family portrait hung on the wall, and my eyes immediately shot to it. They all looked so damn... *happy* in the picture. All eight of them. Together.

Something akin to envy pricked my chest. I had *no* desire to develop a parental bond with Reggie—I already had that with my stepfather who I loved dearly. But watching Adrien talk about his human children with equal love and pride made me burn inside. My mother had been right about one thing. Reggie only became interested in me after I became a werewolf. The man only seemed to care about one thing. His legacy.

But Adrien...

I saw the way he deferred to Sam's wishes, saw how he apologized when he'd overstepped his bounds. The time I'd spent in Reggie's pack had taught me that he was a firm, strict man with little empathy or capacity for feeling. He and Adrien couldn't have been more different, and yet, both were alphas.

"It may be that you are unique. We've never known a human to survive a werewolf attack. However, such attacks are rare—we aren't mindless beasts, after all—and none were born to werewolf parents. So it does raise questions."

I could have argued that. The one who'd attacked me sure hadn't seemed all there in the head.

"And when an attack *does* occur, I can say with the utmost confidence, the victim doesn't turn into a werewolf. Unlike all the colorful stories about our people, we aren't some contagious disease waiting to spread among the masses." Adrien paused. "And then we have you. A rarity. Perhaps your alpha is right. Perhaps the attack activated your latent genes. And if that's the case—"

"What of Brenda?" someone demanded near the back of the room.

Adrien turned to face his pack. I followed his line of sight to find a man weaving through the others. He came to a stop at the front of the group, his fingers now resting on the dining room table. His pale face told me everything I needed to know. Brenda was important to this man.

"Will she survive?" he asked, his gaze aimed at me.

"I don't know," I whispered. "Like I said, I wasn't conscious. But..." I shot Adrien a quick glance. "I'd like to see her, if that's okay? Maybe sit with her? Talk to her?"

The man's chin wobbled, and his eyes shone with tears. Clearly, it was taking him a great deal of effort to remain calm. A part of me wanted to go to him and hug him, promise him she'd be perfectly fine, but I couldn't make such promises. I knew as much about this as everyone else. And honestly, I wasn't one of them. I didn't belong to this pack. So I wondered if my sympathy would be welcome here.

"Matthew?" Adrien asked, looking at the broken-hearted man for an answer to my request.

"Yes, yes, of course," he said. "If you think it'll help."

I honestly had no idea what *would* help. Christina and Sam had thought my experience could offer some insight, but beyond that, I was at a loss.

"Who attacked Brenda?" Sam suddenly asked.

His question seemed to suck the life right out of the room. Everyone stared at Adrien as though they believed he'd have all the answers.

"We don't know that yet," Adrien admitted. "Brenda's brother grew concerned when she didn't come home tonight. He went out to find her and tracked her scent to an alley near the French Quarter. He told us Brenda's blood was still warm when he found her. Meaning—"

"The attack had only recently happened," Sam finished.

Adrien nodded.

"What about Brenda? Have we been able to pick up a scent from her? Anything that might suggest who's responsible?"

"We definitely noticed a scent, but no one was familiar with it."

Sam cursed and whipped a hand through his hair. "Then we have nothing."

"For now," Adrien said, patting Sam's back. "But that doesn't mean we're giving up. Remember, Brenda might still be able to tell us who attacked her."

I bit the inside of my cheek. While I would never forget the night I was attacked, I couldn't recall many helpful details. Because all I could remember was pain and agony as that monster tore into me. Doubtful it'd be any different for Brenda.

"So, what are we doing next?" Sam demanded.

"I have a few trackers out right now. They're starting at the scene, and hopefully they'll be able to hunt this bastard down. Brenda is being attended to by our pack doctor. They're currently upstairs." Adrien stood in front of me. "Did you bring any pack members with you from Mississippi?"

I shook my head. "No. I came back to see my best friend get married and talk to Sam. But I came alone. I apologize for not notifying you of my arrival beforehand. I wasn't aware of that little rule."

Something flickered in Adrien's gaze. "Your father allowed you to come alone?"

"I didn't give Reggie a choice," I admitted. "I wasn't missing my friend's wedding. He suggested I bring a few packmates with me, but I turned down his offer. This is my home. I'm safe here."

"Hmm." Adrien considered my answer, then faced the kitchen. "If it were my daughter, I doubt I would have allowed this. Could Reginald have sent someone without you knowing?"

My eyes widened. "Oh, I don't know. I spent a year with him, but I honestly don't know him well. I'm not sure if he'd be the sort to do that or not."

"He would," Sam said.

I startled. "You've met Reggie?"

"No, but I know of him through reputation."

A good reputation? But the look on Sam's face suggested otherwise.

"I could absolutely see Reginald sending someone without Lucy knowing. She's his heir. He wouldn't allow her to wander between territories without some form of protection."

I bristled. If that were the case, I'd be sharing my thoughts on that with Reggie when I returned to Jackson.

"Wouldn't they need to announce themselves?" I asked.

Sam's head bobbed. "But if Reginald did send someone, then that someone very much did not follow that rule."

"Which raises the question why," Adrien continued.

"No. No, you can't actually think someone from the Mississippi Pack did this? Why would they?"

"Sometimes when a werewolf leaves his alpha's territory, he gets reckless," Sam said. "Maybe this werewolf thought they might have a little fun."

"Fun?" My voice dropped to a deadly tone. "You

think attacking someone and nearly killing them is fun?"

Shock crossed Sam's face. He blinked, then shook his head. "No. Of course not. I'm merely suggesting that this other werewolf might think that."

I touched a hand to my head and sighed. "Sorry. I didn't mean to react like that."

"It's okay," Sam said. "Under the circumstances, I would be surprised if you didn't have any lingering trauma."

Ugh. Sometimes he said the sweetest things, and sometimes he knocked out that sort of drivel. I ignored his comment and instead rubbed my eyes. I was getting tired. Between the travel time to get here, and all the ensuing drama, I needed to sleep. But I still had to visit Brenda tonight before I could do that. I wouldn't be able to sleep without speaking to her first, even if she couldn't respond.

"Lucy, perhaps you could speak to your father, ask if he did send someone," Adrien suggested.

"And if it isn't someone from the Mississippi Pack?" I asked.

"Then we're back at ground zero, I'm afraid."

"I'll call Reggie in the morning," I said. Before I visited Anna.

Adrien clasped my hands in thanks, then

released them and turned to face his pack. "Let's call it an evening. Keep an eye on your phones. I'll send an update once we have one. And please, everyone, keep Brenda in your thoughts. We could use a little luck here tonight."

Everyone dipped their heads respectfully, then filed out of the dining room.

"May I still see her?" I asked.

Adrien pondered my question before finally nodding. "I don't see how it could hurt. And who knows, maybe it'll help."

"Thank you."

"You can head on upstairs. Brenda is in the guest room. Just let the doctor know that I'm allowing the visit."

Sam dipped his head in much the same manner as the others, then took my hand and led me through the house. On the way upstairs, I spied their family photos, and my eyes immediately picked Sam out of each and every one. When I saw one of him in high school, I chuckled at his frosted hair.

Sam's gaze followed mine, but his eyes narrowed playfully. "Don't laugh. I'm sure you have some terrible photos of your youth in your mother's house too."

A smile tugged on my lips. Had my mother not

thrown Sam out on his ass the instant we'd stepped foot inside, he would have seen some interesting photos indeed. Like Anna and I dressed up for talent shows or our prom photos. Maybe next time, I'd be able to show it all to him, and we could laugh together at our silly teenage years.

Sam led me down the hall. At the final door on the left, he grasped the doorknob and quietly turned it. The door opened without so much as a noise, and inside, we found the doctor sitting next to the bed. On the bed was a sight that nearly broke me.

Brenda looked mauled.

Mutilated.

Mangled.

I knew I hadn't looked any better after I'd been attacked. But seeing it in person was gut-wrenching. Was this what Anna had seen? It was no wonder she'd been practically inconsolable when I'd first opened my eyes.

Sam spoke with the doctor while I was staring, then quietly escorted her out.

We shared a look until I finally nodded.

His hand brushed mine as he left the room, leaving me and Brenda alone.

6

ONCE WE WERE ALONE, the first thing I did was take a seat in the chair the doctor had abandoned. It was far from comfortable—little more than a kitchen stool—but it would do. Next, I took Brenda's hand and gave it a gentle squeeze. I didn't know her, but our shared experiences made me feel connected to her, almost like we had this strange kinship. Like an invisible cord tethered us together.

I didn't know anything about Brenda beyond her unfortunate circumstances. Even so, I held her hand, the one part of her that hadn't been savaged. Tears pooled in my eyes as I cataloged the long list of her injuries. With luck, her body would undergo the change and she would heal. According to Anna, I'd healed almost instantly right before opening my eyes. Maybe the same would happen for Brenda. While I didn't love being a werewolf, I liked death even less. I only hoped Brenda came to the same conclusion when—*if*—she woke.

I gauged her age to be around thirty or so, which was tough considering she was riddled with wounds. But if I was right, that put her a little older than me by a few years. I glanced at her left hand and noted her empty ring finger. Not married, then. That didn't mean much these days though. Tons of people didn't marry, even though they were in committed relationships. Matthew, the man downstairs, had looked about the same age. A boyfriend, perhaps?

Sighing, I braced my elbows against my knees and leaned forward on the stool, Brenda's hand still clutched in mine. I wanted to promise her—and everyone else—that everything would be fine. But I had no way of guaranteeing that. Just because I'd gone through something similar hardly made me an expert in the field. So, instead, I drew a deep breath and began speaking, hoping my voice and my words helped ground her to this world and guide her back.

"I know you don't know me," I started. "But I'm the only one who truly understands what you're going through. So I have a story to tell you since *you're* the only person I feel safe telling it to. Strange, right? To feel so connected to someone you've never met."

I chuckled, all while running my thumb across the back of her hand. "They say it's easier to talk to a stranger, so maybe that's all this is. Or maybe it's because you're unconscious and can't offer advice or opinions."

I paused, then drew a deep breath. My eyes focused on the middle of the nearest wall, the bland beige color calming my emotions. "Much like you, I was born human. And then, a year ago, a werewolf attacked me." A shuddering breath rushed past my lips, and the hand that clutched hers started trembling. At least I knew she couldn't judge my momentary weakness. "It all started with my best friend, who's a vampire. The night I was attacked, she was off doing—well, vampire things. That's not important. The point is, she wasn't there when I was attacked. I was in a house with three other vampires, and one of them heard something odd. At first, they thought it was a dog howling in the night. But as it grew closer, they realized it wasn't a dog. Far from it. See, vampires and werewolves don't cross paths often, so my companions weren't prepared when a small pack of werewolves raided the house.

"One moment, all was silent. The next, utter pandemonium. I wasn't like you. I wasn't raised among vampires or werewolves. So, I find the paranormal world downright terrifying, especially because these creatures moved *so* fast, I could barely see them. I could hear them though. I heard my friends fighting, screaming, crying... then glass shattering as they were thrown through windows and doors. Suddenly, I was all alone. That was when I heard a noise."

I shuddered as the memories swept over me. "When I turned toward the sound, I saw it, this hulking beast stalking toward me. Even though Sam and I had met almost a year prior, I'd never actually seen him in wolf form. I wasn't prepared. I nearly wet myself at the sight of this monster. On all fours, he came up to my shoulders, and his breath..." I shivered. I still remembered the rancid scent. "His breath reeked of death. I did the only thing I could think of. I ran. But that thing just stalked me through the house, hunting me. When it found me cowering in my friend's room, I swear, the beast grinned. I knew then that I wasn't leaving that room alive."

I placed Brenda's hand back on her chest and scrubbed my face. Damn, this was harder than I'd expected. I hadn't told anyone this story, not even

Reggie, for fear telling it would break me. But maybe Brenda needed to hear it, to help light her path back.

"The first bite was pure torture," I whispered. "Its teeth... well, you already know. We'll never be able to describe that pain. When the second bite came, so did the claws. The sound of my skin ripping will haunt me for the rest of my life." I stopped before telling her that the sound *still* startled me awake every night. Brenda didn't need to hear that. She'd figure that out for herself when the nightmares came.

"Eventually, the pain faded, and I realized I was dying. The blows came, but I didn't feel them anymore. I just felt cold. And I was so grateful for it. Not to feel, not to know what that *thing* was doing to me. Then, when the darkness came, I rejoiced. I think... I think I even smiled."

I cleared my throat and focused on my task. "I'm sure you felt something similar, which is why I'm telling you this. That darkness, that reprieve, that... sanctuary, doesn't need to be permanent. You *can* come back from this. You have the strength within you to *live*. Matthew is downstairs, and he's so worried about you. I don't know your relationship to him, but I can see he cares about you. For me, it was the sound of my best friend's tears that called me back. I've never told her that. But I could hear her sobbing over me. It broke my heart to know she was in so much pain. So I fought. I rallied. And I came back, changed. You can too. You just have to fight for it. I can tell you're a fighter. You're still alive. You haven't given up. So keep fighting, Brenda. For Matthew, for your pack, for yourself. Don't let this be your final moment."

I slipped my hand back beneath hers and gave it a final gentle squeeze. "It's your choice though. Only you can decide. But I think it would be a shame if you chose the other path."

Finished with my story, I slowly rose to my feet and brushed a stray hair off her cheek. "I really hope you survive this because I would love to meet you."

I touched her shoulder and gave her a sad smile. Staring down at her gave me a greater appreciation for what Anna had gone through. She'd described the process of everything, but she'd never spoken about her emotional state that night. I'd heard a little from the others. They'd told me how it'd broken her to find me like that, but it wasn't something she and I had ever talked about. And I doubt we ever would. Some things were too painful.

I had just turned to leave when I heard it. A sudden quickening of Brenda's heartbeat. I stood rooted to the spot as I watched Brenda's injuries melt away, like magic. The long gashes sealed without a scar, the bruises yellowed, then faded, the piercing fang holes closed... One by one, her injuries vanished. And then, by some miracle, her eyes opened.

Brenda blinked, her gaze a bit hazy as she stared at the ceiling. But after a few breaths, her head rolled to the side.

"You," she whispered, her green eyes almost glowing with life. "Who are you?"

I choked back a relieved sob.

"I heard your voice..."

This time, I couldn't stop the hot tears from spilling down my cheeks. "My name's Lucy, and I'm so glad you're awake. Let me get the doctor for you, okay?"

After a slight pause, she nodded. But as I turned to leave, she reached out and caught my hand. My gaze leaped from her hand to her face.

"Thank you," she whispered, her voice hoarse. "I think I was lost."

I knew that feeling all too well. "Maybe. But you aren't anymore."

"Thanks to you."

I smiled, all the while knowing I hadn't done

anything special. "I truly hope you feel better soon, Brenda."

Her tongue flicked out and dampened her lips, which I took as a sign to fetch her doctor and some water. I knew from personal experience how thirsty and downright hungry she was about to become. According to Reggie, werewolf metabolisms were markedly increased from humans. Considering the amount of food I now consumed, it seemed his information had proved accurate.

I reached for the door, then gasped when it swung open without any help from me. On the other side stood Sam and the doctor, who immediately rushed in to tend to Brenda, glass of water in hand. I felt the weight of Sam's gaze on me, so I met his stare, but the sadness in his eyes nearly shattered me.

Shame burned through my cheeks, and I broke the connection, instead staring at my feet. "Let me guess. You heard?"

"Every word," he rasped.

"And here I thought you had better manners than that."

"You're in a house full of werewolves," he murmured, not unkindly. "It isn't eavesdropping when we have exceptional hearing."

Right. I mean, duh? I definitely should have known better.

All right, so now he knew. Maybe it was for the best. But that thought didn't chase away the lingering humiliation. I'd bared my soul, and I couldn't take back those words. Not that I would, especially considering they'd helped Brenda.

"Hey..." Sam clasped my hand and pressed it to his chest. "Lucy, look at me."

It took me a few moments to muster the courage, but when I did, I was stricken silent by the sight of pride in his warm eyes.

"What you just did was incredible." His other hand rose to cup my cheek. "Brenda's family will never forget it. Neither will the pack."

I nodded, then jumped at the sound of footsteps pounding up the stairs. Sam's arms came around my waist and he eased me out of the doorway as Brenda's family cleared the stairwell. As they raced toward the door, only Matthew paused long enough to look my way. His eyes shone with tears, but his face still carried the weight of everything that'd happened.

"Thank you," he whispered, sweeping me into a crushing hug. "Thank you, thank you, thank you."

I patted Matthew's shoulder, then stepped aside

as he entered Brenda's room, his pace slow as he approached the bed. The rest of her family eased back and parted like the Red Sea to let him approach. Brenda burst into tears and threw open her arms at the sight of him. I barely saw him move before he had her tucked up against him, his head resting on hers. Even from here, I could hear him whispering to her, telling her how much he loved her, and how he'd never let her out of his sight again.

Seeing them together, seeing her awake and alert, seeing her family crowding around her sobbing with relief... I decided right then and there not to be ashamed of my story any longer. If it helped one person, then it was worth telling. And seeing this proved it was worth it. Even if the pack *had* heard every word. What did that matter if it meant helping people?

"You did this," Sam said, his voice barely audible. "Thank you."

Sighing, I stepped farther out into the hall. As beautiful as it was to watch Brenda reunited with her loved ones, I didn't want to intrude on their private moment. A private moment that I was sure would soon extend to the rest of the pack, as they welcomed her into the fold.

"I should go," I said. "It's getting late, and I still

need to find a place to stay for the night. Besides, you guys have your hands full right now."

Sam's hand on my stomach stopped me from descending the stairs. "You didn't make any arrangements?"

I shook my head. "This was very much a last-minute decision. I grabbed the dress, hopped on the next bus, and here I am. I didn't have time to pack anything if I was going to make it to the wedding."

"I see. And you can't stay with Anna?"

"I probably could, but I don't want to. It's their wedding night, and honestly, I'm not in the mood to listen to Vlad and Anna..." I paused, then finished with, "...celebrating their love."

Sam lifted a brow and started chuckling. "Celebrating their love?"

"Well! I can't very well say the S-word!" I whisper-hissed. "There are little ears around, and I was just reminded that you people can hear everything."

Sam's chuckle grew into a full laugh. "Believe me, Claire has heard far worse."

"Doesn't mean I need to add to it."

"Sex is hardly a dirty word, Lucy."

I growled something incomprehensible and gripped the banister, ready to head downstairs.

Sam shook his head, still smiling. "Well, if you don't have anywhere to stay, I guess you'll have to stay with me."

I froze with my foot on the top step, then shot him a sharp look. "What?"

"What, you think I'd send you out into the night with the hope that you find a hotel room?"

"I mean... yeah? Us staying together probably isn't the best idea—"

"Just get in the car, Lucy," Sam said, shaking his head. "And for once, please don't argue with me."

A silent challenge rose between us, one I almost fell for, until I realized how exhausted I was. It'd been such a long day so far. Between the three-hour drive from Jackson to here, the wedding, and Brenda, I was wiped. So much drama for one day. I needed to crash, and the last thing I wanted was to drive around town hunting for a vacancy. January wasn't tourist season in New Orleans, but that didn't mean the city was quiet either. A lot of people escaped the colder northern states for a bit of winter reprieve.

"Are you sure about this?" I asked. "I know things are... awkward between us right now." And that was putting it mildly.

"It's a guest room, not a proposal," Sam retorted.

I flushed at the word proposal. "Okay."

"Okay?" He tilted his head as though he expected me to argue.

"Yeah, okay. If you're alright with me staying at your place, then I accept the offer. But I won't overstay my welcome. It's just until I can find something more suitable."

"Huh." He scratched the back of his neck. "So that's what winning an argument against you feels like."

Despite my exhaustion, I couldn't help but laugh. "If you think that was an argument, you got another thing coming to you."

We descended the staircase together, but my thoughts were a million miles away, picturing us cohabitating. I had to tamp back the mix of fear and excitement coursing through my veins. This was what I wanted. I'd come back to romance him, to show him how serious I was about us. I certainly hadn't expected to stay with him, but I was flexible. I could adapt. So long as he didn't leave the toilet seat up, I was positive we'd survive this brief stint together.

"How long are you planning to stay anyway?" he asked.

I didn't have an answer to that. Until I accomplished my goals? "I'm not sure. Anna and

Vlad leave the day after tomorrow for their honeymoon, and they'll be gone for two weeks. I originally planned to go to Jackson, then come back when they returned."

"But now?"

I rolled my bottom lip between my teeth. "I don't know. I'll need to talk to Reggie before any decisions are made."

Sam nodded. I sensed he had more to say on the topic, but Adrien's appearance at the foot of the stairs distracted us.

"Lucy..." Adrien gripped my hand and yanked me in for a tight hug, smooshing my face against his chest until I couldn't breathe. I now saw where Sam's height came from. "I don't know how I could ever thank you."

I anxiously tapped his shoulder, then wrenched back and sucked in a rasping breath. The man had some strength, that was for sure. Guess he was the alpha for good reason.

"Sorry," Adrien said, chuckling. His expression sobered. "You are incredible, I must say. I'm afraid we all heard your story. It was unavoidable, sadly."

"Yeah, it's been quite a year, one I'm still adjusting to."

He offered me a comforting smile. "My

youngest, Claire, is in a similar situation to you. Not your history, of course, but she's new to all things werewolf, and she's still learning how to control herself. Even for those born into the lifestyle, it takes a while to master everything. If you're willing, I'd like to offer you some lessons while you're here. Perhaps we can help you come to grips with your new reality and teach you our ways."

"I-I'd be honored," I stuttered, stunned by such an offer.

"Excellent. Why don't you pop by the day after tomorrow? Take some time to settle in first. Sam can bring you since I overheard you'll be staying in his guest room."

Warmth scoured my cheeks. Man, *nothing* was private among these people.

"Don't worry, Lucy," Adrien chuckled. "You have nothing to be embarrassed about."

"Come on," Sam said, gesturing for the door. "Let's go before one of my sisters drags you into the kitchen to help her bake."

Horror swept through me, and I dashed toward the door, leaving behind father and son.

"Believe me," I called back over my shoulder. "No one wants that. As Anna has repeatedly said, I'm a menace in the kitchen."

"I'll let Elena know you'll be stopping by soon," Adrien said. He walked Sam to the door, then gave me a quick one-armed hug. "Thank you again, Lucy."

Sam and his father wished each other goodnight, then we were down the stairs and heading toward the car. All in all, tonight had gone well. I'd tackled Sam's family, and now I just had to tackle Sam. Metaphorically, of course.

And maybe a little bit literally.

Okay, a lot.

A lot, literally.

7

THE HOUSE WAS silent the next morning when I woke, except for the sound of Sam's snores through the wall. After I climbed out of bed, I spotted a bag resting just inside the guest bedroom door with a note pinned to it, signed by Elena. Apparently, she'd overheard me telling Sam that I hadn't packed anything, so she'd raided one of her daughter's closets for clothes and brought me fresh toiletries. She must have dropped it off sometime last night after I'd tumbled into Sam's queen-sized guest bed.

I chuckled to myself as I combed through the bag of goodies. Elena and my mother were practically twins. This was something I could absolutely see my mom doing. At the sight of a brand-new toothbrush and toothpaste, I squealed. There was nothing I hated more than morning breath. But at least now, I could handle that situation before tackling the rest of my day.

Scooping up an armful of borrowed clothes and the toiletry kit, I ducked out into the hall and glanced both ways. Sam had given me a quick rundown of his place last night, but I didn't remember much. While he'd been describing the layout, I'd been fighting off a panic attack at the thought of us staying together. In his place. Alone.

Even now, that thought sent my heart skipping ahead.

I'd slept in my underwear last night, which didn't consist of much, considering I'd been wearing a fitted dress. Little more than a sheer, strapless bra and matching panties—if you could call a G-string "panties." After braving a few steps into the hallway, I finally spotted the bathroom. Covering my horrifically bare bottom with my hands, I bolted inside, then locked the door behind me. Regardless of our history, I wasn't ready for Sam to see me *nekkid*. Elena's bag of goodies had included clothes but no clean underwear or bras, so I'd need to go out today and grab new stuff. In the meantime, I'd have to go without. Thankfully, my 36-Bs were used to holding themselves up.

I scrubbed my face clean of makeup—I know, bad me for not doing that last night—then brushed out my hair. Once I had it twisted into a messy bun, I scoured my teeth until they practically twinkled in the mirror. Then I moved on to the outfit. It wasn't anything fancy. Just a pair of yoga pants and a V-neck long-sleeve shirt that framed my scant cleavage. A part of me wondered about Elena's choices. Had she just grabbed a V-neck, not thinking about it? Or had she chosen this shirt purposely with the intent of emphasizing my girls? If the latter, I wasn't sure how I felt about that. Surely Sam's mom wouldn't play matchmaker, right? Except, my mom sure as heck would, and seeing how similar the two women were, it made me think Elena would too. I'd have to keep an eye on her and her wily plans.

Dressed and squeaky clean, I opened the bathroom door, and jumped at the sight of a rumpled Sam standing in the hallway. My minty mouth went dry the instant my gaze landed on him, bare chested and barefoot. In our year apart, I'd convinced myself that my memories were biased. That no one looked *that* good without clothes. But here he stood, proving me completely wrong. His rippling muscles practically winked hello at me. And I wanted nothing more than to say hello back. With my tongue. And my hands.

"Mornin'," Sam rumbled.

His deep voice didn't help me control my lusty thoughts. I blinked and forced my wandering gaze up, up, *up*. Away from the Adonis belt framing his hips, away from his droolworthy pecs, even away from his sinful mouth.

Eyes, focus on his eyes.

It was a struggle, but I managed to obey my own direct order. "Uh, morning."

He lifted a dark brow as though clueless to my confusion. Yeah, right. Werewolves had impeccable senses, including smell. Chances were he could scent *exactly* what I was feeling right now. But if he could ignore it, then so could I.

I hoped.

"Sleep well?"

"Actually, yes. Your bed is so comfortable." Horror widened my eyes. "I mean, your guest bed is super comfortable. Not your bed."

He quirked one of those half smiles at me. "Glad to hear it. And I'm glad you found the bag my mom brought you."

Seeing as how it'd been sitting just inside the

door, I wasn't sure how I could have missed it. "Thank her for me, the next time you guys talk. In case I don't see her."

He nodded.

"When did she bring it by?"

"About an hour or so after we got here." Sam ran a hand through his tousled hair. It took every ounce of restraint I possessed not to ogle his body as he moved. "You'd already passed out. I don't think you even heard me knock on your door."

Nope. I sure hadn't.

"Hungry?"

Oh. Yes. Very much so. But, sadly, he meant for actual food.

"Lucy?"

I shooed those thoughts right outta my head and focused on Sam's question. Food. Right. I mean, were werewolves ever not hungry? "I could eat."

"I'll whip something together once I'm done washing up. How does a buffet-style breakfast sound?" When I nodded, he grinned. "Great. Give me a few minutes."

"That's fine. I need to call Reggie anyway." I shot Sam's guest room a glance. "Is there anywhere I can have a private discussion with him?"

"I soundproofed my attic," Sam said as he strode into the bathroom. "You can use that."

Uh, okay. Trying not to let that sentence skeeve me out, I retreated into my bedroom to grab my phone, then made my way toward the staircase. What kind of person soundproofed their attic? Should I be concerned? I'd watched a lot of horror movies in my life, and the basement and the attic were always the *worst* places a heroine could go. As I reached the cord to pull down the stairs, my mind flashed to *The Grudge*.

My mother had always warned me those movies would screw with my head. Wouldn't she love to hear me admit she was right?

This was ridiculous. First of all, it was bright and early in the morning. And second, even if there *was* something terrifyingly freaky up there, I was undeniably scarier. Poltergeists had nothing on the big bad wolf.

So, with that encouraging thought in mind, I climbed into the attic. The instant my head cleared the doorway, I gasped. My fears and imagination had *nothing* on the actual truth.

Unlike Vlad's liminal attic, Sam had used this space to create his own recording studio. I took in the entire room, noting the expensive stereo equipment, computer, instruments, everything I imagined a recording studio would need, plus more. I'd expected dusty cobwebs hanging from rafters, spiders scurrying across the floor, and bats sleeping in the dark, dank corners. Instead, I found polished wood flooring, a long leather couch that wrapped around the entire room, a gleaming guitar, a massive cello, and other shiny equipment I couldn't put a name to.

"What the..." I whispered.

Was Sam a musician?

I flicked on the light, then closed the stairwell behind me. This room was remarkable. It practically screamed "artist," and I adored it. After a few minutes of reveling, I reminded myself I had to call Reggie. I wanted the conversation over and done with as soon as possible. But afterward, maybe I would explore a little more.

Grabbing my phone, I scrolled through my contacts, selected Reggie's name, then pressed the phone to my ear and waited.

Eventually, he picked up with what amounted to a growl.

"Reggie, it's Lucy."

"I have caller ID," he grumbled into the phone. "Why the hell are you calling me at this godforsaken hour?"

Nine a.m. was godforsaken? Didn't he realize normal people were up and already at work this time of day? Probably not, considering the man hadn't worked a day in his life. Not only did he abandon his children, but he also lived off a sizable inheritance that would support him for the rest of his days and then some. Not that I could talk. Thanks to Anna's successful vlog that I'd managed before I was turned into a werewolf, my bank account was more than happy. With luck, she'd let me return to that job. But right now, my focus was more about repairing our friendship.

"Did you send a few packmates to New Orleans to watch me?"

Reggie unleashed a long sigh, one worthy of an Oscar. I listened as he sat up in bed, then mumbled about how it was far too bright out.

"Well?" I asked when he didn't immediately answer.

"Well, what?"

"Did you send someone here to watch over me?"

"Is that why you're calling? For fuck's sake, Lucy. No. You told me you didn't need protection, and I agreed."

While I was relieved that he hadn't deceived me,

I was also disappointed because that meant Adrien's one lead had turned into a dead end.

"Then no one's left the pack and come here?"

"No, everyone is exactly where they're supposed to be. Why?"

I gave my own sigh, then filled him in on what'd happened last night. I didn't go too far into detail since this wasn't his pack, but I'd given him enough to understand the developing situation.

"Okay. So Adrien has his hands full. What's this gotta do with me?"

"Wow, you're a real crank pot in the morning."

A warning growl rumbled through the line—his wolf telling me to back off. I shrugged, not caring enough to apologize.

"Adrien just wanted me to make sure that there weren't any stray members from our pack causing trouble," I said.

"How kind of him," Reggie deadpanned.

"You understand why he would think that, right? And that I would wonder too?"

"What are you going on about now?"

"Reggie," I snapped, knowing I was pushing my boundaries. "I was the first human turned into a werewolf. I belong to your pack. Then the day I come home to New Orleans, one of their human members is attacked and also turned."

Reggie gave a cold laugh. "Which would lead me to think that *you* are the culprit."

His words lit the fires of hell within me. "What's that supposed to mean?"

"Ugh. Look, it's too fucking early to fight with you. Some of us had a late night, you know? Jesus, why couldn't you have gotten your mother's sunny disposition?"

"Just lucky, I guess," I snapped.

Another long growl. "Knock off the attitude."

"You first," I retorted.

The sound of Reggie's teeth grinding brought a smile to my lips. At least we could piss each other off. That was something, I suppose.

"Listen, kid. I don't know what you want me to say. I didn't send anyone to New Orleans. And I certainly have no desire to start a war with Adrien's pack. So, is that it? Can I go back to sleep now?"

I rolled my eyes and mentally noted that he wasn't a morning person. "Not yet. I'm staying in New Orleans to help out any way I can until the attacker is found."

Reggie's silence didn't bode well. When he

finally spoke, his words were clear and calm. *Too* calm. "You're kidding, right?"

"No." I perched on the edge of the leather couch and stared at the wall across from me. "It's too coincidental that this all happened once I returned to New Orleans. I can't just up and leave now."

"You told me you would only be gone for two days," Reggie barked. "Yesterday and today."

"Are you telling me you can't spare me for a couple more days? It isn't like we had any plans."

"That's beside the point," he snarled. "For crying out loud, this doesn't have anything to do with you, Lucy. So one of their human bitches pissed off a pack member. It happens."

Rage shivered down my spine at his description. And people wondered why I didn't like my sperm donor. "Not according to Adrien."

"Oh, please. Because Adrien's so perfect that his pack doesn't cause trouble? Yeah, right. Werewolves are temperamental and accidents happen. If he wants to find the person responsible, he should look at his own pack before blaming others. You're coming home today, exactly as we agreed."

I drew a deep breath, then closed my eyes in anticipation of an even bigger fight. "No, I'm not."

Reggie went deathly silent. So quiet that for a

moment, I wondered if he'd ended the call. But then he said, "Excuse me?"

"I believe I can be of help here. Maybe you're right, and this doesn't have anything to do with me. That doesn't mean I can comfortably walk away."

"This is about Adrien's stupid son, isn't it?"

My own growl vibrated across the phone. "Watch it, *Dad*."

"I don't know why I was so obsessed with siring a werewolf," he groused. "You've been nothing but a pain in my ass."

"Ditto."

"Get home today, Lucy."

"No." I'd pushed him this far already, might as well keep going.

"Lucy—"

"Am I your heir?" I suddenly asked.

I heard Reggie's mouth click shut. Guess my question had startled him.

"Well?" I pressed.

"You know you are," he bit out. "You're my only werewolf child."

"Why didn't you tell me? I had no idea. Sam had to fill me in on that."

"Because you're not ready for the responsibility that comes with the title," he admitted. "As seen here today. You're undisciplined, emotional, belligerent, and frankly, your control over your wolf sucks."

I almost laughed at his description. Truthfully, he'd described Anna. I was the easygoing one, the loving and doting one, the supporting cast member as opposed to the heroine. But Reggie brought out the worst in me. Daughter or not, he and I butted heads like no one I'd ever met.

"You still should have told me."

"Why? Would it have changed anything?"

This time, my silence seemed answer enough.

"I'll formally announce you as my heir when you get your shit in line. When you can obey the simplest orders."

I bristled at his words. As a human, I hadn't had to *obey* anyone since living with my parents. With Reggie, I sometimes felt like a teenager again, having to live under his control. And I resented him for it. Along with everything else.

"Isn't it the heir's responsibility to protect pack members? To defend them against any perceived threats?"

"Oh for crying out loud—perceived threats to *our* pack, Lucy. Not someone else's. I need an heir, not some idealistic girl with her head stuck in the clouds."

"Nice," I sniped.

"I won't tell you again. Get your ass back to Mississippi now."

My eyes closed, and I drew a deep breath. "No. I'll come back when this matter has been resolved. In the meantime, I'm going to stay."

"Lucy—"

I ended the call before he could utter any other threats. Oh man, he was going to have my *ass* for disobeying. It didn't even startle me when my phone rang two seconds later, his name flashing across the screen. I clicked ignore, then pocketed my cell before it rang again. He could continue calling until the cows came home. I had no intentions of answering and engaging with him further. Especially knowing it wouldn't accomplish anything.

Yeah, he was definitely going to kill me.

Metaphorically, of course.

I hoped.

But at least I had one answer to provide Adrien. No one was missing from the Mississippi Pack. Except me. And I certainly hadn't attacked Brenda. Thankfully, Anna's wedding provided me an alibi if anyone dared to ask for one.

Reggie had been right about one thing though— my staying here did involve Sam. I wasn't ready to leave him again. Not so soon after returning. I had no idea where things stood between us. But beyond that, I truly wanted to help Adrien track down the person responsible for attacking Brenda. It felt like kismet somehow. Like this was my chance, *finally*, to exact vengeance on the wolf who'd attacked me.

I might never step foot in England again, meaning I might never track down the bastard who'd tried to kill me. But I could help here and now. And maybe capturing this wolf would provide the closure necessary for me to move on. It sounded silly in my head, but I knew I couldn't leave without it.

Rising to my feet, I strolled over to the ladder and opened the access. The scent of breakfast wafted up the stairs, and my stomach rumbled appreciatively. Reggie's and my conversation had put me in a sour mood, but maybe some eggs, toast, and bacon would improve my disposition.

After all, bacon was the way to every girl's heart.

I FLOATED down the stairs on a cloud of delectable scents. Breakfast had always been my favorite meal, and I didn't see that changing any time soon. There was something about omelets, bacon, pancakes, waffles, muffins, and hash browns that made my tummy one happy camper. Everything a growing werewolf needed. Breakfast was uncomplicated and unpretentious, unlike dinner, which always seemed to put on airs. And yes, perhaps I was reading too far into my meals, but I was entitled to my opinion.

I glided into the kitchen with my nose lifted in the air, savoring all the different smells. From the looks of the heaping meal, Sam wasn't only a musician but also a gourmet cook. And a gorgeous one at that. Apparently, he hadn't deigned to dress himself before starting breakfast. A shirtless and barefoot man cooking me breakfast? Someone should call 911, because I was about to die of happiness.

I stood near the doorway and watched as he moved fluidly through the kitchen, gathering ingredients and dishware without breaking flow. He piled the goodies onto two plates, then loaded up his arms and turned, his mouth crooking into a half smile when he spotted me watching.

"Still hungry?"

"Famished," I mumbled. And thirsty. So, so thirsty. Except, he was the tall drink of water I couldn't drink. Yet.

I trailed after Sam to the table situated near a large bay window and took the closest seat. I tucked myself in just as he lowered the plate in front of me. I had to remind myself to take my time, to eat like a civilized human, if I could even remember what that looked like. My past year with Reggie had consisted of eating my meals alone. Sperm donor yes, pleasant company no. We didn't converse much beyond what little basic training he'd provided. And I had no intentions of changing that.

Sam seated himself across the table with his own plate, then poured himself a giant glass of orange juice. I did the same once he finished with the jug, then waited for him to take the first bite before I followed suit.

Okay, so maybe there was a bit of awkwardness still. We'd never really shared a meal before, so it was to be expected. Hopefully, we'd quickly overcome it.

I scooped up a forkful of scrambled eggs and dove in, relishing in the deliciousness.

"So, how'd your call with Reginald go?" Sam asked as he cut into his pancakes.

"About as well as could be expected. He was in a mood since I called him before the crack of noon."

Sam hid a smile behind his glass as he took a sip.

"But he claims he didn't send anyone to watch me, and that no one is missing from the Mississippi Pack."

"And you believe him?" Sam asked.

I nodded. Reggie's exasperated tone had rung true.

"Okay then." Sam dug into his sausages with a pensive expression. "Then that takes us back to square one."

I waited to swallow before continuing. "I made plans to visit Anna today, but afterward, I'd... I'd like to stay, if that's okay with you? I want to help your pack with the investigation."

Sam frowned. "That's not usually how things are done. Packs remain separate from one another. And this has nothing to do with yours."

"I know. But I feel responsible, if that makes sense."

Sam lowered his fork to the table and stared at me, his sharp amber gaze locked on mine. "Why would you feel responsible?"

I sighed. I wasn't even sure if I could put my feelings into words, but I needed to try. "Was your father correct when he said none of your human-born members had ever been attacked by a werewolf before? That seems... unlikely to me."

"Not that unlikely, actually," Sam said. "Our human-born don't attend pack events too often. Some join because their family is involved, but truthfully, most just go about their normal lives. Why do you ask?"

I shrugged, then took another sip of juice. "I just find it strange that this"—I waved at myself—"has never happened before. But then I'm turned, and now, a year later, it's happening again."

"Coincidental?" Sam asked.

I rolled my eyes. "You and I both know there's no such thing."

"You already know that word has spread about

your circumstances. It's not just my pack that knows what happened to you. Werewolves gossip like teenage girls."

"Teenage boys gossip too," I corrected him. "So, if everyone knows, does that mean Brenda's attack is connected to mine?"

Sam seemed to consider my question. "I don't think we can completely rule that out. While you two have never met, you were both human-born, and now you're both werewolves. Perhaps someone is trying to replicate the scenario. But we also have to consider that this was just a brutal attack with the intent to kill. Maybe it's merely a miracle that Brenda survived."

Maybe. Or maybe this was *all* connected. I didn't relish the thought, but it was one we needed to take into consideration. The timing was a bit off, but that didn't mean it wasn't feasible. "What if Brenda's attacker is the same wolf who attacked me?"

Darkness flickered in Sam's eyes. Guess he didn't like the idea any more than I did. "The one from England?" When I nodded, his jaw tightened. "It's possible. Right now, we can't rule anything out. Not without more evidence. But if it's him..." Sam's hands clenched into tight fists, and for a moment, I thought I caught the sight of claws.

I reached across the table and covered his hand.

The thought that this might be the same wolf who attacked me set my blood boiling. If it *was* him, I sure as hell wasn't leaving New Orleans. Not until I had that bastard's head pinned to my wall.

"Guess we'll find out," I said. "I would hate to leave only to learn that the attacks truly are related."

"You're staying then?"

"Yeah. At least, I'd like to. Until we find some answers, anyway. If only to reassure myself."

Sam's brow creased as he contemplated me. He steepled his hands together and rested his index fingers against his bottom lip. "And if nothing comes of this? If it was a random attack?"

"Then I suppose I have no reason to stay," I murmured, ignoring the sting of my own words.

Sam's expression didn't change. "Is Reginald okay with this plan of yours?"

Laughter slipped past my lips before I could contain it. "Oh, not at all."

"And that doesn't concern you?" Sam asked.

"Why would it?"

"Because he's your alpha. You're supposed to obey."

I waved a dismissive hand in his direction.

Sam's mouth tugged at the corners. "You're a horrible heir, you know that?"

"Sure, but I could have told you that already. I don't really dig the whole alpha vibe, to be honest."

"You don't say," he teased.

I shrugged. "When you're raised human, and female no less, the idea of blindly obeying someone, especially a father figure, doesn't sit well. It makes me sick to think about it, to be honest."

"Too bad you can't transfer to my pack," Sam suggested.

An invisible fist closed around my heart. "Is that... something you'd want?"

As though realizing what he'd suggested, Sam shrugged and returned to his breakfast. "If it kept you from causing trouble, sure. But since you're an heir, that's not an option."

I rolled my eyes. Typical male werewolf response. Reggie had brought it to my attention more than once that my obedience left much to be desired. I always blew him a sarcastic kiss and stalked off whenever he brought the topic up. Sorry, not sorry. Maybe those born into the lifestyle were raised to trust and obey their alphas, but not me. Anna always pushed me to think differently, to question the patriarchy, and, where applicable, to stomp it into oblivion.

"Anyway, as I said, I'd like to stay."

"If that's your wish," Sam said.

"Even if that means staying here with you instead of at Vlad and Anna's?"

"I figured that was what we were discussing," Sam casually said, as though we were chatting about the weather.

"And you're okay with that? I don't want to overstay my welcome or make you feel like you have to accept this. I'm sure Vlad and Anna wouldn't mind me staying at their place. I've stayed there before."

"Lucy." Sam lowered his fork once more and pinned me with a frustrated stare. "I said it was fine. I meant it, okay?"

"Okay," I whispered.

Clearly, it wasn't fine. But I didn't know how to back out without seeming ungrateful.

As though sensing my discomfort, Sam sighed and rubbed his brow. "Sorry. I didn't mean to snap at you."

I nodded, accepting his apology. "Thank you for breakfast," I said, eager to change the topic.

"Of course."

"You didn't need to go through all the effort though. If I'm staying here, I'd like to make myself useful. So I can make us food—"

"I'd rather you didn't," Sam said.

When my head rose, I found him watching me with a mischievous twinkle in his eye.

"Didn't you say you're a menace in the kitchen?"

I burst out laughing. "Right. Well, I do know how to feed myself. I just... happen to order in a lot."

Sam joined in with my laughter. "Let's just agree right now that I'll make all the meals. You can buy the supplies, if that works for you."

Now that was an arrangement I could agree to. Gourmet meals without any effort? Um, yes, please. "Definitely."

"Perfect. The only other thing I ask is you tidy up after yourself and please, don't bring any guests back to the house without my knowledge."

"Of course."

Sam's head bobbed as he scooped up the remaining scrambled eggs and devoured them. Once he swallowed, he chugged the rest of his orange juice and rose from his chair. "I'm heading to my father's later this afternoon. I can drop you off at Vlad's along the way if you'd like."

"Oh, that'd be great, thank you."

Another polite nod, then he vanished from the kitchen, his steps padding up the stairs. As I listened to him enter his bedroom, I realized I hadn't asked him about his music equipment. Conversation for another time, perhaps, now that I wasn't leaving.

I SPENT the majority of the morning reacquainting myself with Anna's vlog and subsequent social media profiles. Prior to becoming a vampire, her following had been insignificant. Enough to provide her some fun money throughout the month, but nothing serious. After she'd become a vampire, people had instantly glommed onto her, and she'd risen to fame. She'd appointed me her business manager, a job I'd completely abandoned along with everything else. From the looks of it, Anna had been handling things fine herself.

I hadn't looked too closely during my time away, mostly because it'd been a painful reminder of what I'd done. But now that I was back, I wanted to ensure everything was running smoothly. Which it appeared to be. Her social media accounts were up to date, and she had a consistent publishing schedule. Before I'd left, she'd reached five point five million subscribers. Now, she was up to seven. Needless to say, she didn't need my help. But I hoped she wanted it. Not only did I need my job back, but I also wanted to be there for her, in any way I could, to prove to her I wasn't going to disappear again.

Images and videos of her wedding were already live, and comments were rolling in. People were fawning over Anna's gown—which was all they could see—and the reception. It brought a smile to my lips to see the success she'd accomplished. Fame and fortune had always been her life's ambition. I'd never cared much for notoriety, but the money certainly made me happy.

Afterward, I unpacked the bag of clothes Elena had sent and took stock of what I needed. Which pretty much just consisted of underwear. I'd have to remember to thank Elena the next chance I got.

By the time I was done settling into Sam's guest room, it was two in the afternoon. I had a few more hours to kill before Anna woke and wasn't sure what to do with myself. I was considering searching for a good book to read when Sam's footsteps caught my attention. I perched on the edge of my bed and listened as he strode past. Next came the distinct sound of him pulling down the attic stairs.

Excitement stirred my blood, and I rose from the bed. Was he heading up to play one of his instruments? I crept to my door and inched it open. A quick peek showed him vanishing into the attic. But he'd left the stairs down. A silent invitation, perhaps? Or did he always leave the stairway open? He lived alone, so it wasn't like anyone else would be spying on him.

I stepped out of my room and tiptoed through the hallway.

A few moments later, the sound of him tinkering with his guitar trickled down the stairs. It took me a couple of seconds to realize he was tuning the instrument. I wasn't a music aficionado. Far from it. In grade school, I'd played the recorder, and then the alto saxophone for one semester in junior high. That was the full extent of my musical career. Anna had always told me I had a nice singing voice, but it wasn't anything special. I could carry a tune, but I'd never be that person who belts out a soulful song.

Eventually, the random sounds of his guitar turned into actual music. I had no idea what song he was playing, but he sure knew what he was doing. Guess that answered my musician question.

I leaned against the wall and listened as he played. The notes swelled in my ears, and I closed my eyes, imagining him bent over the guitar, his fingers expertly strumming the strings. For some reason, the image turned me on. Surely talent like that would carry into other interests.

The notes changed as Sam continued into another song. This one more soulful than the last. Since he didn't like pop music and I didn't listen to instrumental, I couldn't place the tune. But it didn't matter. Just because I didn't know it didn't mean I couldn't enjoy it.

I lost track of time, and it wasn't until he stopped playing that I remembered to move. He hadn't invited me up, so I had to imagine he wouldn't like me eavesdropping. So when I heard him place the guitar back on its stand, I tiptoed back into my room and closed the door.

A heartbeat later, Sam knocked.

I scrambled onto my bed and grabbed my phone. "Come in."

When the door opened, he found me sprawled against a bunch of pillows, pretending to read an e-book.

Sam perused my room, then hiked a thumb over his shoulder. "You ready? I thought we could head out now."

Right. His music had actually made me forget

about my plan to visit Anna. I scrambled to my feet, my cheeks flush with heat, then slid my phone into my back pocket. "Uh, sure. Yeah."

With an amused chuckle, Sam cocked his shoulder against the doorframe and hitched his thumbs in his back pockets. "I'm guessing you heard."

I tucked my hair behind my ears as I pretended to look for my purse. "Heard? Heard what?"

"Lucy," he said, laughing. "It's not a big deal. If I cared, I would have sealed the room."

Embarrassment flooded my face as I turned toward him. "Sorry. I just didn't want you to think I was creeping on you or something. Obviously, I saw your guitar and all your equipment earlier when I was talking to Reggie. When you went up there, I was curious."

"And?"

And? And what? I lifted a brow to silently convey that question.

"Did you like it?" he asked.

I blinked as I considered his question. Did he actually care about my opinion?

When I didn't immediately respond, his face fell. "I know it wasn't Spice Girls or the Backstreet Men—"

I burst out laughing. "Backstreet Boys. Not men."

"Yeah, them, whatever, but—"

"No, Sam. It was great. Seriously. You were great. I didn't know you could play like that."

"Yeah, well..."

He didn't need to finish that sentence. I understood the insinuation. I didn't know because I'd never given two craps about his interests. My gaze dropped, and I nodded.

"When did you start playing?" I asked.

"Years ago. When you have five baby sisters who all love pop music"—he winked at me—"you gotta find some way to maintain your sanity."

"Why did you choose the guitar? Why not the piano if you like classical so much?"

"Because pianos are difficult as hell to move around," Sam said, laughing. "I love listening to people play the piano, but my heart has always belonged to the classical guitar. I used to sneak out to the jazz clubs when I was younger. My father was on a first-name basis with a few of the owners, who would call him to come pick me up when I lost track of time."

"Did your dad ever get mad at you for that?" I asked.

"Nah. He said it was better than anything else my friends were into. One of the rules for us werewolves is no sports. We're too fast, too strong, too agile. People would notice. So football wasn't an option for me. My friends were all on the varsity team, and afterward, they would party. I had no interest in that, so my dad saw no need to worry himself about my adventures."

I chuckled.

When neither of us immediately spoke, I drew a deep breath and braved a step toward him. "I like this," I said. "Learning about you. About your past."

A shadow flickered in his eyes before he tossed me a disarming smile, then pushed off the door frame. "Right. Well, we should probably get going. Anna will be awake soon, and I don't want you to miss any time with her." Then he turned and marched downstairs.

I stood in my room a heartbeat longer, confused as to what the heck had just happened. That shadow worried me. Maybe Sam wasn't ready to trust me yet. And that was fine. I'd win his trust back, no matter how long it took.

9

THE SUN still sat high in the sky when Sam and I finally pulled up in front of Vlad's mansion. At first glance, not a single light blazed in the house, telling me Anna hadn't yet woken. Made sense. Unless things had changed, she typically rose between three and four in the afternoon, which was early compared to other vampires. She couldn't withstand direct sunlight—no vampire could—but she could enjoy a quiet afternoon before Vlad eventually woke at nightfall.

Sam put the car in park, then together, we stared out the window. I'd forgotten how massive Vlad's estate was. Wetlands brimming with wildlife surrounded his home, but last I'd visited, I'd been human and couldn't hear all the animals. Now, my werewolf hearing picked up on everything within a few miles' radius, including the two gators *wrastlin'* in the distance.

"I told my dad I'd stop by after dropping you off," Sam said, breaking our silence. "What time do you want me to pick you up?"

Hmm. I had no idea how long this visit would be, considering Anna left tomorrow for her honeymoon. And seeing as how Anna never packed in advance, I had to imagine she had quite the to-do list.

"Can I text you once I have the answer to that?" I asked. "Anna and I didn't get much of a chance to talk last night, so this might be a long visit. I could always ask one of them to bring me back to your place."

Sam nodded, then leaned down and peered out my side window. "Doesn't look like anyone's awake yet."

Yeah. And seeing that it was only two-thirty, I had quite a bit of time to kill.

I stared at Vlad's front porch and sighed. "You know, I used to just sit in their living room and wait for her to wake up, and it never used to bother me. When she became a vampire, I reorganized my entire life around hers. I slept during the day, woke when she did... everything was about *her*. I used to consider this mansion my home."

"And now?" Sam asked.

"Now..." I fiddled with my fingers in my lap and considered his question. "Now, it feels weird. Like I'm intruding. I mean, they're married, and they've been living together without me for a year. I don't feel like I'm part of their relationship anymore. Guess that much time apart changes things."

"You two will always be best friends," Sam said in a soothing voice. "But you and Anna are heading down different paths now. She's a vampire and married to the infamous Dracula, and you—"

"Are a werewolf and the heir to the Mississippi Pack," I finished. Meaning this really wasn't my home anymore, much to my dismay. Reggie naming me his heir might have changed my location, but it didn't change where my heart lay. New Orleans—and Anna and Sam—would always own that part of me.

When I didn't immediately reach for my seatbelt, Sam flipped the ignition and killed the engine. I shot him a quick glance, my brows arching in question.

"How about we go for a run?"

"A run?" I repeated, my attention drifting out the

front windshield. Dread settled in my stomach. I had a feeling he didn't mean in human form. "Where? Here? Now?"

"Sure. Vlad's place is about as secluded as it gets. There's no one nearby to see us, and it'll kill some time until Anna wakes. Two birds, one stone."

"But your dad—"

"There's no immediate rush," Sam said. "He just asked me to drop by so he could give me an update."

"That's important, Sam. Far more important than us going for a run."

He shrugged, his gaze averted. "If my father had any new information regarding the attack, he would have called me. Trust me, it's not a big deal. I told him I'd be over around late afternoon, early evening. So we have time. Besides, doesn't a run sound better than sitting silently in Anna's house waiting for her to wake up?"

To him, maybe. But it definitely didn't sound better to me.

I gnawed on my inner cheek and tried to figure out how to reject his request without raising suspicions. The thought of running with Sam terrified me. So much so that my damn heart was pounding a deafening rhythm in my chest.

Sam faced me, his brows knotted. "Why is your heart beating so fast?"

Damn werewolf hearing.

"Um." I drew in a trembling breath. "So, here's the thing... I, uh... haven't..." A jittery breath rushed past my lips. I sucked in another, then ran my hands over my hair. "So... I've only shifted like..." My mouth suddenly went dry, and I stumbled over my words. The wolf pressed on my thoughts, encouraging me to say yes, to let loose and run. Only my fear kept the beast tamped back, trapped in the dark recesses of my mind, where it couldn't control me.

"Lucy?" Sam asked.

I quietly cursed, then blurted out, "I've only shifted twice."

Sam stilled. "What?"

"I-I don't have control over... that part of me yet. The wolf, it's..." I shook my head and started over. "Reggie said he'd help me learn, but he hasn't had a lot of time. He's always busy with the pack, and—"

"What?" Sam demanded again, his voice deafening in the small confines.

I winced at the sound and dropped my head back against the seat. "I'm sorry, I should have better control, I know, but—"

"You have got to be kidding me." A furious snarl escaped Sam's twisted lips. "You're his pack! He has a responsibility—twice? You've been a werewolf for a year, and you've only shifted *twice*?"

My heart skipped a beat or two. "I'm sorry—"

"Don't apologize," he barked. "This isn't your fault. It's his." Sam lifted his hands and took a calming breath. He closed his eyes and shook his head. "Sorry. I'm not mad at you, Lucy. I'm mad at Reginald. His primary responsibility is protecting his pack members and the public. You were with him for a year, so you should have shifted a hell of a lot more than twice. That's..." Sam unleashed another terrifying growl and gripped the steering wheel until his knuckles bled white. "Let's go."

"Go?" My head shot up like a startled rabbit. "Go where?"

"You need to practice. And since you have some time to kill, we're going for that run."

"Right here?" I squeaked, ever the frightened little bunny. "Right now?"

Sam's narrowed eyes told me, yes right here and right now, and that there'd be no arguing about it.

A faint whimper slipped past my lips. Shifting terrified me. It involved giving myself over to this beast, this monster that took over every aspect of me.

What if I lost control? What if I hurt someone? What if I hurt Sam? I couldn't handle that.

Sam gripped my hand and gave a comforting squeeze. Something must have given my fear away. My scent? The rapid hammering of my heart? My sharp breaths? The answer was D—all of the above.

"Do you trust me?" Sam asked.

"Of course," I said without hesitation, though my voice was raspier than normal.

"Good. I won't let anything happen to you," he promised. "You're safe here. And I can help you learn how to control yourself."

"Control the wolf," I whispered. "That's what I'm afraid of. It isn't me—"

"It is you, Lucy. You are the wolf. The wolf is you. And until you start accepting that you two are one and the same, you'll continue to struggle."

Easy for him to say. He'd been born this way.

Sam popped open his door and slid out into the Louisiana winter air. I shivered, then followed after him, my arms wrapped protectively around my middle.

"We won't be long," Sam said. "We'll shift, go for a quick run, then come back. I won't push you beyond that."

I gave a jerky nod, all while staring at the

marshes in the near distance. I couldn't focus on Sam, couldn't bear to look at him for fear he'd see right through me. He'd know I was a coward and he'd wash his hands clean of me.

"Lucy." His commanding voice nearly brought me to my knees. When I didn't respond, he circled around the front of the car and took my hands. "Trust me."

I finally met his gaze and felt my body respond. I sucked in a full breath, then another, and another for good measure.

"Come on," he said, leading me around Vlad's house.

My teeth scored my lip. Was it me, or did they seem sharper already? The damn wolf was always at the ready, always poised to take control. If I so much as gave it an inch, it took a mile, evidenced here as it fought to steal my mind.

"Breathe, Lucy," Sam said, his hand squeezing mine.

Once we were out of sight of the road, Sam stopped, then turned to face me. His hands released mine and swept up my arms and over my shoulders to cup my face. His gentle touch nearly ruined me. Memories of us crashed to the front of my mind. We hadn't yet spoken of that night, the one where I'd finally caved to my desires and slept with him. I had a feeling it wouldn't be a welcome conversation, considering the accusations I'd flung at him before escaping to England.

"Focus on me," he said.

I blinked and locked gazes with him, forcing my memories away. Now wasn't the moment. Not when a lurking beast was surging to the front of my mind. With a frightened gasp, my hands gripped Sam's forearms, and I held on for dear life.

"Do you want to undress first?" he asked. "I promise not to look."

Any other day, such a comment might have made me laugh. He'd seen me naked and enjoyed every curve I possessed. He'd touched and tasted every inch of me. But the thought of stripping bare before him right now freaked me out. This wasn't as fun as sex.

"Will they shred if I don't?" I asked.

He glanced down my length. "It's all pretty stretchy. Hard to say if they'll survive or not."

My eyes fluttered shut, and I drew a deep breath. "I don't want to ruin your sister's clothing."

"They have plenty. Don't even worry about that."

"Anna... Anna might have some I can borrow after."

He nodded. "If that's what you want. I can also leave and give you some privacy."

"No!" My eyes snapped open, and I squeezed his arms. To his credit, he didn't even wince. "Stay. Please, stay."

"Okay. I'm not going anywhere. You just tell me what makes you most comfortable."

"Clothes on," I mumbled. "On is better. On is..."

"Safe?" Sam asked. He ducked his head and caught my gaze. "It's okay, Lucy. Just breathe. You've got this. Try not to fight it. It's easier when you don't."

Anxiety crept across my skin like ants. Or maybe that was the start of the shift? I couldn't tell.

"Shh," Sam whispered, brushing my hair back from my face. His eyes brightened with his wolf, his irises illuminating with a preternatural glow. "Keep breathing and focus on my words."

I gave a rigid nod.

"We are one with our wolves," Sam said in a soft tone. "There is no us and them. The wolf is a part of you. You need to accept that and stop hiding from the truth."

A weak laugh slipped past my lips. "Who says I'm hiding?"

"That's what you do, Luce," Sam teased, all while one of his thumbs stroked my jaw. I practically whimpered with need, my skin warming from his touch. "You run. You hide. You ran from Anna when she became a vampire. You pushed me away once you learned we were mates. You ran after we slept together. You ran after you became a werewolf."

I hated that he spoke the truth. Running was something I'd always done. My greatest weakness. I was a coward. But I was working on that, trying to improve, and correct my past mistakes.

"I don't want to be afraid of the wolf anymore," I whispered.

He nodded, his mouth curving into a slight smile. "That's great. Now prove it by shifting."

My body trembled with the thought.

"Close your eyes," Sam murmured.

I did.

"Do you see the wolf?"

I nodded. It stalked toward me in my mind, its massive paws eating up the space between us. My first instinct was to banish it, to force it back into the darkness, to maintain control of myself. But I tamped back that impulse and instead stared the beast down.

The wolf cocked its head, its ears upright as though gauging my reaction, as though it expected me to reject it. When I didn't, a small wolfy grin spread across its face, and it sat, still watching.

"You need to embrace her," Sam continued, his thumbs now caressing my cheeks.

I drew comfort from his touch, allowing it to center me.

"When you two finally join, it'll be like nothing you've ever felt before," he said. "The feeling is euphoric."

Nodding, I kept my focus trained on the animal. Sam said I had to embrace it. So, I reached inward toward the wolf, offering it my hand. In truth, we'd never acquainted ourselves before. From the first moment I realized that thing was in my head, I'd been hiding from it.

"Feel the wolf flow through you," Sam commented. "Feel yourselves becoming one. When that happens, you'll feel that rush that signals the shift."

I nodded, more to myself than Sam. I remembered that feeling—scalding adrenaline coursing through my veins. A feeling that suddenly crashed over me. I gasped and mentally retreated, terrified of the coming change.

"No." Sam's hands smoothed down to my shoulders. "Don't pull away. Embrace it."

Embrace it. Right. No more running. I stood my ground and watched as the wolf inched closer. In my mind's eye, the beast held my gaze, as though determined to see who would look away first. But I refused. I needed to master this, if only to stop being so afraid.

A hairsbreadth apart, the wolf peered up at me, its crystalline green eyes a reflection of my own. I stared into the limpid pools and smiled. I knew those eyes as clearly as if I were staring in a mirror. It helped calm my battered nerves and helped me take that final step, the one that let us merge.

The wolf vanished from sight, but I felt it inside, burrowing deeply into my soul. Heat spilled through my veins, and I gasped, my head falling forward. Distantly, I was aware of Sam's voice, calling my name, soothing me, promising me everything would be all right.

The first crunch of bone came a heartbeat later. I cried out from the force of it and collapsed onto all fours. The second snap left me breathless. Thanks to the adrenaline rush, it hadn't hurt as much as the first, but I still felt it. And every single broken bone that followed. Reggie had told me the pain would lessen the more I shifted, but apparently, I hadn't reached that point yet.

"It's okay," Sam whispered. "It's normal. It'll fade."

Another wave swept through me. My arms snapped inward while my legs cleaved backward. My shoulders jerked down while my rear shot up. Faster and faster the change came over me, my bones breaking and realigning, forging me into a different form entirely.

When finally it stopped, I shook free of my shredded clothing and stood on four legs. Pride swelled through my chest. I did it. I accepted my fate and shifted. I was a wolf!

Wide-eyed with wonder, I lifted my furry, black head as a goofy canine grin spread across my face.

I had done it.

And then...

I started sneezing.

SAM JUMPED BACK, his eyes wide with surprise. "Lucy?"

Another sneeze. Then another. And another.

Ugh! I'd forgotten about this part. My allergies. I'd never had a dog growing up because I couldn't be within a few feet of them without descending into an epic sneezing fit. The first time I shifted in Mississippi, Reggie had busted a gut laughing when the fit began. That was the moment I learned I was allergic to myself when in wolf form.

I shook my head and let loose another string of sneezes, then snuffled a breath through my snout.

"Are you..." Sam paused, then tilted his head.

When a grin started to spread across his face, I

yipped and nipped at his thigh. Not funny. So not funny.

"Anna once told me you were allergic to dogs." He bit his lip to keep from laughing. "She asked if that would be a problem when we first met. I was more offended by her question than anything else, but oh my god, you're allergic to yourself."

That grin spread. Oh, I was going to bite him in the ass if he kept this up. If I could stop sneezing, of course.

Another spell came over me, and with every sneeze, I hopped backward.

"Oh my god," Sam repeated. He leaned over and lost himself to the laughter. When he lifted his head to meet my gaze, I spotted tears in his eyes.

Glad someone found this funny because I sure as hell didn't. I snorted another breath through my stuffy nose and shook my head, hoping desperately to clear my sinuses. How the hell could I even use my nose if I couldn't breathe?

Eventually, Sam's laughter waned. He straightened and stared down at me, his cheeks flushed and his eyes shiny. I, however, simply sat there, glaring at him. Even as another small sneeze snuck past my lips.

"I'm sorry," he said, still chuckling. "But that has to be the funniest thing I've ever seen."

My eyes narrowed, and a low growl rumbled deep in my chest.

"We'll have to see if we can find you some Claritin or something," he commented. "Maybe get you some allergy shots?"

Shots? As in needles? Oh. Hell. No.

I shook my head as fast as I could, then huffed quietly.

"Well, we'll need to do something," he continued. "We can't have you sneezing up a storm every time you shift into wolf form."

I glared. Then glared some more. When my mouth opened, a string of wolfy noises came out.

"Argue with me later," Sam said. Shaking his head, he quickly shucked his shirt and pants, tossing them to the ground next to me. The boxers had to go next if he intended to shift without ruining his clothing.

Manners dictated that I turn away and give him privacy. But you know what? No. Call it revenge for laughing at my allergies.

Sam clucked his tongue at me, then slipped his thumbs beneath the waistband. Funny how my mouth instantly went dry, and my heart kicked into overdrive at the sight.

A voice screamed in my head, one I recognized as my own, and it chanted bad idea, bad idea, bad idea. Look away! I averted my gaze the instant he started sliding down his boxers. Regardless of our history, I wasn't ready to see him in his full glory. Not yet. Not without doing something oh so stupid. I wanted to get to know him first, wanted to prove to him that I was in it for the long haul, and not just to jump his bones again.

But damn... he had some fine bones.

I focused on the individual blades of grass surrounding me. So green. So pretty. And exactly what I wanted to stare at. Nothing else of interest here to catch my eye. No siree, Bob. Nothing but marshlands and gators to hold a girl's attention.

Sam's shift was smoother and quicker than mine. He barely grunted in pain as his bones realigned and he took on wolf form. It wasn't until he stood before me that I finally tore my eyes away from the grass and stared at him. I'd never seen him in wolf form before, and holy assbuckets, he was beautiful. Whereas my coat was black with flecks of white, he was white with flecks of black. The ying to my yang. He towered over me, his bulk at least twice that of mine. And then there were his eyes. A pair of beautiful amber gems staring back at me.

With a gentle huff, Sam leaned forward and booped my nose with his. I gave a wolfy laugh, yet another sneeze, then gestured for him to lead on. He was the one who wanted to go for a run, after all.

He led me into the marshes, our paws sinking into the soft, wet terrain. It didn't bother me like it would have if I were wearing shoes. The sensation of wet paws was completely different.

As we traversed through the marshes, my mind started wandering, cataloging everything that had just happened. The thing I found most interesting was how unafraid I was. I'd never managed to find this kind of calm back in Mississippi. Or acceptance. Changing into wolf form had utterly terrified me. I also never had this level of control. The beast wasn't fighting for dominance. It seemed content to simply be here.

Was that all thanks to Sam? It wouldn't surprise me if it was. Reggie was the definition of a shit teacher. Rather than encourage and inspire, he badgered and cussed me out. He seemed to be from the "tough love" generation, believing that taunting someone helped them learn. But Sam listened, and his soothing presence had kept me calm. He'd given me the ability to accept the wolf—my wolf—instead of fighting it. And as a result, here we were. Trotting happily through the marshes without me losing control.

As though sensing my thoughts, Sam shot me a glance over his shoulder and lifted a wolfy eyebrow. I nodded, silently reassuring him that all was well in my head. In fact, it was the quietest it'd been in the past year. My wolf and I had come to an arrangement, one that benefited us both.

Sam slowed his pace and settled at my side, his shoulders coming to my head. He nuzzled my neck once, then gestured for me to follow. I barely had time to glance at the indicated path before Sam bolted into a run and vanished into the trees.

After yet another sneeze, I took off after him, playfully chasing him through Vlad's grounds.

Now this I could get used to.

Run ragged and nearing exhausted, Sam led me back to Vlad's house. I couldn't tell how long we'd stayed out there, chasing each other's tails and hunting gators, but the sun rode low on the horizon.

Not quite setting, but near enough that I knew Anna had likely been awake for a while.

As we approached the porch, the door swung open, and a shadow hovered in the foyer. Even with my allergies, the scent of vampire permeated my nose.

"*Hey, girl,*" a voice echoed in my head.

I yipped and jumped a mile, adrenaline once again coursing through my veins. Once my nerves settled, I climbed the porch and stole a glance inside to find Anna hiding near the shadows. Out of sight of the sun, but visible to those who knew where to look.

"*Sorry,*" she said with a laugh, her voice still booming in my head. "*It's not like I can knock before entering.*"

Geez. So this was what it felt like to communicate silently with her. Anna was the only vampire Vlad knew of who could speak with animals. It'd come in handy a year back, when she and Vlad were warring with the Queen of Vampires. Nothing like rousing an army of rats and ravens to fight for your cause.

"*Why don't you come on in? I still have all your clothes here. You can shift back and get dressed.*"

I wasn't sure how this worked, so I simply thought the words. "*And Sam?*"

"I'll let him know that he can do the same and head on out. Is he coming back to pick you up?"

"Only if you or Vlad can't give me a ride."

"We got you," she said, flashing a toothy smile my way.

Her gaze flicked to Sam, and I watched the two of them silently communicate. After a few moments, his head bobbed. We shared a brief glance before he turned and headed around the house.

"Ask him to wait a few secs before he leaves," I said.

Anna raised a brow but nodded.

I dashed into the house, toward the room Anna and I had once shared here. *"Is everything where I remember it?"*

Anna's soft affirmation rang through my head even as I scrabbled up the stairs. Marble flooring was hell on paws, and my claws could barely find purchase. I skidded across the floor, then bolted into our former room. Interestingly, I barely had to think about shifting back into human form before I felt the tingle spread through my limbs. My wolf—and damn, did I need to get used to that—relinquished its hold on my body and simply vanished back into the darkness. Was this what it was supposed to be like? More of a partnership than an outright war?

I shook my head and inwardly scolded Reggie. The jerk-face had a lot of explaining to do. To think, all this time, it could have been so much simpler if he'd simply explained things instead of yelling or swearing.

But those were thoughts for another time.

I climbed to my feet, then rooted around through the drawers. My clothes all remained, tucked away, exactly as Anna had said. Guess I didn't need to go to the store after all. Underwear, jeans, tops, socks, everything exactly as I'd left it.

I quickly pulled on an outfit, then wrenched open the closet to steal one of Anna's leather jackets. Once fully dressed, I left the bedroom and descended the stairs, gripping the railing for a bit of extra balance. My equilibrium took a bit of time to adjust, and I didn't want to risk tumbling down the stairs, not that it'd kill me. Still, I'd already ruined one outfit today and didn't need to ruin another.

Anna hadn't shut the front door, so I flew through it and came around the corner to find Sam leaning against the side of the house, arms crossed over his massive chest. A flutter of disappointment twisted my lips at the sight of him dressed. A girl could hope, right?

His gaze slid to me as I approached. He lifted a

brow in question. "Anna said you wanted me to wait a few minutes before leaving."

I nodded, a bit breathless from my mad dash up and down the stairs. "I just wanted to say thank you."

"And that couldn't have waited until tonight?" he teased.

I chuckled, then tucked my now loose hair behind my ears. I'd need to find another elastic to keep it out of my face. "Figured no point in waiting. But seriously, Sam, thank you. I didn't know it could be that simple."

"Well, today was just the start. You took a massive step in allowing your wolf to join with you. But there's more to learn."

Undoubtedly, but I still felt as though I'd tackled a huge milestone. "I don't think you realize just how much of a mess I am up here." I tapped my head. "The past year has been rough. And now I see how useless Reggie is. You taught me more in one afternoon than he has in twelve months. And I feel more like myself than I have in a very long time."

Sam pushed off the house and closed the distance between us in three steps. "Have you talked to anyone about what's been going on with you? A professional, I mean."

I bit my lip and shook my head. "Who would I

talk to? Humans know about vampires, but they know nothing about our kind. I can't just walk into a therapist's office and proclaim that I'm a werewolf."

"We have people, Luce. Our pack members do integrate with society. Members who are doctors, therapists, artists, you name it. We have a massive support system in place for just about any scenario."

"We do?"

He sighed and raked a hand through his hair. "I know you're more accustomed to vampires. But we aren't like them. We aren't solitary creatures who spend an eternity alone. We live human lives and have human jobs. We just turn furry every now and then."

Instead of empowerment, I felt a sense of helplessness rise within me. Clearly, I knew nothing about our community. All thanks to Reggie. He'd let me believe that this was something I had to figure out myself. How did such an asshole become alpha? And what the hell did he gain by keeping me ignorant? I shook my head and combed my hair back from my face, wishing I hadn't broken my hair tie during the shift.

"Listen, my dad offered to help you," Sam said. "So tomorrow, just let us do that. You'll learn everything you need to know here. And when you go back to Mississippi..." A shadow darkened his face.

"I can kick Reggie's ass," I said, choking back my own emotions. I didn't want to go back to Mississippi. Not now, not ever. It seemed pretty obvious that Reggie and I would never have a father-daughter relationship. And thank goodness for that. I didn't need someone like him in my life.

"Sure."

Sam's voice sounded so dejected. Fear caged my tongue, so I couldn't ask what was bothering him. Especially when I already suspected the answer. That wasn't a conversation either of us were ready to have. We were mates, so it seemed fair to assume he didn't want me to leave. But I had responsibilities to the Mississippi Pack, thanks to Reggie. And Sam had his responsibilities here. How people made these mate bonds work, I had no idea. But I guess we were going to find out the old-fashioned way.

"Hey." I reached out and snagged Sam's hand, winding our fingers together. "Regardless, I just want you to know that I appreciate everything you're doing for me. I know it can't be easy, considering our past, but I really am grateful."

His thumb traced over my knuckles, and he gave a small nod. "Of course."

I turned and started heading back to Anna. Sam didn't follow, but he also didn't release my hand until the very last second. I rounded the corner of the house, then paused and glanced back, only to find him silently watching me. Our eyes connected, and something tangible leapt between us. Something I couldn't explain but completely understood.

A slow smile spread across my lips, and my heart skipped a beat when Sam's did the same.

That was the moment I knew: This thing between us was more than a mere mating bond, and I would do whatever it took to win him back.

11

"You should have kissed him," Anna singsonged the instant I stepped inside and closed the door.

Laughter bubbled up my throat. Of course she'd overheard everything. My nosy best friend didn't understand the first thing about privacy. "Thanks for your opinion."

"I'm just saying..." Anna turned and strolled into the nearby living room.

I trailed after her, then gaped when I took in all the changes Anna had made over the past year. This room used to be full of uncomfortable furniture, needlessly fancy lighting, and a ginormous fireplace no one ever used. Now it was a real living room, with a sofa, decorative side chairs, stacked bookshelves, and adornments that accented the room. She'd even moved the fireplace and changed it to gas as opposed to wood burning.

"Wow," I whispered.

"Oh, yeah." She paused and studied the room with her hands perched on her hips. "Looks a bit more modern now, hey? Less stuffy old vampire."

I chuckled. "Stuffy old vampire describes your husband to a *T*."

"Hey now. He's not all stuffy. Not where it counts, anyway," she said, winking.

"Gross, Anna. I don't need to know about your sex life."

She shrugged, then sprawled on the nearby couch and kicked her socked feet up onto a wooden table. I had to imagine Vlad would cluck his tongue at her if he could see her now.

"The TV is voice activated," she said, waving a dismissive hand toward it. "As is the rest of the house, including the lights."

I nodded. That was pretty normal these days, so it didn't surprise me in the slightest. "It looks great."

"Thanks." She paused and tilted her head. "Where are you staying? Since you didn't come back here last night."

"Um, with Sam, actually," I said as I took a seat on the matching loveseat.

"Really?" Her eyebrows jumped upward. "You're staying with Sam? Your mate?"

I didn't respond.

"Things didn't seem that great between you two at the reception, so I'm just a bit confused."

"We chatted a little. I apologized."

Anna's expression softened. "Good. I'm glad."

"But we didn't get beyond that. We were interrupted. Unfortunately, a werewolf attacked one of Sam's pack members last night." I met Anna's gaze and winced. "A human."

Anna slowly sat up, her fingers clutching the side of the sofa. "Wait, what?"

"Yeah. And, Anna... she changed. Just like me."

"Holy shit," Anna breathed. "You're not kidding, are you? No, you wouldn't kid about something like this."

I shook my head. I absolutely would not joke about something so serious.

"Then you're no longer the only human-born to be changed."

This time, I nodded. "There's two of us now."

"Holy shit..." she repeated. "Holy shit, Lucy! I

don't even know what to say. This is incredible. And sad. And amazing. And—"

"Let's stick with sad," I said. "A woman was attacked and nearly killed."

"Yes, of course, but, Luce, you aren't the only one anymore! Do you know what this means?"

I blinked. "No, what?"

She scoffed and scooted to the edge of the couch, her elbows braced against her knees as she stared me down. "It means that those of you who were born human can be changed into werewolves. We wondered if you were a special case. But clearly, you're not."

Anna's words trickled into my brain. It wasn't news that there were now two of us, but she was right about something. Brenda's change meant I wasn't a special case. When I'd first been attacked, Vlad and Anna had wondered if there was something unique about me. Now we knew otherwise.

"You're right. Oh my god, Anna. You're right, I'm *not* a special case."

She frowned. "I thought we already established that?"

Pieces startled sliding together in my head. "We

did. And you're right. There's two of us who were human-born and now are werewolves."

"Are you having a stroke?" Anna asked. "Can werewolves even have strokes? Girl, we just said there are two of you now, remember?"

I shot to my feet and started pacing the living room, my mind spinning. I started muttering to myself, running through the events as we knew them.

"Or maybe an aneurysm," Anna continued. "Hey, Luce? You okay over there, girl?"

"I think I'm having an epiphany," I said. "Just give me a second."

Anna leaned back on the couch and tucked an arm behind a cushion. "By all means, epiphinate away."

"That's not a word," I muttered.

"Prove it."

"Shh," I whisper-hissed. "I need to think." I stalked across the room, needing movement to think. "Sam and I were discussing the possibility that Brenda was purposely attacked."

"Aren't all attacks purposely done? It isn't like the werewolf tripped over his tail and just happened to maul someone on the way down."

I rolled my eyes. "I just mean it wasn't random. Okay, hear me out."

"Thought I already was?"

"My attack happened because the queen ordered her werewolf lackeys to hunt us down, right?"

Anna winced but nodded.

"I wasn't meant to survive. But plot twist, I did. And not only did I survive, but I also became a werewolf."

"Now you're just restating events," Anna commented.

"Shh. Epiphany, remember?"

"Right, I apologize."

"So, I turn, and the werewolf community goes *le gasp*, our first human-born werewolf!"

"I bet they even said *le gasp*," Anna teased. "All melodramatic, like off a telenovela or something. Wait, what do the French call a soap opera?"

"Shut up, you're getting off track," I muttered. "Sam said word spread among the packs. So what if someone—our attacker—decides to give it the ole college try. See if lightning can strike twice?"

"Why not, indeed," Anna drolled.

"Would you stop?"

She shrugged, but the small grin on her face

inspired one of my own. Trust Anna to keep this conversation light and breezy.

"So, now there's two of us."

"Which has already been established. What's your point?"

"That *is* my point. There's *two* of us. What if they're doing this simply to create more werewolves?"

Anna froze on the couch, her gaze leaping to mine. "What?"

"There has to be an underlying reason. No one would randomly orchestrate an attack just 'because.' They had to know there was a risk, that they might kill whoever they chose as their victim. That's a pretty heavy thing to do on a whim."

"Okay, so say they wanted to create more werewolves..."

"Then that leads us to why. Why would they feel the need to create more werewolves?"

Silence stretched between us as we each considered the options. I couldn't think of many beyond wanting to grow their pack or heck, gain numbers to start a war. But that one seemed super farfetched. Who the heck would werewolves even go to war with? We certainly wouldn't go after vampires. They outnumbered us greatly. As did humans. Of the three, we had the least numbers.

I gasped when the pieces slammed together. "Humans and vampires out populate us," I whispered. "Maybe that's why! To put us on equal footing."

"But humans don't know about werewolves."

"Yet," I said. "Maybe this person thinks that's going to change. Maybe now that vampires are public knowledge, they're concerned that werewolves are next. They want to grow their—*our*—numbers so that we stand a chance if humans ever come after us."

"That's a pretty big assumption, Luce," Anna said.

I nodded, all the while chewing on the tip of my thumbnail. "Maybe I'm wrong. Maybe they want to change human-borns just for the hell of it, to 'fix' us."

"Those are two very large maybes."

"Yeah. Until we catch this guy, we can only speculate."

"Well, don't get ahead of yourself. One attack doesn't create a pattern."

"But it isn't just one attack. It's two, remember? Me and Brenda."

"Playing devil's advocate here, we still don't know that your attack had anything to do with this."

"We don't know that it doesn't, Mrs. Lucifer."

"That's Mrs. Dracula, if you don't mind," she said, winking.

I flopped onto the couch next to her. "You know me, I don't believe in coincidences. And neither do you. It would be foolish to assume I'm not connected. Can you think of any other reason why someone would attack Brenda?"

"I don't know, personal vendetta? Revenge? Maybe she wasn't meant to survive."

"Sam suggested the same thing."

"It's just as viable an explanation as your two wild theories."

I chuckled.

"Look, I know you're desperate to understand all this, but sometimes shitty things just happen with no rhyme or reason. People are attacked every day, murdered even. It's possible that Brenda's just a lucky survivor. I mean, look at me. I went through something similar, remember?"

"Yeah, I know. But if—"

"Luce, I get what you're trying to say, I honestly do. And I think it's worth investigating." She reached for my hand and gave it a quick squeeze. "But not by you. Let Sam and his pack handle this."

I reared back. "What?"

Sighing, she scooted closer to me on the couch and took my hands. Her face showed nothing but kindness, but I could see the concern in her eyes, feel the anxiety thrumming through her body. "You've been through a lot this past year. I honestly think it'd be best if you let someone else handle this."

"That's rich, coming from you," I said, frowning. "You didn't let anyone else handle your issues with the queen."

"I didn't have a choice," Anna said. "You do."

"You expect me to turn my back on all this?"

"Why not? It's not your mess."

"But—"

"Luce, I lost Camilla. She's dead because of me and everything that happened to me."

Her words were like a splash of cold water.

"And look at you. You're a werewolf because you came with Camilla to help me. Our choices don't just affect us. They affect everyone in our lives. I'm begging you. Don't involve yourself. Let Sam's pack handle it. It's their responsibility, not yours."

Rendered speechless, I simply stared at Anna, shocked at the turn this had taken. This wasn't the

Anna I knew. I'd always called her the impulsive one. She leaped headfirst into everything, regardless of the situation. Cautioning me to take care, to walk away—that wasn't like her. At all. I knew Camilla's death had hit her hard, but I hadn't expected this.

"Anna..."

A half smile tugged at her lips. "I know. Maybe I've finally grown up. Or maybe I just don't want to see you go through what I did." Sadness flickered in her eyes, but she blinked it away. "Now, what do you want to do? We could watch a movie till Vlad wakes up?"

A movie? She wanted to watch a movie? While I struggled with this epiphany? I needed to call Sam and tell him my theory, needed to make sure he and the pack were prepared in case it happened again.

"Luce." Anna's voice pulled me from my thoughts. I lifted my head and found her staring at me. "Come on. We haven't seen each other in a year. Let's do something together. Then you can go do whatever it is you're gonna do, and I can pack for my honeymoon."

I nodded, still thrown by this strange turn of events. I wasn't used to Anna being so levelheaded. But she was right about one thing. We hadn't seen each other in a year, and this was our time together. My theory could wait until I saw Sam tonight.

THE CALL CAME MID-MOVIE.

At the sight of Sam's name flashing across the screen, I frowned. I couldn't think of a single reason he'd be calling. Concerned, I tapped Anna's thigh and gestured toward the television, then quickly swiped across the screen to connect the call.

"Sam?"

"Are you still at Anna's?"

I froze at the sound of his grave voice. "Yeah, we were just watching a movie. Why? Is something wrong?"

His breath rushed through the speaker an instant before he said, "There's been another attack."

My heart lurched into my throat. Another attack, another victim. So much for Anna's theory that Brenda was a random attack.

I slid to the edge of my seat and rubbed my brow. "Another human-born?"

He grunted. Then cursed under his breath.

I should have called him earlier to tell him about my theory. Not that it would have changed anything, considering we had no idea who was responsible for these attacks. Not yet anyway.

"My father requested your presence," he growled. "He wants to talk to both you and Brenda. See if there are any consistencies in your stories—"

I nodded even though he couldn't see that. With three victims, it was becoming difficult to write mine off. Yes, I'd been attacked on the queen's orders, but that seemed irrelevant now. Circumstantial, even. What mattered was the result. Someone was attacking human-borns here, turning them into wolves. The chances of it being the same wolf who attacked me were slim to nil, considering the England alpha had regained control of his pack after the queen's death, but that didn't rule out a copycat.

"I'm on my way now to come and get you," Sam said. In the background, I caught the sound of him opening his car door and sliding inside. "I'm sorry, but this takes precedence to your visit with Anna."

"No, it's okay," Anna said, seeing as how she could hear the conversation. "My condolences to your pack."

"Thanks," Sam muttered. "Luce, be waiting at the door."

"Okay. How's your pack member doing?"

"His injuries are extensive." His voice faltered. "But so were Brenda's."

"His?" I repeated. "The victim is male?"

"Yeah. It's a break in pattern."

"If we're discounting Lucy's attack, then you don't have a pattern yet," Anna interrupted. "You have two victims, one of each gender. Build your pattern around that. Treat Lucy as an outlier, at least until you know more."

I shot her a startled look.

"Sorry." She leaned back against the couch. "I've been listening to a lot of true crime podcasts lately."

"Twenty minutes, Lucy," Sam reminded me.

Then he disconnected the call without another word. I stared at my cell phone and contemplated recent events. I truly didn't believe I was an outlier, as much as Anna wanted to believe otherwise. All evidence pointed toward me being the first attack. What I wanted to know was why now, a year later? Had it merely taken that long for word to spread? Or had there been other attacks that had failed while they perfected their method?

Sighing, I rose from my seat and aimlessly wandered toward the fireplace, staring at the flames.

"Does anyone care to fill me in?" Vlad asked, seemingly appearing from nowhere.

Anna beamed with happiness and approached her husband, bidding him a good evening with a contented kiss. Then she quickly caught him up on everything that had happened since I'd arrived. Once finished, Vlad expressed his sympathies but had nothing else to contribute. As Sam had once told me, vampires lived solitary, eternal lives. They tended not to involve themselves in matters they deemed unimportant.

"Try not to worry," Anna said.

I scoffed under my breath. Sure, don't worry. Like it was that simple. Someone was hurting people. I didn't belong to their pack, but that didn't stop me from caring. Like me, these were innocent people who were being punished for being born human.

"So there's three of us now," I pondered aloud. "I wonder if Brenda has a personal connection to this new victim, other than being packmates. Lovers, maybe? Or close friends? Siblings? Roommates? Could it be a family thing?"

"All questions you can ask when Sam picks you up," Anna said.

I spotted the look on Anna's face, then nodded. I got the hint without her saying the words. Time to focus on her instead of the developing situation.

Regardless of everything, I'd come here to repair things with both Sam and Anna.

"When do you guys leave?" I asked her, forcing a change in conversation.

She grinned at me, clearly pleased by my efforts. "Tomorrow night. It'll take us a few nights to get to the Isles since we can't travel during the day."

"Do you have arrangements for daylight hours?"

Anna chuckled. "Actually, tourism has really taken off for vampires. Remember how when we first came out to the public, businesses started cropping up with synthesized blood products?"

I nodded.

"Well, that's extended into almost every industry out there. Airbnb now offers vampire accommodations with UV ray-proof windows, stocked with bottled blood, and some even have coffins for those who prefer to remain traditional."

I snickered at the image she presented.

"Even the airports have vampire-approved accommodations in case of delayed flights or whatnot. The planes aren't quite equipped yet, but I've heard talk of proposals to install UV-proof windows to provide a safe flight for all."

"Wow."

"Crazy, huh? Soon, the sun will be little more than an inconvenience."

I nodded. Strange how much the world had changed in such a short amount of time. In two years, we'd gone from absolutely ignorant about the paranormal to designing a world around them to accommodate their—our—special needs. It made me wonder how the public would react to werewolves and if they'd launch businesses to best suit our needs. Like shiftable clothing. Now that would be nice.

"How much do you have left to pack?"

"Just a few random things. Toiletries and such. But I can take care of all that tomorrow."

I gave another slow nod.

"Luce, come on." Anna patted the seat next to her on the couch. "I know your mind is preoccupied. And I know you're struggling right now. But Sam won't be here for another twenty minutes or so."

"Right. Sorry. My brain is just everywhere right now."

"Understandably. Maybe I can help distract you. Tell me about Mississippi."

I blew out a long breath. "There's not much to tell. I absolutely hate my sperm donor. Reggie is a piece of work, alright."

"I figured, considering he abandoned you and

your mom. Good people don't do that."

"Yeah."

"What about your pack? Are they nice?"

I wiggled my hand. "Some. Some not so much. The inner members are all really close to Reggie, so they were excited to hear that one of his daughters would be joining. I have no idea what they think about me being the heir though."

"You're the heir?" she asked, her eyes widening.

"Oh, yeah. Reggie made that decision without asking me first. I just learned about it recently, actually."

"Asshole," she muttered.

"Definitely a dickwad."

Her lips curled upward at my choice of insult. "And your mother? How's she handling all this?"

"Better now that some time has passed. She wasn't too happy about any of it in the beginning."

"Understandably. She and I spoke a few times while you were away, but never about you. I think we both understood that was a forbidden topic."

"I apologized to Sam for running away, but I never apologized to you," I said. I reached for Anna's hand and gave it a squeeze. "Sam pointed out that I run away when things get difficult. And things got really difficult."

She nodded.

"I shouldn't have bolted like that. And I certainly shouldn't have hidden from you for so long. I know you don't hold a grudge, but I do want to say I'm sorry. I'm trying to be better. Trying to be stronger. Sam helped me with my wolf today, and already I feel like I'm on the right path."

Anna leaned in and hugged me. "You're my sister. No matter what happens, I will always be here for you. I love you."

"I know," I said, parroting her favorite line from Star Wars.

Anna laughed, then leaned back.

The sound of an approaching car perked our ears. "That'll be Sam."

"Please be careful. With everything." Anna swept me in for a second hug. "I'll be home in two weeks. When I return, you better be here, alive and well. And preferably, doing Sam."

"Anna!" I scolded.

She laughed, then nudged me off the couch and toward the front door. "Go. Don't keep him waiting. But remember what I said. Be careful. I love you."

"I love you too," I said.

With a final smile, I slipped out the door and headed for Sam's car.

12

Sam's strained mood kept me silent as he drove us back to his father's house. Every now and then, I braved a glance. And every time my eyes landed on him, he tensed, his hands gripping the steering wheel until the leather stitches nearly popped. He kept his gaze on the road, but I sensed his focus was more on me—gauging my reaction, perhaps?

After a few minutes of us playing eye-tag, I finally gave in. I pulled on the seat belt to loosen it, then angled my body toward him, tucking my feet under my butt. Sam shot me another look, his mouth still a flat line.

"Alright, let's hear it."

His fingers tightened, and I swear, the poor steering wheel groaned in pain.

"Sam."

"His name is Daniel," he said.

Four little words, yet they told me everything I needed to know. This Daniel must have meant something to Sam. I heard it in the tremor of his voice, saw it in the tightening of his jaw. I'd never noticed it before, but Sam had a slight tic that pulsed near his jaw, one that was rapidly flashing right now. A sign that he was beyond pissed.

I took a moment to catalogue my thoughts. Daniel. Male. A deviation from Brenda and myself. Did gender matter? Probably not. But we'd soon find out.

"He was found in his house by his mother," Sam continued, his voice thick with emotion. "They'd planned to meet tonight, and when he didn't show, she went to his place to check on him."

I nodded. I didn't ask if Daniel still lived. Sam had said his name is Daniel, not was.

"Any change in his condition?" I asked instead.

"Not yet."

"He's at your father's?"

A single nod.

Unable to take it any longer, I braved resting a hand on Sam's thigh. He didn't jump, but I felt every muscle beneath my palm tense. His narrowed gaze briefly flicked my way before he forced his eyes back on the road. But he didn't move away. If anything, he seemed to inch closer to me, as far as his seat belt would allow.

I didn't offer any empty platitudes or promises that Daniel would be fine. We didn't know that for sure. Brenda and I had survived, but it only took that one time to prove me wrong. Instead, I offered companionship and sympathy, enough that his mood seemed slightly improved by the time we pulled up in front of his father's house.

Yet again, cars littered the driveway and street. And I caught sight of silhouettes moving in front of the house windows.

Sam killed the engine but didn't open the door. Instead, he turned toward me, his face a grim mask. "Daniel was once my best friend."

A lump formed in my throat. I was intimately familiar with this scenario. I still remembered the night I'd found Anna in that back alley, clutched in Vlad's arms and covered in blood. The sight had taken fifty years off my life. The next three nights had been the most harrowing I'd ever faced, wondering if she'd wake, despite Vlad's assurances that she would. To see Sam going through this now brought tears to my eyes.

"I need to find this asshole," Sam growled. "Before they hurt someone else."

"And we will." We had to. "What have you learned so far?"

"Nothing. I asked my father to wait until you arrived."

"Me?" I squeaked. Why me? I had no place in Sam's pack.

"To save us the hassle of repeating everything over and over again. You're the last to arrive, so let's go."

He shoved open his door, and I scrambled to do the same. This time, he didn't wait for me to catch up before leading me inside the house. It was like entering a strategic war room. People gathered in groups, some hovering over a table covered with a map, while others stood nearby with cell phones pressed to their ears. A single woman sat at the back of the room, her purse clutched in her hands, and her face as pale as a ghost. I didn't need to read minds to know she was Daniel's mother. Elena sat next to her, a silent comforting presence. When she caught sight of me and Sam, she offered a slight smile, then turned her focus back to Daniel's mother.

It was all a bit overwhelming. So many werewolves crammed into one space, all anxious to find the person responsible for these attacks.

"Ah, Lucy." Adrien straightened and pushed away from the table. "Come on in. We've been waiting for you."

"So Sam said. Sorry to keep you waiting."

"Not at all. The last members arrived only minutes before you."

Phew. Relief loosened my muscles. Muscles that quickly tightened again when we entered the dining room to find the rest of the pack once again staring at me.

"Very well," Adrien said. "May I have everyone's attention, please." I liked that he'd added the please, even though it wasn't needed. He carried about him a sense of leadership, one that commanded the attention of every last werewolf present. Including me.

"Let's get started. I received a call from Daniel's mother, Maria, around eighteen hundred hours. She'd grown concerned when he hadn't arrived for their scheduled plans. After a few unanswered calls, she decided it best to check on him in person. When she arrived, she noted his front door had been broken open. Maria entered Daniel's residence and immediately scented blood."

Then Maria was a werewolf. I made a mental note for myself and continued listening.

"Maria found Daniel on the second floor, alive but badly injured. It's clear he was attacked by a werewolf, much like Brenda. Maria immediately phoned me, and I dispatched a team to not only assess Daniel's medical condition, but also to retrieve him and bring him here. He's upstairs and currently in critical but stable condition."

Meaning the pack doctor was also here.

"What did the team find?" a voice chirped from somewhere near the back of the room. "Any evidence at all?"

Adrien sighed. "The team picked up an unfamiliar male scent, but the trail ran cold a few miles away from Daniel's residence, where it vanished into the marshlands."

Even I cursed at that one. Clever way to mask one's odor.

"Joseph is the team leader and has memorized

the scent. With luck, we will be able to track down this perpetrator."

"Any other leads?" another asked.

Adrien shook his head. "At this time, we are still investigating. I summoned you all here to discuss how we, as a pack, will proceed."

If possible, the tension in the room spiked.

"As this is our second member attacked in as many nights, I believe the best path is to declare a prolonged state of emergency. So far, the victims all appear to be human-born members. Therefore, all human-born members must, from here on out, pair up with a wolf-born member. I do this not to restrict your rights or cause you any grief but to protect you. I don't wish to see any more of our members harmed. Elena has created a spreadsheet and numbered everyone off. Please refer to it to find your partner." Adrien began circling the dining room table. "I know this is an inconvenience, but we must protect our own. It will be up to you and your partner to handle your living arrangements. Compromise is key here. We understand this situation isn't ideal, but we must all do our part to protect one another."

A low murmuring broke out among the pack members, so much so that Adrien turned and pinned them all with a severe look. One that immediately had them quieting down.

"If for some reason your pairing isn't acceptable, please speak with Elena. She will do what she can to change your partner. But I caution you, only extreme circumstances will be taken into consideration. If you wish for a new partner simply because the two of you don't get along, tough. Am I clear?"

"Yes, Alpha," came the pack's response.

Adrien faced me and Sam, and for a brief moment, I caught sight of the emotions he wanted to keep hidden from the others. Shadows bruised the skin beneath his creased eyes, and his mouth flattened into a familiar grim line—the same look Sam had worn not moments ago.

"I've specifically paired you two together," Adrien murmured. "I want you to work closely with Joseph. Find this asshole. Find him and put an end to this mess."

Even I knew what he meant, and my stomach dropped at the implication.

"What about the girls?" Sam asked. "Izzy and Monique?"

It took me a moment to recall those familiar names, but then I remembered our conversation last night regarding Sam's five sisters. Adrien had stated two were born human. A nagging fear crept into my bones. The thought of Sam's sisters being vulnerable made it hard to breathe.

Adrien shot me a knowing look, his emotions clearly in tune with mine. "Monique is still too young to go unsupervised. So she'll remain by your mother's side. And we paired Izzy with Gabriel."

Relief loosened Sam's shoulders, which told me everything I needed to know about this Gabriel.

"She'll hate every moment of it," Adrien continued. "But he'll tear apart anyone who lays a hand on her."

"Good." Sam nodded while carding a hand through his hair. "That's good. And hopefully, this won't last long."

"That's up to you two and Joseph," Adrien commented, his glance turning stern. "Catch him. End this. For our family and everyone else's too."

Sam turned and glanced into the hallway, his gaze straying toward the stairs. "I need to see him. But tell Joseph I want to speak to him before he leaves."

"Of course. He'll be waiting." Adrien dropped a hand on Sam's shoulder, his expression softening as he stared at his son. Not that Sam saw it. I did though. Their love for one another brought a smile to my lips. It reminded me of my father, my true father —the one who'd raised me. I didn't biologically belong to him, but I knew that man would go to hell and back for me. And from the looks of it, so would Adrien.

Sam started toward the stairs, then paused at the first step and glanced back at me. "You coming?"

"Oh..." I murmured. "I can, I mean, if you want to be alone with Daniel, I completely understand."

With a hint of a smile, Sam gestured for me to follow before he headed upstairs.

"A moment, Lucy, please," Adrien said.

I paused.

"Sam mentioned you shifted today. I wanted to offer my congratulations. But I'm concerned about your training with Reginald."

Who wasn't?

"Is this sort of thing common in his pack? This lack of preparedness?"

I lifted a shoulder. "I don't know. No one has joined the pack since I arrived. But I can tell you his people are certainly well trained. I don't like the man, but he does seem to have everything under control."

"Except you?" Adrien asked, his head cocked as he considered me.

I choked back a laugh, knowing now wasn't the appropriate moment. Instead, I nodded. "Yeah, that seems about right."

"I trust that you know what you're doing?" Adrien pushed. "Here, I mean. With my son."

Knowing Sam could hear us, heat flushed my cheeks. "No, sir. Truthfully, I haven't the foggiest idea."

To that, Adrien did chuckle. "Well, I suppose I should appreciate your candor."

I started toward the stairs but was stopped by Adrien's hand on my shoulder. I lifted my gaze to his, my brow morphing into a frown at the sight of his scowl.

"Don't hurt him again," Adrien stated.

I forced a swallow. "That is the last thing I want to do."

"Good. Now, off with you. My son is waiting."

And listening too, most likely. Ah well. I'd just have to accept that nothing would ever be private in my life again. C'est la vie.

Before Adrien could delay me further, I jogged up the stairs and followed my nose to a different guest bedroom. Sam sat inside the room, next to who I assumed was Daniel. After seeing Brenda, Daniel's condition didn't shock me, but I did feel a wave of sympathy as I slowly entered.

"Can you fix him?" Sam asked, his voice barely more than a breathy whisper.

"Fix him?"

"Like you did for Brenda."

"Oh, Sam." Every bone in my body urged me to fold my arms around his shoulders and hold him close. "I didn't fix Brenda. I just… gave her a reason to fight."

"Can't you do that for Daniel too?"

I stared down at Sam, my throat welling shut. I had to cough to clear it before speaking. "No, but I think you can."

"Me?"

"Yeah, you. Go on, take his hand."

Sam hesitated for a moment, then did exactly as I said. I stared at their joined hands, one pale, the other dark.

"Now talk to him. Give him something to hold on to, something to fight for."

"That easy, huh?"

"No. There's nothing easy about this." I rested my hands on Sam's shoulders and offered whatever silent encouragement he needed. "All you can do is try. It can't hurt."

Sam shifted in his seat, then adjusted his grip on Daniel's hand and leaned forward, my hands slipping off his shoulders. When he started speaking, I backed up to the door, wanting to give them a little privacy. But it didn't stop his words from reaching my ears.

"I never did tell you that I forgive you," Sam said. "And I should have. But I want you to know I've thought about you. And that I miss you. I miss causing trouble with you. I knew the second you and Grace saw each other that you were destined to be together. I should have forgiven you immediately. Even I know there's no ignoring the mating call. But I was stubborn and so full of pride. All I saw was my best friend stealing my girl."

Oh shit. Guess that meant Daniel and Brenda weren't lovers. I crossed that off my mental list.

I glanced at the door, my back to Sam as I tried to give them privacy. I would have heard him from anywhere in the house, but a semblance of privacy was better than nothing.

"I should have told you." Sam leaned forward, his head bowed over their hands. "So you need to fight this. You need to wake up so that you can hear me apologize for being such a stubborn jackass. And don't tell me you're not interested in seeing that."

I almost chuckled.

"I'd also like to know where Grace is. She should be at your side right now, causing one hell of a ruckus, ordering you to wake up. You know she wouldn't stand for this sort of laziness. Napping on the job, I mean really."

I couldn't help but smile.

"So, you better wake the hell up. That's an order. And since I'm the heir, you can't refuse me. You hear me? There will be no dying for you today."

Sam heard Daniel's heartbeat quicken the same time I did. We both straightened, but it was Sam's relieved laughter that allowed me to relax. Geez, I wasn't cut out for all this drama. But I did turn and watch as all the wounds healed and vanished from Daniel's russet skin.

Sam leaned back in his chair and gave another laugh. He hadn't seen this part last night. Quite miraculous when you think about it. One moment, Daniel had possessed the pallor of a corpse, and now, he seemed to practically glow with life.

Daniel's eyelashes fluttered against his cheeks, then his eyes opened. His head turned on the pillow, and he lit up at the sight of Sam sitting next to his bed.

"Damn. I must be dead," Daniel rasped.

Sam gave a playful growl. "Nah. But you came darn close. Glad to see you awake."

"Awake, huh?" Daniel lifted his hands and studied them in the pale-yellow bedroom light. I guess he saw what he needed because he lowered them onto his stomach, then turned to face Sam. "So, glad to hear you finally forgive me."

"What? You actually heard that?"

Daniel gave a hoarse chuckle. "Who couldn't hear you? And to answer your other question, Grace is in Texas, visiting her mother."

"Oh, I doubt that," Sam said. "Mom's probably already called her. And if I know Grace, she's hauling ass to get back here, ready to whoop you for scaring the hell out of her. Nothing could keep her away from you."

"Not even you," Daniel said, laughing.

I sucked in a sharp breath through my teeth. That seemed a dangerous joke to make at the beginning of a reconciled friendship. Call me cautious, but I would have stuck to safer jokes for the first little while.

Daniel clutched his ribs and groaned, even as he continued laughing. I shook my head. Strange creatures, men were. One moment fighting over a woman, then best bros the next, as though no time had passed between.

"I'm sure my old man already knows you're awake." Sam slapped his hands on his thighs, then pushed to his feet. "I'll let the doctor check on you and double-check to make sure someone has, in fact, phoned Grace."

"Thanks, man," Daniel said. "It was weird. I could hear you, but I couldn't answer." He stared down at his own body and grimaced. "So what, I'm, like, a werewolf now?"

"Just focus on getting better," Sam said. "I'll check on you in a few days, see how you're feeling."

A light tap on the door behind me ended their conversation. I moved out of the way just as the doctor nudged it open.

"That's our cue," Sam said. "Feel better soon." Taking my hand in his, he led me out of the room, his relief practically palpable.

We hadn't taken five steps away from the guest room before Sam released my hand, cupped my shoulders, and dragged me into his chest. His arms tightened around me, almost to the point of painful, but I didn't complain. Not with the feel of him pressed up against me.

I sank into his embrace, my eyes fluttering shut as

I rested my head against his chest. His heart hammered against his ribs, beating nearly perfectly in tune to my own.

"Thank you," Sam murmured, his breath ruffling my hair.

I didn't respond. I didn't need to. Instead, I simply hugged him, knowing that this was a moment I would never forget and one I would always cherish.

13

Joseph stood at the foot of the stairs, clearly awaiting us. Once we started the descent, he jerked his head to the side, silently indicating for us to follow him. He led us into the living room and took a seat on the nearby couch. Sam sat across from him on the loveseat. A bit unsure of myself, I debated standing behind the couch. As though sensing my anxiety, Sam grabbed my hand and gently pulled me down onto the seat next to him, his thigh brushing mine.

My skin flushed, and I averted my face if only to keep Joseph from spotting my cheeks. Not that it mattered. Every nose in the house could likely tell exactly what I was feeling right now. Including Sam.

People kept telling me there were upsides to being a werewolf, but this wasn't one of them. I truly hated that everyone could smell my emotions.

"Let's hear it," Sam said, leaning forward with his elbows braced on his thighs.

"We arrived at Daniel's place a little past eighteen-thirty. We assessed his wounds and determined him stable enough to move. Three of my team members brought him here while the other three—myself included—remained on scene to investigate. The front door had been busted open. Nothing was touched on the main levels. The attack occurred on the second floor, outside Daniel's bedroom. The house itself seemed undisturbed, which seemed strange considering the nature of the attack—"

"Explain."

I shot Sam a glance and found him stern-faced, studying Joseph intently. From the looks of it, he'd slipped into full heir mode.

"There were pictures hanging on the walls," Joseph said. "In an attack such as this, violent and brutal, I would expect to find everything in disarray. These sorts of attacks aren't clean or easy. Except none of the pictures were disturbed. Everything was in place. Daniel, on the other hand, had been savaged. How does someone attack another and injure them so severely, to the point of near death, without messing up the scene?"

Sam leaned back, silently contemplating Joseph's question. "So they contained the attack somehow."

Joseph nodded. "Based on what we've seen, I think it's safe to assume that mauling is necessary. We all know from experience that a single bite isn't enough to change a human—"

"How do we know that?" I asked.

"Accidents happen when we're first learning how to control ourselves," Sam said. "We've seen human members bitten before."

"I thought you said none of your human pack members had ever been attacked by a werewolf before?"

"Attacked, no. Bitten, yes. Mistakes occasionally happen, but they're never more than tiny nips. No one has ever been mauled or nearly killed because we teach our wolf-born from a very young age how to control themselves."

"Therefore," Joseph said, "I would theorize that the only way to change a human-born is by injuring them severely, but not to the point of death. Perhaps that's what it takes to activate their latent werewolf genes."

"Which we would never have guessed," Sam continued.

"Until—"

"Until me," I whispered. It was exactly as I'd feared, then. I was the catalyst and the source of all this. The more we learned, the more it cemented my theory—which I still needed to pass on to Sam. "My attack taught the packs that human-borns can, in fact, be changed."

"It seems logical to assume there were likely other experiments done before now," Joseph continued. "Which could explain why it's taken so long to reach this point."

"Experiments?" I asked.

"Tests to see what exactly sparked the change in you. Bite locations, moon phases, et cetera. Eventually, they must have connected the dots that we're only now connecting. That the victim must be near death in order to activate the gene."

"That's... horrific," I murmured. "And sadistic."

"Often, vicious attacks such as these occur in the heat of the moment. The police call them crimes of passion. But that doesn't appear to be the case here if the scene remains in pristine condition."

"No broken pictures, shattered glass, broken

lamps. The front door had been busted open, but that was it."

"Suggesting our attacker has a great deal of control."

"Or that they put a lot of planning into this," I said. "Methodical."

"Which also implies that Daniel was a specific target."

"Perhaps the attacker incapacitates the victim first," Joseph suggested. "Then proceeds to inflict damage."

"That would explain how the scene remains undamaged."

A shiver spider-walked down my spine. To think someone could be so cold, it gave me the chills. I'd watched documentaries about serial killers and the like, but this entire situation terrified me a hell of a lot more. Likely because it was more personal to me.

"The only thing we don't yet know is why," Sam mused. "Why bother with any of this? What's the purpose behind these attacks?"

"I might have an idea regarding that," I said. "What if this is about increasing our numbers? From what I understand, both the vampires and humans outnumber werewolves. What if someone thinks turning human-born is a good idea because it'll strengthen us? Turn all the human-borns, and maybe we won't be at the bottom of the hierarchy anymore."

Sam stroked his chin and nodded. "That's a solid theory. I'll run it by Adrien and see what he thinks." He turned to Joseph. "Have you learned anything else from Brenda's scene?"

"Very little, unfortunately. Hers was in public, albeit secluded. We questioned nearby businesses, but no one heard a thing."

"Further implying the attacker first incapacitates."

A small blessing, to be rendered unconscious before the attack. I might have preferred that. I still suffered nightmares that featured the creature's eyes staring at me in the darkness.

"We were able to catch the scent of a werewolf at both scenes. However, it's unfamiliar to those on my team."

"Suggesting a member from another pack."

"Not the Mississippi Pack," I supplied. "Reggie assured me he isn't missing any members."

Sam shot me a sympathetic look, one I easily interpreted.

"You think he's lying?" I asked.

He let loose a long sigh, then leaned back and slung an arm over the back of the couch. "It's something we need to consider. If Reginald is planning something, I hardly doubt he would tell you about it. It's not like you two have a close relationship, and don't forget, you have a history with me."

Perhaps I should have risen to Reggie's defense, but honestly, I barely knew the man. Even after a year together, I knew nothing about him, other than him being a deadbeat dad. Which didn't exactly give him a gold star in my books.

"Maybe I can dig a little deeper. I made a few friends in the pack while I was there. I could call just to check in, ask how everyone is doing, that sort of thing. Feel out if anyone is AWOL."

Sam contemplated my suggestion with a slight nod. "Good idea. In the meantime, I should check out Daniel's place."

Joseph straightened. "You think I missed something?"

"Not at all. You're the best tracker we have. I just want to get a whiff of this person's scent myself."

"Fair enough," Joseph said. "My team and I plan to return to Brenda's neighborhood, see if we can pick up anything we missed the first time."

Sam rose to his feet. "Sounds like we all have our assignments then." He extended a hand toward me, one I took without hesitation, and helped me stand.

Together, we headed for the front door, only to be stopped by Elena and Adrien. I focused on Elena while Sam filled Adrien in on my theory. Exhaustion dimmed her eyes, but she offered me a beaming smile.

"Will I see you tomorrow?" she asked me. "Adrien mentioned some lessons?"

Right. In all the chaos, I'd forgotten. After a second to change gears in my head, I nodded. "Yeah, that'd be wonderful, thank you."

"It won't be quite this loud," she said, giving a sad chuckle. "This place isn't always this busy. It's just with recent events..."

Her pale face made my heart stutter. I couldn't explain it, but I felt this need to hug her. Just the thought of being heir gave me hives. I couldn't imagine what it must feel like to be the alpha's wife. So much responsibility.

She blinked, then forced another smile. "Anyway, tomorrow. Ten, okay? I can't get Claire to wake up any earlier than that, and I wouldn't want you sitting around waiting on her."

"Ten," I confirmed.

She pushed open the front door then waved us out. "Go on now, you two. And Sam?"

He glanced over his shoulder with a raised brow.

"Be careful, my boy."

A soft smile claimed his lips. He leaned in and gave his mom a hug—and no, my ovaries did not give an eager nudge. Not at all.

"I'm always careful, Mom," he said before ducking out of the house.

I moved to follow him toward the car, but Elena's hand came down on my forearm, halting me. Sam continued forward, completely unaware that I'd been waylaid by his mom.

"Adrien told me," she murmured just before closing the door, likely so Sam didn't overhear us. "About you two. That you're mates."

Oh, shit. I braced for the scolding. To see the disappointment in her eyes.

"He also told me about your history. Your mother, your... sperm donor? Is that what you call him?"

I chuckled.

"I'd like to speak to you about this a little more tomorrow, if that's okay with you? A little girl talk. There are things I think you need to know."

Anxiety prickled across my skin.

"Don't look so scared!" she said, laughing. "It's not like I'm going to force you two to get married or anything. I just think we should talk. It sounds like your education on these matters is lacking."

"Oh," I breathed. "I think I understand it."

She gave me a knowing glance. "No, my dear. You don't. But worry not, I'll teach you the mating ways."

Oh god. Because that was exactly what I needed. I was suddenly flashing back to my high school days when my mother forced me to endure the birds and the bees spiel. But considering all Sam's family had done for me, I couldn't refuse. They could have just as easily thrown me out on my ass as punishment for how I'd treated Sam this past year.

"Tomorrow?" she confirmed, waggling a very mother-like finger in my face.

"Tomorrow."

"Good!" She leaned in and pressed a quick kiss to my cheek. "Then scoot. Sam's waiting."

Still slightly horrified by this conversation, I jogged down the stairs and hurried to Sam's car. He stood next to the driver's side door, arms braced on the roof, and gaze trained on me. I ignored the silent question in his eyes, then ducked inside. No, I most definitely wasn't going to tell him what his mom and

I had just discussed. That was a new level of embarrassment I just wasn't prepared for.

♦

I'D NEVER GIVEN THOUGHT to how eerie crime scenes were. Except, this wasn't officially a crime scene, not truly, considering the pack hadn't reported the attack to the police. What would they say, after all, when the victim suddenly healed? But that didn't make Daniel's house any less disturbing.

Joseph hadn't lied when he'd described the state of the scene. Everything sat in pristine order. Even the nearby hallway table remained upright, with none of its knick-knacks out of place. The only thing that didn't fit was the blood. And there was so much of it. So much that my stomach lurched, and I had to turn away. I'd been spared this sight after my own attack. Anna had immediately moved me into my own bedroom with strict instructions to remain there until they'd cleaned the house. I'd chosen to remain in my room until it was time to leave the country and come home.

"You don't need to be here," Sam told me.

I clutched my stomach but shook my head. I just needed a few moments to acclimate. A coppery stench filled the hallway, one I recognized as blood. But beneath it were hints of something else. I couldn't place it. An emotion, yes, but not one I'd ever smelled before.

"Interesting," Sam mused.

I finally turned, but kept my gaze averted from the pool of blood soaking into the carpets. Daniel would need to rip it all up and start fresh. Heck, I'd probably even sell the place. Too many memories.

"Usually, at a scene like this, we can detect lingering scents like fear and anger. But that's not what I'm picking up on."

I was intimately familiar with those two scents, enough so to note their absence as well.

"What I smell is desperation," Sam continued.

"Desperation?"

He faced me, his expression morphing into something more akin to curiosity. "No fear, perhaps because Daniel was unconscious?" Sam turned to study the hallway. The stairs were behind us, Daniel's bedroom in front of us. "Could the attack have been a surprise? The door was busted open, but maybe he hadn't heard it? Distracted by something, perhaps? Music?"

Sam opened the door to our left. Not a guest bedroom like Sam's place, but a computer room, complete with a plush chair and a nifty pair of noise-canceling headphones.

"He was gaming," Sam concluded. "And completely oblivious to the monster in his house."

"He ends the game," I said, helping Sam fill in the blanks. "Leaves the computer room to head to his bedroom—"

"But he's attacked in the hallway. Struck from behind perhaps. Goes down without a fight, without even realizing what'd happened."

"Then the wolf..." I gulped. "Does his thing." I stared at the stained carpet and fought to control my stomach. "So, that leaves the question, why? Why tonight? Why Daniel? Why here? Just, why?"

"All good questions, and ones we don't have answers to yet."

"Those aren't my only ones. You mentioned you could smell desperation. But if Daniel didn't know he was about to be attacked, does it belong to the attacker then?"

"Possibly. But why would they be desperate?"

"No one's dead, so not a serial killer. But maybe someone desperate to cause harm? Or desperate to increase the werewolf population?"

Sam ran a hand down his face, his own

exhaustion peeking through. "I also don't recognize the wolf's personal scent."

"Meaning it isn't someone you know."

He nodded. "I know the scent of everyone in my pack. When we're initiated, it's part of the ceremony."

I remembered that from Reggie's pack and my initiation.

"One more question," I said. "Back at your parents' house, you mentioned a woman named Grace?"

Sam's mouth slid to the side. "Daniel's mate."

"She's in Texas?"

"That's what he said."

"So that means this was all timed accordingly. I assume Grace is a werewolf since Daniel is—was—human, and they're mates."

Sam nodded, then slipped his hands into his back pockets and strode to the stairs. "It's possible. It lines up, after all. Wait until the human is at their most vulnerable. Waiting for Grace to leave would have given them their best shot at success."

"Then that means the attacker was watching them. Waiting for the right moment. Hunting them."

"Seems a safe bet."

I considered that. "What about Brenda?"

"She was attacked on her way to her brother's."

"And he's a werewolf too?"

"Yes."

The pieces were slowly coming together. "Then you guys have someone who is intimately familiar with your pack. Someone who knows your families, knows your humans, and knows the perfect moment to strike."

Sam froze, his foot halfway to the first step. He shot me a startled expression, perhaps impressed I'd made that conclusion. One he hadn't made from the looks of it.

I winked. "Not just a pretty face."

He snorted. "I've always known that."

Cue my swooning heart.

"That suggests it might not be someone from the Mississippi Pack," I said as I started toward the stairs.

Sam fell silent for a few moments, his hand sliding down the railing. When he reached the middle landing, he said, "Check anyway. Just in case. Best to cover our bases."

"So if it isn't someone from your pack, but it's someone who knows your pack, where does that leave us?"

Sam blew out a breath, then shrugged. "Hell if I know."

"But all great questions to ask your father and Joseph. Maybe they can help us piece this together."

"Maybe. In the meantime, we should go. It's getting late. And I don't know about you, but I'm starving."

Despite our grisly surroundings, I laughed. When weren't werewolves hungry? "I could eat."

"Should we pick something up on the way home?"

Considering the time, cooking didn't seem the best option.

Together, we climbed down the remaining stairs then strode out onto the porch. We were discussing our food choices when Sam came to a rigid stop. Before I could ask what was wrong, he gripped my hand and tucked me behind his back, then lifted his chin and sniffed the air. His nostrils flared with every breath he inhaled.

I inched closer to him, my own wolf sensing a disturbance in the force. Curious, I also drew in a deep breath, sampling the plethora of fragrances surrounding us. It might be winter, but New Orleans never lacked smells. Unfortunately, it didn't take me long to establish exactly what Sam had picked up on.

There, beneath the crisp January night air, was the scent of a werewolf.

And not just any werewolf.

The werewolf. The one we were looking for.

Sam whirled around. He cupped my cheeks and scanned my face, as though committing it to memory.

"Stay here," he said in a brusque voice.

Then in a flash, he was gone.

I STOOD on the porch and peered into the
surrounding darkness. Thankfully, my eyes were far
sharper than they were as a human, but that didn't
mean I could see perfectly. The growing and moving
shadows still hindered my sight.

My sense of smell, however, wouldn't let me
down. I stepped off the porch and lifted my chin,
inhaling deeply. Sam's scent practically smacked me
in the face, and there beneath it was the attacker's
familiar odor. But if I wasn't mistaken, there was a
third trail. Softer. Almost imperceptible.

I drew another breath and started tracking the
markers. Where Sam turned left, I went right. This
scent certainly belonged to another wolf, but one I'd

never sampled before. Could there be two wolves working together? And if so...

My heart leapt into my throat.

Sam was heading into a trap.

Cursing, I stole a quick glance around and found the neighborhood as silent as the night. It was late enough that most had gone to bed. And those still awake were likely glued to their televisions. Not a soul graced their porches.

Now or never, I told myself.

I couldn't let myself think about the next step. If I did, I'd talk myself out of it. So before my brain took control of my actions, I dove back into Daniel's yard and started stripping, discarding my clothes in a pile next to his slightly decrepit fence.

My wolf started prancing in my head, eager now that it understood the plan. She—not it—trotted forward, her tongue lolling out of her mouth as excitement danced through her paws. I paused and silently drew attention to the scent I wanted to track. She pranced in one spot, keen to get this party started.

This had better work.

If I lost control of her—*me*—and Sam was injured, I'd never forgive myself.

"You hear that?" I whispered under my breath to

the impatient beast. "Do not let me down on this. That's our mate out there."

Her gaze sharpened at the word mate, and I swear, she lifted a lip in a growl. Not threatening, but reassuring me that she could do this. Our mate could be in trouble. And we—I—was the only one nearby who could help him.

It was difficult, retraining myself to think of the two of us as one entity. But we were. We shared one body, one mind. I couldn't keep talking about her in third person. She was me, and I was her. And we needed to work together.

In my mind's eye, I stepped out of the way and allowed my wolf to come forward. The shift began almost instantaneously. I ignored the sound of snapping bones and focused on breathing, on remaining calm. The pain would pass. In fact, the less I fought, the less it hurt. And within moments, I stood on four legs while the wind caressed my furred head.

I took a second to orient myself, then I lifted my snout in the air and sniffed. A decision I immediately regretted when I descended into a sneezing fit. I really needed to take care of this little problem. One sneeze could be all it took to alert the other werewolf to my presence.

Fighting off another fit, I tipped my head back and snuffled the air again.

There it was. Beneath the sneezes and the familiar aroma of New Orleans, the scent. So subtle. Almost invisible. But I could sense it.

They were close too. Watching me? No, too far away for that. Most likely keeping tabs on their partner—Sam's target.

My sinuses tingled, and my eyes welled with tears as I held in the sneezes, but I couldn't let them escape now. With my nose to the ground, I began tracking, following their trail through the neighborhood and around the back of the houses. The scent of marshland grew stronger, but that didn't surprise me. The entire city reeked of it. The key was separating the other wolf's smell from the stronger scent of wildlife—and beignets.

Movement to my left.

My head snapped to the side, and I crouched low, listening. Something was easing through the grass, their steps slow and purposeful as they gained distance away from me. I sucked in another breath just to confirm I was still tracking the other wolf. And I was. Evidenced by the annoying tickle in my nose. No. I couldn't sneeze right now.

Holding my breath, I crept through the grass

myself, careful of each and every step. Mindful as a hunter. If I gave away my position, they'd bolt.

My target paused, so I did the same, one leg still hovering mid-air. I took that moment to file away everything I could. I couldn't make out the coat color, but the scent was purely male. And from the looks of it, he was massive. Far larger than me. Terrifyingly so.

Then I heard it.

Yelling. Shouting. Fighting.

My heart slammed into my chest.

Sam.

It had to be.

My target must have heard the same thing. He bolted forward, no longer caring about stealth. I did the same, pouring every bit of strength I possessed into my legs, grateful that the adrenaline surge seemed to tamp back my allergies. I couldn't let this wolf catch up to Sam. Couldn't let him be surprised by the attacker's accomplice.

I pushed harder, my muscles screaming as I ran, all the while listening for Sam's voice. Their fighting grew louder with every step I took. But most importantly, I felt myself gaining on my target. He was quick. I was quicker. Every step brought me closer to him.

A heartbeat later, Sam came into view, just in time to watch him heave a massive body into the air and slam him onto the ground. Unfortunately, Sam's back was to us, making him vulnerable.

My gaze shot to my target, now crouching as though preparing to attack. My focus leapt back to Sam, still utterly oblivious to our presence.

No!

The word reverberated in my head, and a second before the other wolf could lunge, I leaped, paws outstretched and jaws gaping wide. My target pivoted, only now sensing danger. But it was too late. The other wolf barely had a chance to turn toward me before I landed, smashing into his side. We tumbled to the ground, limbs flailing, teeth snapping.

Something sharp grabbed hold of my scruff, and I snarled, ripping free. I struck out with my front paw, smacking the other wolf in the head, then lunged for his exposed throat. My teeth had just grazed my opponent's fur when it darted out of range, then pivoted and snapped back, embedding its teeth in my front upper leg.

I screamed in pain and thrashed, fighting to free myself. Too slow, untrained, inexperienced. Those were the words dancing through my head. I'd only shifted three times before this. And I'd certainly never fought in wolf form—hell, not even in human form. I was as docile as they came.

"Lucy!" Sam shouted.

I didn't so much as glance his way. I couldn't allow myself to be distracted. Not now. Not with this hell-beast ripping into me. I needed free! But I couldn't move, not with my front leg caught between his jaws. And pulling only caused more damage. No, I needed to think.

I couldn't get free. So I needed to distract him. Needed to force this jackass to release me.

Before I could talk myself out of it, I opened my mouth and engulfed as much of the wolf's head as possible, then clamped my jaws down. I felt my fangs pierce the side of his head, felt him start thrashing, panicking, yipping. My leg slipped from his grasp, and relief washed through me for a brief second before the deep-seated pain kicked in.

I ignored it as best I could and bore down tighter, digging my teeth deeper and deeper. Maybe I could crush his head, maybe I could—

Sharp pain sliced through me.

Crying out, I released the wolf and stumbled back, only to see his claws had gored my side. I staggered at the sight of the dark blood in the moonlight. Distantly, Sam cried my name once more, but neither of us could reach the other.

The other wolf towered over me, blood streaking his face and madness glowing in his eyes. His lips peeled back, exposing a pair of enormous fangs. Fear rippled through me. I'd been an idiot to think I could take this guy, to think I could help Sam.

As though taunting me, the wolf's mouth spread into a strange grin seconds before he lunged and raked his claws across my chest. I scrambled backward, searching for a way around him, to get to Sam, to escape this wolf's clutches. But every time I dodged, he was there, blocking my path.

"Lucy, run!" Sam shouted.

My gaze shot to Sam to find him caught in his own battle. It was clear from his position that he was trying to reach me, trying to help, but his opponent kept him trapped. Kept us separated. The two struck at each other, their punches practically thundering in the night.

Sam's eyes caught mine. "Run."

I shook my head. I might have been able to run before, but not now. Not with this injured leg that could hardly bear any weight. And I refused to abandon Sam here. Not with these two brutes looming over us.

No. I couldn't run. But I could be smarter. This jackass thought he had me cornered and bleeding. And he did. But he'd grown cocky. He loomed over me, his head held high. And that was all I needed. Well, that and my leg to work just long enough for one last attack.

I placed it on the ground and bit back a pained whine. Flames of agony burned through me, but I refused to let it distract me. Both Sam's and my life depended on this moment.

The wolf's muscles bunched beneath him, preparing for his last attack. But I couldn't let him land that blow.

Instinct took control of me the second the wolf lunged.

I somehow managed to duck to the side, surprising both of us. But rather than pause to soak in that success, I pivoted and attacked. There, right in front of me, was his unguarded throat. The second my jaws clamped around it, I held on for dear life.

Even as he roared and snarled and thrashed.

Even as he slammed me into the ground.

Even as he rolled us over and over, his claws raking my sides, my legs, anywhere he could land a blow.

And all the while, I squeezed.

And squeezed.

And squeezed.

Just when I thought I couldn't hold on any longer, his movements grew less erratic, and his thrashing eased. He collapsed onto his side, his chest rising slower and slower. Still, I didn't release him, too afraid that he'd recover and tear me to pieces. Instead, I draped over his body and gripped harder.

I wasn't sure how long I laid there, but eventually, a gentle hand touched my shoulder.

"It's done, Lucy, he's gone. Let him go," came Sam's soft voice.

But I didn't. I couldn't.

Because that was the moment I realized the wolf's chest hadn't risen once in the last minute, the moment I realized he was dead, and I'd killed him. With a horrified gasp, I limped off the body and shifted back to my human form. Naked and covered in blood, I dropped to my knees and started crying.

*

ARMS SLID beneath me and lifted, so gentle, so careful. I bit my lip to keep from crying out. Every inch of me hurt, but my heart ached the most. I'd just killed someone. With my own bare hands—or rather, teeth. I'd seen death before, thanks to my vampiric best friend. But I'd never killed. It felt like I'd just lost a part of myself.

Tears ran down my face as Sam draped his shirt over me, hiding my bare body from any prying eyes that might spot us. Then he kept to the back alleys and the shadows as he carried me past Daniel's house to his car. His steps were careful, as though he feared jarring me, and I was grateful, considering my injuries. I hadn't braved glancing at my arm yet, but I already knew it wouldn't be pretty.

Sam didn't bother to stop for my clothes. Instead, he carefully loaded me into the passenger seat, then slid over the hood and hopped into the driver seat. He fired up the engine, gripped the steering wheel, then tore out of there like a bat out of hell.

The instant we were on the road, he lifted his hips and dug a cell phone out of his back pocket. A few taps later, he had the phone pressed to his ear. I listened on my end as Sam updated his father, including the location of the body, and told him to get a team out there as soon as possible before anyone discovered it. Then he disconnected the call and tossed his phone on the back seat.

Only when we stopped at the first traffic light did he turn to face me, his eyes aglow with his wolf. From the smell of it, his emotions were running high right now. But then again, so were mine.

"Are you okay?" he demanded in a gravelly voice.

I gave a jerky nod. "You?"

"What the hell were you thinking?" His fingers tightened on the steering wheel. "You could have gotten yourself killed!"

"You needed help."

Sam didn't insult me by countering my statement. Instead, he growled under his breath and turned back to the road, his gaze never straying from the lane.

"You should have let me handle it," he snapped, his foot pressing down on the gas pedal. If he kept this up, we would get pulled over for speeding. But I wisely kept my mouth shut. "You should have done what I said and stayed put."

"And then you would have been facing two werewolves," I argued, though my voice broke a little. This was not the conversation I wanted to have right now.

Sam ground his teeth, then cursed. "I would have preferred that."

I startled, then winced at the fresh wave of pain.

"You would have rather faced those two brutes yourself? You would have died."

He snarled softly. "But you wouldn't have had to do... that."

Kill someone. Hot tears sprang to my eyes. I dashed them away with my good arm, then stared out my window.

"I can't lose you, Lucy," Sam suddenly whispered.

It took a second for those words to sink in, but when they did, all the pain and anguish vanished. "What?"

He shook his head, unwilling to repeat the sentiment. But I'd heard it. I knew I had. My racing heart told me I knew exactly what he'd said.

I slowly moved my injured arm, trying not to cry out, and rested my hand atop his on the gear shift.

He jumped in his seat, then shot our joined hands a stunned glance. Without a word, he turned his hand over and gripped my fingers so hard, I hissed. His hand instantly loosened, and he muttered a quiet apology.

"We're a mess." I gave a watery laugh.

"It's fine. We'll go back to my place and clean ourselves up."

That so wasn't what I meant, but I didn't have

the energy to correct him or dig deeper into our relationship tonight. Not after... that.

"What happened to the other werewolf?" I asked, referring to the one he'd fought.

"Ran when he saw you had the other pinned."

"Seriously? He ran?"

"Took one look at you and bolted."

Okay. Not what I'd expected. "You didn't pursue him?"

Sam threw me an incredulous look, like I was insane for suggesting such a thing. "You were hurt. I wasn't about to leave you there alone."

Warmth spread through my chest, soon followed by dread. While I appreciated his concern, him staying had cost us the chance to put an end to this entire situation tonight. I would have survived, but maybe the next victim wouldn't.

"Did you recognize him at least?" I asked.

"No," Sam ground out. "I didn't have a clue who he was. You?"

"I never even caught a glimpse of him. I was a little busy."

Sam gave a rigid nod. "Then we're back at square one."

"Well, not quite. We have the guy I—" I cleared

my throat. "Maybe we can send his picture out to all the packs and identify him."

Sam muttered something, then released a long breath and relaxed his shoulders. An attempt to calm his wolf, possibly.

"How did you know about the second wolf?" he finally asked.

"When you left, I picked up his scent and tracked him. He heard your fight and was racing to intervene. So I had to do something."

"You could have died," he said again, as though I didn't already realize that.

"Same could be said to you."

He shot me a withering glare. "I'm—"

"What?" I interrupted him. "You're what? Stronger, faster?"

"Yes!"

Sadly, I couldn't argue that. So, instead, I raised my chin and stared at him from my tiny corner of the car. "Then teach me. Help me become stronger and faster so that next time—"

"Next time," he scoffed.

Thankfully, he didn't try to tell me there wouldn't be a next time. I wasn't sure how I'd take that sort of controlling statement.

"Next time," he repeated.

He glanced my way once more, but this time his eyes were softer, as though logic and reasoning had finally returned to him. After a few seconds, he finally nodded, then stared back out the windshield.

"Next time, you'll be more prepared," he finally said. "Trained on how to fight, where to strike, and how to react. I'll design a plan with my father tomorrow. A workout regimen to build some muscle. Then we'll work on your fighting skills."

Something loosened in my chest, and I found it a bit easier to breathe. Maybe because Sam hadn't pulled any controlling alpha crap on me.

"You clearly don't have any issues shifting anymore," he continued.

"No, that part's easy now. Thanks to you."

"Good. That's the first obstacle cleared." He stole another glance, his eyes trailing down my half-clad body. Thankfully, his shirt covered my more vulnerable bits. Not that I was thinking about sex right now. "How are you feeling?"

"Better," I said. "The pain isn't as bad."

"We heal fast," he said. "So long as our wounds aren't lethal, we can heal anything rather quickly. Except for any wounds made from silver."

"Reggie briefly mentioned that we're allergic to it."

Sam nodded. "Wounds made by teeth and claws, we can heal. A few more minutes, you'll be back to normal."

I winced at that. Because while I might heal and return to normal, the wolf I killed was straight-up dead. And there was no coming back from that. I tried telling myself that he deserved it. Brenda and Daniel deserved justice. But deep down, I knew better.

15

Sam eased me up onto his kitchen counter and took a moment to inspect my wounds. A quick glance showed the puncture wounds on my arm had mostly healed, while the slashes across my chest and the gouges on my side were still seeping through Sam's T-shirt. Thankfully, the pain had started to fade. One upside to being a werewolf, at least.

"May I?" Sam asked, pointing at his shirt. When I raised a brow, he chuckled. "I need to see the wounds underneath."

"Underneath?" I squeaked.

"You know, I have seen you naked before, Lucy."

Oh, doggy. Heat flamed my cheeks, and my hands rose of their own accord to twist the shirt in my palms. I wasn't ready for that. I plucked the collar away from my neck and peeked at my own chest, still slick with blood. Well... shit.

Reggie had already explained to me that nudity didn't bother werewolves, considering they often shifted in front of each other. But the same couldn't be said for me. Not yet. I was just getting comfortable in my own skin again. I wasn't ready for anyone else to see me. Not until I felt like me again.

Sam's index finger caught my chin and he lifted. "It's okay if you'd rather not. I can give you the first aid kit, and you can patch yourself up. Whatever works for you."

Relief loosened my muscles. A voice in my head urged me to knock it off. Sam had already seen all my bits before. So it wasn't like there were any secrets between us.

Time to be brave and take that first step.

I grasped the edges of his massive shirt and started to lift the hem. I paused when I reached my thighs, then threw all caution to the wind and eased the shirt over my head.

To his credit, Sam didn't utter a word. He even managed to keep his gaze north of my breasts to show me he wasn't some randy teenager excited to see some bewbs. Finally, he broke our connection, and his eyes swept south to inspect the damage.

When he finally took everything in, his mouth twisted.

"Not pretty?" I asked.

He shot me a droll look. "You're beautiful, and you know it." He grabbed a clean cloth from inside the first aid kit and doused it in warm water. He wrung it out, then cupped my side with one hand and pressed the cloth against the wounds, slowly cleaning them off.

I hissed but kept my hands to myself instead of batting his away.

"I gotta say, your doctoring skills are far better than my mother's." I chuckled. "She used hydrogen peroxide for everything."

Sam lifted his gaze and gave me a wicked grin. "I do enjoy playing doctor."

I couldn't help but laugh, even though the movement jarred aches I hadn't had a chance to take inventory of yet.

"Hydrogen peroxide isn't necessary for werewolves. We're invulnerable to all diseases and infections. I'm just here to help clean you up and make sure these wounds don't need further attention."

"Like stitches? Do we ever need those?"

"Rarely," he said. "We usually heal too fast, and believe me, you don't want your wounds healing over stitches."

"Then when would stitches ever be necessary?"

A grim expression shadowed his face. "I've only seen them used once, and it was because the injured wolf had been doused with silver. It slows our healing abilities to human speed."

Sam stroked the cloth across my upper chest, cleaning off the remaining blood. When he pulled the rag back, I glanced down to find four garish wounds gouging my flesh. I winced at the hideous sight of them. But thankfully, they'd stopped bleeding. Which meant they'd be gone in a few more minutes.

Without a word, he moved to my other side and studied the puncture wounds. "These are almost healed too."

"Good."

He took a step back from me and cleared his throat. "Right. I'm all done. And you're all clean, so..."

My teeth scored my bottom lip, and I nodded. "Thank you." A watery laugh slipped past my lips.

"This was my first fight as a werewolf. It was pretty scary."

"For you and me both," he murmured.

But before I could delve into that comment, Sam vanished, like mist in the night. Just gone. I sat atop his counter, buck ass naked, and stared into the hallway. Damn. I wasn't sure I'd ever seen him move that fast. And all to avoid me?

I hopped off the counter and took a moment to inspect the rest of me. Other than a few aches and pains, I was good to go. No nasty stitches or gauze needed. Just, boom, healed. Every time I thought I'd fully adjusted to being a werewolf, something happened to prove otherwise.

I left the kitchen and headed upstairs to my room, where the bag of clothing Elena had provided me awaited. At some point, I needed to return to Anna's and pack more clothes for myself. Thankfully, I knew where they kept a spare key for emergencies. Digging through Elena's bag, I fished out a loose-fitting hoodie and what looked like soft pajama pants. The outfit wouldn't win me the Oscar for best-dressed, but after tonight, I deserved a bit of comfort. I slipped into the clothing then gazed longingly at my bed. Sleep beckoned, and lord knew I needed it.

But just as I was about to crawl between the covers, soft music drifted downstairs.

I paused with one knee on the mattress and listened.

Sam must have retreated into the attic. To calm himself with music, perhaps? And if I could hear it, that suggested he'd left the stairs down. Did that mean I could go up and listen? I didn't want to invade his space, but I also desperately wanted to watch him strum that guitar. Watch his fingers fly across the strings, hear him pour his soul into his music.

Decision made, I slipped out of the guest room and started toward the stairs. Such beautiful music drifted down, and I found my hand gripping the ladder before I even thought about it. Something called to me. Something I couldn't ignore. This deep pulsing need to climb the ladder and be with him.

I quickly ascended and quietly climbed inside. Sam sat on one of the leather couches, his back to me as he played. I tiptoed toward him, eagerly listening. His musical preferences were quite different from mine, but there was a beauty to his that pop music seemed to lack.

So lost within himself, Sam didn't seem to hear

my approach or even acknowledge my presence until I laid a gentle hand on his shoulder.

His music came to an abrupt stop. He lowered his guitar onto the couch, then turned to face me, his body settling between my legs. For the first time ever, our heights were reversed, and warmth spread through my stomach as I gazed down at him. Here before me sat this devastatingly beautiful man, someone capable of strumming my heart, and I'd rejected him. Like a fool.

Smiling softly, I caressed his stubbled cheeks with my palms, then swept my hands through his hair, all the while losing myself in his eyes. I saw the question within, the hesitation—even a bit of fear. I couldn't blame him. I'd burned him more than once already. Maybe he wasn't willing to give me a third chance.

But there was only one way to find out.

With my heart in my throat, I leaned down and brushed my lips featherlight against his. Sam froze, though I heard his fingers grip the leather couch. When he didn't move, I braved a second kiss, just as gentle as the first, emboldened now that he hadn't pushed me away.

Sam's hands finally moved and came to rest on the back of my thighs, his thumbs moving in slow circles. Every nerve in my body came alive as though waiting for this moment. As though to say finally.

Our lips had barely parted when I stole a third kiss, this one more demanding. This time, when our mouths came together, I parted my lips and touched his with my tongue. Sam sucked in a sharp breath as he reciprocated, welcoming my kiss. And just like that, I was a goner. I lost myself to him, reveled in the feel of his lips pressed against mine, of his fingers digging into my thighs. He tugged me closer, pulled me flush against the couch, his chest pressed against my hips. I fought to hold still, not to push him too far, because damn it, I wanted everything right now. I wanted him on the couch, on the floor, against the wall. I could barely think past my body's needs. But I had to rein it in. Had to control myself. Had to show him I wanted more from him than just sex, considering that was all I'd given him last time.

It took more strength than I thought I possessed to break from the kiss. Sam's eyes slowly opened, hazy with longing, his mouth a bit reddened. The sight of him all lust addled nearly had me falling into his lap. But I knew if I gave into that most base desire, it would ruin all my efforts. I needed to stand firm on this.

I smoothed Sam's hair back once more,

determined to show him that I wasn't frightened this time, then leaned in and kissed his brow, his nose, his mouth, before stepping back.

Sam stared at me, his gaze almost predatory as I backed toward the ladder.

"Good night," I whispered.

It took him a few swallows before he managed a gruff, "Night."

I forced myself to take my time climbing down, to show him that I wasn't running. Only when I closed myself in the guest bedroom did I press my fingers to my mouth and suck in a shuddering breath. My skin tingled everywhere he'd touched, and my girly bits were screaming at me for walking away. But it was the right choice. I knew it with every fiber of my being.

From here, we'd only grow. Strengthen our connection, our bond. And when he was ready, we'd take that final step. Then and only then. Whereas I... needed a cold shower. A long one.

🦇

"KEEP UP!" Sam shouted back at me, his feet running in place as he waited for me to catch up.

I sucked in a painful breath, my chest nearly

imploding with the effort. I wasn't a runner—far from it. Anna's and my idea of working out consisted of weightlifting wine bottles on a Saturday night. But Sam and his father thought differently. According to them, if I intended to train, I had to learn the basics first. Which meant running, apparently. And a lot of it. I didn't need to glance at my phone to know we'd been at this forever. My lungs and legs told me that all on their own.

"Come on, Luce," he encouraged. "Only a quarter mile to go."

"I'm pretty sure...," I wheezed, "you said that... already."

He shot me a devilish grin, then pressed forward. At least there was one upside to being left in the dust —I got to ogle his perfectly shaped ass and those wonderfully sculpted legs. The scent of desire smacked me in the face, and I might have laughed if I had any breath left. Thank goodness Sam had long since lapped me. I would have died from embarrassment if he picked up on my emotions right now.

Last night had left me feeling rather restless.

The cold shower hadn't done anything except make me long for a hot, hard body to press up against. And this morning, seeing rumpled, fresh-out-of-bed Sam had tormented my already aroused body. Forcing myself to wait seemed to be more punishment for me than him. Wasn't it supposed to be the other way around? Except he looked chipper almost. Certainly far more energetic than me. I just wanted to pounce on him, whereas he seemed content watching me sputter for air.

Sam started jogging backward, his gaze tracking me. There was a diabolical twinkle in his eyes that didn't inspire confidence. Clearly he had something nefarious planned.

He ambled over to me, his legs still moving, and pointed in the direction of his parents' house. "Tell ya what." He leaned his head down, his breath fanning my sweaty throat. Sweet baby Zeus, I was about to combust right here on the street. "Beat me back to the house, and you can choose our meal tonight."

At the bored expression on my face, he laughed.

"Not good enough? Okay..." He tapped his chin, effortlessly keeping pace next to me. "Beat me back to the house, and—"

"You have to play me a song of my choosing, even if that means singing."

Sam stared at me, as though that'd been the last thing he'd thought I'd suggest. An evil grin snaked across my face. I liked this bet. He didn't say anything about how I had to beat him. And already, I had an impish plan forming in my mind.

"Okay," Sam finally said, clearly not believing that I would win. "You got yourself a deal. On three?"

I nodded.

"One."

Grinned.

"Two."

And attacked.

Before the word three left Sam's lips, I swept a leg under his, exactly as I'd seen Anna do many times before when she'd first been learning to fight as a vampire. With a startled gasp, Sam dropped to the ground.

Then I took off.

I had to be quick. Faster than the time it would take him to scramble to his feet and chase after me. I pumped my arms and legs as fast as I could, reveling in the feel of the air streaming against my sweaty face. I'd already made it half a block before I caught the sound of Sam's playful curse. His feet hit the pavement and quickly started closing the distance between us.

I refused to lose this bet. Sam was going to sing

for me, even if it meant destroying my body in the meantime. I was a werewolf, I'd heal. What were a few torn tendons and muscles compared to Sam serenading me?

Every bone in my body seemed to groan in protest. No, I couldn't give up on myself. As though sensing my need, my wolf ventured to the forefront of my mind, her head cocked. I instinctively reached out to her, not to shift but to borrow from her. To be that little bit stronger, to run that little bit faster.

I felt my pace quicken, and an excited cry slipped past my lips. I was going to win this!

Adrien and Elena's place came into view just as the burning in my legs grew to a nearly unbearable point. Don't give up! I wasn't some meek little human anymore. I was a wolf, a beast, a predator. And I could run.

When I reached the bottom of their sidewalk, my knees had the audacity to wobble. I choked back a gasp, mentally steeled my legs, and pushed harder. Their door was inches away. Inches!

I outstretched my arm and practically flung myself up the porch. My fingers grazed the door a mere heartbeat before Sam's.

Laughing sure was hard without any breath, but I somehow managed. My entire lower body went boneless, and I sank to the porch, stretching everything out. I couldn't stay still for long, even I knew that. I needed to get up and keep moving before stretching out my abused muscles. But I could give myself this single moment.

"Jesus." Sam sprawled next to me, his hands resting on his rapidly rising chest. "Where the hell did that come from?"

I turned my head and caught his gaze, chuckling at the sight of his burning red cheeks. Seemed I'd given the boy a run for his money. He might look like Superman, but right now, I felt like Wonder Woman. I'd kicked his ass.

"You cheated, by the way," he said.

"Cheating implies I did something wrong," I countered. "You never stipulated any rules. Therefore, I did nothing wrong."

Amusement curled his lips. "Technicality."

"Life is built around those," I teased.

"What does that mean?"

"I don't know." I laughed, then forced myself to stand. "I can't think right now."

Sam chuckled, then struggled to his own feet and followed after me, stretching out his arms. When he started pivoting his hips, I had the grace to look away.

Didn't need the whole neighborhood to know that I had a wicked hard-on for him.

The front door opened, and Elena stepped out onto the porch. "You two done abusing each other?"

"We were running," Sam told her.

"Like I said, abusing." She shot me a knowing look. "I've been patient and let you change the schedule to take her for a run. It's my turn now."

"What?" Sam tucked his arm behind his head and stretched out his triceps. "No, I told her I'd start showing her how to fight."

"That sounds like tomorrow's problem," Elena chirped. "She promised me some girl time."

Ah shit. I glanced at Sam and shrugged. "She's not wrong."

"Besides, your father wants to speak with you. He was able to put together a composite of the werewolf you described. He wants to run it by you to make sure there aren't any tweaks needed before he sends a copy out to nearby packs. Hopefully, we get some answers."

The smile vanished from Sam's face as we were both reminded about the developing situation.

"And Claire has been nagging me all morning about you. So go spend some time with your sister, then see to your father."

I pressed my lips together to keep from laughing. The man was almost thirty, and his mother still told him what to do.

Sam shot me a glare as he stomped past, as though sensing my thoughts.

"And don't forget about tonight," I told him. "I'm thinking something from Pink."

His glare turned to a frown. "Something's pink?"

Laughter burst from my lips. "No, not something. Someone. Pink. The artist."

He blinked, then shook his head. "I have no idea what you're talking about."

"That's okay. I'll introduce you, and then you can serenade me."

He paled, which only made me laugh harder. But that laughter died when I glanced up and caught the smirk on Elena's face. I swear, stars were twinkling in her eyes and wedding bells were chiming in her ears.

16

"Sɪᴛ, sɪᴛ, sɪᴛ," Elena urged as she tucked me into the kitchen table. "I bet you need something to drink after that run. What would you like? Tea? Water?"

"Tea's fine," I mumbled, gripping the edge of the table for dear life. I so wasn't ready for this discussion or to get this personal with Sam's mother. I felt like a thirteen-year-old girl again, sitting in front of my mother and discussing sex.

Elena poured me some sweet tea, then placed the glass in front of me before taking her own seat. An easy smile spread across her face as she folded her hands. "So, first things first, how are you?"

I quirked my head. "Uh, I'm fine, thanks. How are you?"

"No, hun. I mean after last night. How are you?"

My mind flashed to Sam's and my kiss, and I stuttered out a ragged breath.

"It's not easy killing someone," Elena continued.

Oh! I shook my head to clear my thoughts, then almost laughed at myself. Right. Of course that was what she'd be inquiring about. Not the kiss. I cleared my throat and nodded. "I'm doing okay. Better than last night. It helps knowing they would have killed us if given the chance."

Elena gave her own little nod. She held my gaze and took a sip of her drink, then she placed the glass down on the table and said, "Well, tell me about yourself."

I blinked. "Pardon?"

"Come on now. I want to get to know the woman who is my son's mate. That shouldn't surprise you."

It took a second for my head to switch gears. "No, of course not. What would you like to know?"

"Adrien told me you grew up not too far from here, in a small town called Perish?"

I nodded. "My mother moved us there when I was young. After Reggie left us, she felt like she needed a fresh start."

"And your mother is human?" Elena probed.

"Yes, both her and my stepfather are."

"I see. And your stepfather, he's a good man?"

"Better than Reggie," I ground out. I reached for the glass of tea and gently spun it in my hands, giving my poor fingers something to do during this inquisition.

Elena chuckled, then repositioned herself. "Yes, I've met Reginald. I dare say he wouldn't be my pick for father of the year."

That made me laugh. "No, certainly not."

"I also understand your mother hid your werewolf genetics from you until recently?"

I felt a sudden urge to defend my mother. "She didn't feel it necessary to divulge that information, seeing as how I am—was—human. She didn't even know that I knew about werewolves until she met Sam."

"I'm sure that must have surprised her," Elena commented.

"She threw him out." I winced, hoping I didn't paint my mother in too harsh a light. "My mom is a wonderful person. Very loving. And perhaps a touch overprotective. She loves me more than anything and would do anything to keep me safe. When I introduced my parents to Sam, my mom reacted out of fear and asked him to leave. That night she told me everything."

"Well, not everything."

I frowned.

"It seems to me like you're still rather confused about what it means to be a mate."

"Oh. No, that I understand."

"Really?" She quirked a brow. "Then how about you explain it to me, and we go from there."

I sighed, slightly flustered by her probing.

"Just humor me," she said when I didn't immediately start talking.

"There's not much to say," I said. "The mating call helps werewolves seek out a strong partner, someone they're compatible with to produce strong offspring. Beyond that—"

Elena held up a hand. "That information came from your mother?"

"Well, yes, and Sam's told me a bit about it too."

"My dear, it's no wonder you're hesitant."

"Sorry?"

Elena cocked her head and regarded me. It felt like she was trying to peer into the depths of my soul. "Finding your mate is about so much more than finding the best partner to reproduce with. It's about finding your equal, finding your perfect other half."

My frown deepened. "That sounds like soulmates, like vampires. I was told that we were different from them."

"Ah." Elena leaned back in her chair and lifted her own glass to her mouth. She took a sip. "Yes, vampires do have a bit of an advantage in that when they find their soulmate, everything falls into place. It has something to do with their intrinsic magic, which no one's ever been able to explain. But for us, our mates are still our equals. It just takes a little bit of effort on our end to develop the deeper connection or the emotions, if you will."

She smiled and rested a hand on her chair's armrest. "Let me tell you, when I first met Adrien, I thought he was an arrogant prick who wanted nothing more than to solidify his place within the pack. He was the heir when we met, and his father's golden boy." She chuckled, clearly lost to her memories. "He thought that I would fall at his feet and fawn over him. Why shouldn't I? He was the future alpha, right?"

I grumbled something incomprehensible about men.

Elena laughed. "Exactly. It didn't take long for me to clear up that little misunderstanding. See, our wolves select our perfect partner for us. It's less about destiny and magic and more about our nature. Yes, reproduction is involved, but the bond truly does go deeper than that."

"But my sperm donor—"

"Is an exception to the rule, I assure you," Elena commented. "There are some like him, who like to plant their seed wherever they can. If Reginald abandoned you and your mother, I promise you, they were never mates. They were simply…"

"Fuck buddies?" I whispered, using a phrase I knew Anna would use.

Elena had the grace to snicker at the expression. "Sure, we can go with that."

"My mother said they were mates."

"Which is likely what Reginald told her." Elena repositioned herself, then sighed. "He isn't the best role model or example, I'm afraid. And your mother has fed you quite a bit of incorrect information—which isn't her fault, of course. She can only share from her perspective. But I fear Reginald lied to her, fed her the story of them being mates simply to get into her bed."

As if I needed another reason to dislike the bastard. I already knew this was information I'd never pass on to my mother. I didn't need to cause her any pain by suggesting she'd been taken in by Reggie's schemes.

"I understand why you left after you were attacked," Elena continued. "Your entire world imploded. You needed to gain control of your life. But from Sam's perspective—"

"I bailed," I whispered.

Her head bobbed.

"I understand that. I'm working on fixing our relationship as best as I can."

"And if he decides you two shouldn't have a relationship?"

The thought cleaved my chest in two. "Then I'll leave. I just want him to be happy."

She smiled, and I had the feeling I'd just passed a test. "Then you finally understand what it means to be a mate. It isn't about popping out children. It's about forming a relationship, becoming a partner to someone. It's about growing and forging a life together. The mate connection is far stronger than any relationship you'll ever experience. And if you nurture it, it'll take care of you. I love Adrien more than anything in the world, and I would do anything to protect him, much like he would for me. If you think you and Sam can have that, then this is your chance."

Her words warmed my stomach. I'd come back to Louisiana for Anna's wedding, but things changed the moment I saw Sam. Almost like everything in my life had clicked back into place, like all was right with the world again.

"There is one small issue, though," I said. "I'm the heir of the Mississippi Pack."

"Yes, that does complicate matters. But it's not impossible. However, you and Sam need to sort that out together."

"If he still wants me."

"Sweetheart." Elena reached across the table and took my hand. "I've never seen him light up with anyone the way he does with you. Believe me, he still wants you."

Last night's kiss flashed in my memory, bringing a smile to my face.

"Ah, you should see your face right now." Elena beamed at me. "I have no doubts the two of you will work this out."

I wish I had her confidence. The kiss last night had bolstered mine, but we still had a long way to go before we reached our happily ever after.

Before Elena could say anything more, the front door popped open, and Sam stomped inside with his father at his side. Thankfully, they'd gone to the garage to have their conversation—by Elena's request, of course—to give us some privacy.

Rising from her chair, Elena rounded the table, then bent down and kissed the top of my head. In my ear, she whispered so quietly I wasn't sure Sam would hear, "Welcome to the family."

Heat flamed my cheeks, so I quickly glanced down before Sam noticed anything out of the ordinary.

"Well, it seems we've learned the identity of Lucy's mysterious wolf from last night," Adrien said as he entered the kitchen. He strode to Elena and brushed a gentle kiss across her cheek, then placed a photo on the counter.

I rose from my chair with my glass in hand and approached the picture, the tea sloshing as my fingers shook. It wasn't the face of a wolf staring back at me. It was the face of a man.

"He was a wolf when he died," I murmured.

Sam's comforting presence pressed against my back as he said, "If we die in wolf form, our bodies shift back to human."

Tempted to lean against him, I instead touched a finger to the photo and memorized my victim's features, not that it would help me sleep at night.

"Why?" I asked, referring back to Sam's statement.

"No one knows. Likely something to do with the magic leaving our bodies. The amount of time it takes ranges between individuals too, but generally, it happens within a half an hour of our death."

I stared at the man's portrait, and my gut gave a twist. He looked like a regular sort of guy. Just a normal Joe Blow from the streets. Nothing about him stood out to me or screamed killer.

"So, who is he?" Elena asked.

Adrien cleared his throat. "His name is Damon Hart. He originally belonged to the South Arkansas Pack."

"Originally?" I parroted in a quiet voice.

"Well, according to Damon's alpha, he split from his pack a few months ago. No one has seen or heard from him since."

My brows furrowed. "I didn't know you could leave your pack."

"Normally, no. But Damon didn't give his pack, or the alpha, an option. He told them he was leaving, then poof, vanished. The alpha had people searching for him, but they never ventured beyond state lines, so they never found him."

"Why would he just leave?" I asked, fighting to understand this person's motives.

"Another question no one had an answer to. But if I had to hazard a guess..."

The room fell silent as we all waited for Adrien to finish his sentence. When he didn't, I tore my gaze off the photo and stared up at him. I had my own theory, such as increasing the werewolf population, but I wanted to hear Adrien's now.

"I think he left his pack to form a new one."

"A new pack?" Sam grunted. "That doesn't make sense. Most werewolves already belong to packs. Sure, there are a few rogues here and there, but they keep to themselves."

Adrien shook his head. "Damon's alpha told me that Damon had challenged him a few times in the last year or so. He dreamed of taking over the South Arkansas Pack. Except, he didn't have enough mettle to win the fights." His gaze briefly flitted to mine. "My theory is that he—and this partner of his—are attacking the human-born in order to change them. Then, once they're turned into wolves—"

"They could recruit them," Sam interrupted. "Daniel and Brenda haven't been inducted into our pack as official members yet, and therefore—"

"Could choose to join another pack," Elena finished.

My eyes leapt between all their faces. What they were suggesting... it was... "That's insane," I blurted. "Who in their right mind would join the pack of someone who savagely attacked them?"

"Well, some may not see it that way," Elena murmured. "Some of the human-born hold grudges that they weren't chosen as werewolves. We know genetics play a factor, but for some, it's this epic—and nebulous—mystery. Why was their sister chosen over them? Or their brother? Their cousin?"

"I can think of a few in our pack who would give anything to be turned into a werewolf," Sam said. "The risk of death would be worth it to them."

An icy shiver chilled me.

"They'd be so grateful, they'd even agree to join a new pack. One formed of former human-born."

My mouth fell slack as I listened to Sam and his parents discuss this theory of theirs. Everything made sense, but I just couldn't wrap my head around the violence of it all. Brenda and Daniel had nearly died. Hell, so had I. Anna was adamant that I had died. My heart had stopped beating, she said. Who would risk their lives just to be able to shift into a wolf?

I exhaled, then slowly walked back to the kitchen table and took a seat.

"Do we know who the other wolf was? Damon's partner?" Sam asked. "Did my description help at all?"

"No, and that concerns me. The South Arkansas alpha wasn't aware of anyone matching the description you gave. He didn't know of any other wolves that Damon was close to either."

I perched my chin in my hand and struggled to bring up my memories from last night. In all the excitement, I hadn't caught even a single glimpse at the man Sam had fought. I hadn't picked up a scent either, likely due to the wind. So I had nothing to contribute to that issue.

"Then we keep searching," Sam said. "We need to find this other wolf before he hurts someone else."

"Do you think he'll continue on this path without Damon?" Elena asked.

"Who knows."

The kitchen slipped back into silence while I pondered this entire situation. Something was bugging me about it, something that just didn't quite feel right. And I couldn't put my finger on it. We had a rogue wolf gone AWOL, trying to form his own pack, with a partner we knew absolutely nothing about.

"Why haven't they reached out to Daniel or Brenda if their goal is to start a new pack?" I asked.

"Perhaps because they've been sheltered here," Adrien said. "I haven't allowed them to leave the house, as a precaution, until I know they can control themselves."

I slowly nodded. "Assuming all alphas took that measure, it seems this plan of theirs is flawed."

"It could be that they're just in the testing stage still," Sam suggested.

"Testing stage?"

"Well, they may not even want Daniel or Brenda. Their attacks may be nothing more than attempting to replicate your results."

Anger churned in the pit of my stomach. I hated this. We weren't experiments, for crying out loud. Brenda and Daniel had almost died because of all this. I couldn't even contemplate the carelessness and recklessness that went into planning something like that.

It took every fiber of my being not to rush out of the house and track the other wolf down. To crush his throat between my teeth as I had Damon. To show him that their stupidity had cost them their lives.

"Lucy." Sam's whispered voice snapped me back to the present to find him crouched before me, kneeling on the kitchen floor. He held my hands in his, and I hadn't even noticed.

"Sorry," I murmured. "I just…"

"Just what?"

"This is because of me, Sam. The queen might have been the one to order my attack, but because I survived, there are now psycho weres out there mauling and damn near killing people. It's my fault."

"This is *not* your fault," Sam snarled, flashing his teeth. "The blame rests solely on Damon and this other wolf. They are the ones responsible. Not you. You did nothing wrong, you understand me?"

"But—"

"Hey…" He released my hands and cupped my cheeks. "Listen to me. You were not responsible for your own attack, nor are you responsible for Daniel's or Brenda's. Much like them, you're a victim in all this."

I gritted my teeth to stop my chin from wobbling, then nodded. Sam's words soothed a bit of the anger within, but not enough. I still wanted to rip the other wolf apart.

"My question," Elena murmured, "is why now? Lucy was attacked a year ago. So why wait this long?"

"Hmm." Adrien considered her question with a slight frown. "The timing may be irrelevant. Perhaps it just took those two some time to find each other. I can't imagine there are many who would willingly partake in such a plan. Right now, the most important thing is identifying the other werewolf. I'll send Sam's sketch composite to the other packs and hope for the best."

Sam clasped my hand and rose to his feet, pulling me up beside him. "Let me know when you hear something."

"Are you two heading out?" Elena asked.

He glanced at the microwave clock, then nodded. I did the same, surprised to see we'd spent the entire day here. "I think so. I'll check in with you two tomorrow."

Elena smiled at her son as she stretched up onto her tiptoes to brush a kiss against his cheek. She hugged me next, her mouth brushing my ear as she said, "Remember what we discussed."

Embarrassment flooded me, chasing away the lingering rage.

I caught Sam watching us, a knowing expression

on his face. But I ignored it and instead dashed for the door. Sam trailed after me, chuckling under his breath. Somehow, I suspected he knew exactly what his mother and I had chatted about today. And wasn't that just horrifying.

THE INSTANT we stepped foot inside Sam's house, I shot him a grin before marching upstairs. My mood had taken a bit of a rotten turn since deciding this was all connected to me, and I needed something to cheer me up. Namely, Sam serenading me. I wanted Pink, Katy Perry, Kesha, heck, even Miley Cyrus would do. I honestly didn't care. I just wanted Sam behind his guitar, singing me a song. Anything to take my mind off all this.

I listened for the telltale creak of his steps following me upstairs, then wrenched open the attic hatch. My hands found the rungs, and up I went. Once inside, I made for the couch and flounced down onto it, folding my hands in my lap.

Sam was a little slower, clearly less enthused than me. When he finally joined me, he picked up his guitar and quickly tuned it. Somehow he even made that look good. What I would give to be those strings beneath his fingers. I wanted him to strum my body until I made beautiful music.

"So?" he asked as he seated himself in a nearby chair, the guitar placed on his lap. "What silly song do you want me to play?"

My mouth twisted as I contemplated his request. Dozens of songs rose to mind, some I was sure he must have heard at some point. It was impossible to escape them, especially considering movies relied heavily on hit songs. But that didn't mean he knew how to play any of them. And if this was the only opportunity I had, I didn't want to waste it.

So I changed tactics.

Leaning forward, I braced my elbows against my knees and met his stare. "Do you know any modern music? Or does your library consist of all instrumental?"

"I know... a few," Sam admitted.

My curiosity piqued when a bit of color flushed his cheeks. Oh, this had to be good. If he was blushing, it had to be a truly embarrassing song.

"Tell me which song you're thinking of right now," I said.

Sam sighed and scratched his nose, his elbow bumping the guitar body. He fixed its position, then averted his gaze. "I do know one Lewis Capaldi song. It was something I heard one of my sister's singing, and the lyrics caught my attention."

Much like the proverbial cat that found the cream, I sat back with a Cheshire grin. "Then that's the song I want you to play for me." A win-win in my book because I loved Lewis Capaldi's music.

Sam gave a small cough. "Um, no, I don't think—"

"I won the bet, didn't I?"

"Yes, but—"

"Then it's my choice. What are you embarrassed about? Lewis's music is gold."

Sam's eyes slipped close as he drew a deep breath. I was about to ask him what was wrong when he straightened in his chair and started strumming.

After a moment, he paused and met my gaze. "Just remember, you asked for this."

My grin widened. Surely, it couldn't be that bad. I hadn't heard him sing yet, but I had this feeling that Sam's voice would melt butter. There was something about the way he spoke and his deep, rich tone that told me all I needed to know. So long as he wasn't tone deaf—which I assumed not since he knew how to play the guitar—we'd be fine.

Before I could offer any encouraging words, he struck the first chord. Instantly it became music, his fingers expertly flying across the strings. I melted into the song, but it was nothing compared to the moment he started singing. My eyes flew wide, and I stared at him, my heart hammering in my chest. The words fell from his lips in a rich, baritone timbre that sent a shiver through me, lifting the hairs on my arms.

He moved into the chorus, and my damn heart skipped a beat. "Before You Go" was one of my favorite songs, but I'd never connected to the lyrics, not until now. I sucked in an unsteady breath when Sam lifted his head and speared me with his gaze while he sang.

Somehow, I just knew he'd learned this song because of me. The heart-wrenching lyrics hit too close to home. And as he sang, pouring his soul into every note and word, tears sprang to my eyes. It wasn't only that Sam was a talented singer and musician, but also the emotion he plucked from deep inside me. Emotion that rendered me speechless.

When the traitorous tears slipped down my

cheeks, I dropped my head and knuckled them away, a bit embarrassed by my reaction. The purpose of this had been to cheer me up, not to make me cry. But I couldn't stop picturing him learning this song after I'd left, a means of escape from his own grief.

Sam's voice faded, and the music stopped. "Luce?"

A gruff laugh rose from my throat. "Sorry. I didn't mean to let it affect me like this." My head rose, and I caught his gaze. "Why did you learn that song?"

Sam's fingers slackened against the strings, and he sat back, blowing out a heavy breath. "I'm not quite sure. Primarily because it's one of the only pop songs I know, but also because..."

When he didn't continue speaking, I lifted a brow. "Because?"

"Because I resonated with it." He sighed, then raked his free hand through his hair. "After you left, I questioned everything. What I could have done differently, what I could have said, the different steps I could have taken to help you. I knew our bond terrified you, but I always assumed you'd adjust and get over that fear. But you didn't."

I forced myself to swallow.

"The night we slept together, I thought for sure

that everything had worked itself out. That you'd realized our connection was more than physical. That you understood how I felt for you. But then I woke up, and you were gone. Like gone, gone. Across the ocean, gone. And I couldn't follow. I had no idea what to think or how to act. When Anna told me you guys were coming back, I was so relieved. Except, instead of calling or coming to see me, you vanished. That was the moment I realized how badly I'd fucked up."

I sucked in a raspy breath. "Sam, no—"

He shook his head, silently pleading for me to listen. "A few days after I realized you weren't coming home, Sophie was at my parents' place, and she came in singing this song. The lyrics struck deeply and made me realize that I'd been so caught up in myself that I hadn't realized how badly you were hurting. I let you down, Luce. I wasn't there for you when you needed me. Don't get me wrong, I was still angry you took off like that, but I was also angry at myself for letting it happen."

"No, Sam. You did nothing wrong."

He gave a disgruntled laugh. "I did everything wrong. That first day when I stepped inside Vlad's house, all I could smell was you. Your scent nearly drove me mad. You were best friends with a vampire, so I immediately thought you could handle the news that we were mates. I should have been more delicate, taken the time to let us get to know each other first. If I had, I would have seen that you were far more afraid of our mating bond than I realized. Then when Anna was taken to England, and you came to me looking for comfort, I let us sleep together, thinking that would solve all our problems. But that only made things worse."

I shook my head.

"And then you were attacked." His voice caught, and he had to clear his throat. "And you didn't even reach out to me to tell me what happened. I had to hear about it all from Anna. That was a low moment for me. That you didn't trust me enough to tell me what had happened. I drove you away."

My chest ached with each word.

"When Sophie came in singing this song, it just clicked with me. So I learned it, if only to help me deal with my own emotions."

I slid off the couch and dropped to my knees in front of Sam, his guitar a barrier between us. I cupped his cheeks and gazed into his eyes. "You did not drive me away. I drove myself away. I ran instead of reaching out for help from my loved ones."

"Lucy, you'd just been turned into a werewolf,

something we all thought impossible. It wasn't a surprise that you ran, but rather that you ran without letting anyone know where you'd gone."

"We could sit here and blame ourselves for everything that's happened. Or we could try and fix everything." I smiled softly. "Sam, you are a good man. Never doubt that. I never should have run out on you, and I certainly shouldn't have gone to freaking England like that, not right after sleeping with you. It was cowardly to bail like that. And that's why I've come back now. To tell you I was wrong, and to make things right between us, to tell you..." I sucked in a sharp breath and swallowed the words that'd nearly escaped.

But Sam wasn't stupid. "To tell me what?"

I bit my bottom lip and debated my response. I could—should—be honest. That was why I'd returned, after all. To fix this entire mess and to prove to Sam that I wanted to be with him. Lying wouldn't accomplish either of those goals.

So, with a deep breath, I faced my fears head-on and said, "To tell you that I want to be with you. Be your mate."

Sam blinked, stunned into silence.

"And I'll totally understand if you're not ready for that. But I thought you should know what I want," I rambled. "I don't know yet how we'll make this work, seeing as how we're both heirs to two different, and geographically undesirable, packs. But I'm willing to figure something out—no, I want to figure something out. Need to figure something out. This last year without you has been miserable and—"

Sam looped a finger in the collar of my shirt and pulled me forward, effectively silencing my rambling with a kiss. I might have laughed, but the feel of his lips pressed against mine elicited other emotions. Lusty, deliriously happy emotions that lifted a heavy weight from my shoulders.

I could only assume that Sam kissing me meant he wanted to be my mate as well. And that made me so happy, I almost shifted, just so I could howl at the moon. Reality butted its ugly head a moment later, reminding me not to get too invested until I damn well understood the situation. That was the whole point of this, wasn't it?

I begrudgingly broke from the kiss and leaned back, scanning his face for any hint of what to expect from my next question. But the man hid his emotions well.

"Before we go any further," I hedged. "I need to know... Does you kissing me mean we are, in fact, mates?"

"You already know we're mates," he murmured.

I rolled my eyes. "That's not what I mean, and you know it. Does this mean we're together now? I don't want there to be any confusion about this. I'm in this for the long haul, so I need to know if you are too."

Sam leaned in and brushed the gentlest kiss against my mouth. "I've been playing for keeps since the day you and I beheaded that vampire together."

Laughter burst from me. "You sweet-talker, you."

His lips found their way to my cheek, then started to trail down, down, down, until they found my neck. Oh, the neck. My danger zone. One that completely frazzled my brain. Sam had learned that the first night we spent together, and apparently, he'd logged that away for future information. When his teeth scraped my collar bone, I damn near jumped out of my skin.

He gave a manly chuckle as his fingers inched up my waist. When his thumbs brushed the underside of my bra, he paused and leaned back. "Are you sure about this? I don't want to push you if you aren't ready."

Oh, I was more than ready. I was willing and able and eager.

With a wicked grin, I grasped the hem of my

shirt and ever so slowly started pulling it over my head. I removed my bra next, and made sure to arch my back just enough to thrust my chest forward. And from the instant smoldering of his eyes, he noticed.

Sam's hands encircled my waist, and he laid me back on the attic floor, the chilly wood making me gasp. He grunted, then fumbled around on the couch until he produced a blanket, one he tucked beneath me.

"Better?"

"Mm," I hummed.

Sam hovered above me, his gaze drinking me in as though recommitting me to memory. "I missed you. So much."

"I missed you too. At the time, I didn't want to. But you were always in my thoughts, and I couldn't shut them out."

"I'm not sure how to feel about that," Sam said, a crease forming between his brows.

Chuckling, I lifted his hand and placed it back on my side, then began slowly inching it upward, all the while holding his gaze. "I'm glad I couldn't get you out of my head because then we wouldn't be here, and we wouldn't be together. And that would be a travesty."

Sam's mouth quirked in a crooked grin. He dipped his head but paused a hairsbreadth from my mouth. "Are you still on birth control?"

I gave a nod, so grateful right now that I'd never stopped taking it. "I also haven't been with anyone since we last slept together."

Pleasure rippled across his face. Desperate to taste him, I threaded my fingers through his hair and pulled him down. The instant our mouths came together, fire ignited in my body. I was suddenly starved, and he was the meal. I wanted to devour every inch of him.

I arched my whole body up against him, then looped a leg around his hips and pressed us together. The feel of him, hard and ready, was so damn hot I nearly combusted on the spot.

"Sam..." I rasped against his mouth.

He pulled back with a questioning look.

"I don't want to go slow. Not this time. Let's save slow for next time."

His expression darkened, and without a word, he reclaimed my mouth in an almost bruising kiss that left me gasping for breath. Yes. This was what I wanted. For a year, I'd been fighting it. After twelve months, a girl had needs. And those needs were demanding attention right now.

Sam tore my pants and panties off in one solid rip. I silently bid them adieu, then lifted his hands and placed them on my breasts. The feel of his calloused palms caressing me nearly undid me right there. I moaned and arched into his touch, all while fumbling with the fly of his pants. The damn button eluded me for longer than I appreciated, but once I had it open, I shoved his pants down and ripped him free of his boxers. Then I happily freed him of his shirt, my eyes immediately drinking in his abs.

God, the sight of him. I'd thought the image I'd built in my head had been exaggerated, but nope. Not at all. He was everything I'd dreamed. And I wanted that dreamworthy dick buried in me so fast, I nearly screamed with impatience.

"Not yet," Sam whispered against my mouth.

Before I could argue, he swept down the length of my body, placing gentle kisses along the way. Hadn't I just told him I didn't want to go slow? I was about to force him back up and climb on him myself when his mouth landed between my legs.

I gasped, my hips flying off the floor.

Sam wasted no time. He unleashed his wickedly talented mouth and tongue on me until I found myself begging for him to finish me. Heat built within me, like stoking a flame. The next thing I knew, my hands were fisted in the blanket beneath me, and I was crying out with pleasure. I'd nearly forgotten how fast Sam could make me come. No one else had ever been as accomplished as him when it came to working my body. It was like he could hear my thoughts and knew exactly what to do to pleasure me. Part of the mating bond, perhaps?

The orgasm slowly faded, and I found myself staring up at Sam. While I'd been lost to ecstasy, he'd repositioned himself between my legs. He brushed his length against my core once, then twice, teasing my already sensitive clit. The instant I cried out, he entered me in one smooth thrust. My head fell back, and I moaned, reveling in the silky feel of him moving within me.

This was how it should always be. I felt so complete with him, like everything lacking in my life was finally fulfilled. And I knew it was because of him, because of our bond.

Lifting my hips off the ground, I met his every thrust with one of my own. The sound of our bodies coming together echoed through the attic. Luckily it was soundproofed. At least the neighbors wouldn't be able to hear us. Not that I cared right now. The only thing I cared about was getting that dick of his in me as deeply as possible.

Seemed Sam was of the same mind. But he also seemed to have another goal, one he accomplished after a few well-timed strokes with his fingers. Another orgasm slammed into me, this one more powerful than the first. Even though my eyes were closed, it was like I could see every color known to man.

Sam's mouth crashed down on mine, swallowing my cries. I felt his pace stutter, felt him swell within me, and knew he was almost at the finish line. I reached down and cupped his balls, adding a little bit of pressure. From the sound of his grunt, he liked it. Not a moment later, he broke from the kiss with a ragged groan and dropped his head, the tips of his hair brushing my throat as he succumbed to his own climax.

When finally he lifted his head and our gazes met, I started laughing. To think, this was what I'd been avoiding for the past year. Suffice to say, I was insane.

"Normally a guy doesn't like it when a girl laughs after sex," Sam teased.

"Don't worry, I was laughing at myself for being so stupid for running from you."

"Ah. Well, I won't argue that."

I jokingly slapped his shoulder. "How about we move this somewhere more comfortable?"

Sam winked. "Is the attic floor not cutting it for you?"

"Let's put you on the bottom and see what you think."

"I definitely won't complain about that," he teased.

Sam slowly rolled off me, and I immediately missed the feel of his weight. I already knew we were great in bed, but tonight put my memories of us together to shame. Every inch of me tingled with blissful happiness.

Sam seemed just as satisfied. He laid next to me, hands tucked behind his head as he stared at the ceiling. But there was this little grin spreading across his face that meant the world to me. There was something about seeing my mate thoroughly fulfilled that pleased me. A little high that came with knowing my partner was explicitly happy because of me.

If I were a cat, I might have purred. Instead, I tucked into his side and stretched, all the while imagining myself luxuriating on a soft pillow-top mattress. Next round needed to end there. Not on a wooden floor.

Sam turned on his side and studied me. "Hungry?"

"Always," I teased, trailing a finger down his chest.

He caught my hand and lifted it to his mouth, nipping at my fingertips. "I meant for food."

"Ah, well, I meant for dick."

Sam burst out laughing. "Now, that you learned from Anna."

"I can be crude too. Sometimes."

Sam lifted a dubious brow.

"Okay," I said, laughing. "I learned that from Anna."

"Do you want something to eat?"

"Nah." I stretched again, head to toe, relishing the tiny ache between my legs. My body felt thoroughly used, and I loved it. "Don't wanna move."

"Well, I would make you the food, silly."

"Don't want you to move," I said, playfully pouting.

I was about to sprawl on him, not only to make my point but to hopefully entice him into round two, when his cell phone blared to life, vibrating on the couch cushion.

Sam groaned and rolled over. When he grabbed

the phone, I caught his father's name stamped on the screen and frowned. It was after midnight.

"Dad?"

"Sam."

The sound of his father's distressed voice had me slowly sitting upright.

Sam's heart quickened. "What's wrong?"

"It's your sister. You need to come home. Now."

18

My GAZE LEAPT to Sam's face, and I watched as the contented bliss from moments ago faded into a cold awareness as he demanded, "What happened?"

"Just get here."

The call disconnected.

Sam and I sat in silence, anxiety eating away at my nerves. When Sam didn't move, I jumped into action. I grabbed our torn clothing and piled them on the couch. I'd need fresh clothes from downstairs, but I could handle that. His had mostly survived. Only his boxers had died a happy death, but he didn't necessarily need those right now. What I couldn't handle was Sam's pale face.

"Sam." I cupped his cheek. "Sam, we need to go. You need to get dressed."

He turned his head toward me, his gaze almost blank.

"Hey..." I touched his hair, his face, his shoulder. "Are you with me? We need to get dressed and go."

A slow nod. He reached for his shirt and pants and began to dress. In the meantime, I bolted downstairs and dressed, then grabbed the car keys, Sam's wallet, and my purse. I checked my phone but found no missed calls. Either his family knew we'd be together, or this was a family-only matter. I hated not knowing what was wrong. Hated not knowing how to help. All we could do was get there as fast as we could. Something in my gut told me that we couldn't delay.

When Sam's feet hit the stairs, relief flooded me, and I reached for the wall to help steady me. I couldn't explain why, but I had this foreboding sense that we were on a clock.

"I have the keys," I said, ushering Sam out of the house.

We hurried to the car, and I pushed him into the passenger side. Now didn't seem the best time for him to drive, evidenced by his vacant expression.

Seemed I wasn't the only one whose senses were screaming.

I bolted around the vehicle and practically lunged into the driver's seat. I fired up the engine and tore out of the neighborhood, speeding beyond the posted limit. I didn't give a damn about the rules right now. Sam's father had sounded grim. Worse. He'd sounded devastated. I couldn't let myself think any further beyond that.

The ten minutes it took to drive to his parents' place had to be the longest of my life. Sam's too, judging by the way he gripped the edge of his seat. The second I parked and turned off the engine, we jumped out of the car and sprinted up the sidewalk.

The front door already hung open, and Elena stood within, framed by the dim hallway light. The sight of her face turned my stomach. Something very bad had happened. I paused at the entry and gripped Elena's hand. If she'd been human, I might have broken it. But thankfully, she merely squeezed back.

"It's Izzy," she whispered.

I heard the sound of metal groaning seconds before I realized Sam had broken the porch railing. "What happened?"

Oh, damn. His voice was heavy with his wolf. That was why he'd been so quiet and absent-minded on our way here. Strong emotions often brought out the worst in us, which seemed to be the case right now.

"She was attacked," Elena said. Her hand flew to her mouth, and she turned her head away from the light to shield us from the sight of her crying.

My heart shattered. "She's okay, right? Was she attacked like the others?"

Elena's head bobbed.

"Okay. Okay." I released a slow breath and gathered my thoughts. "Then she'll be okay. She'll become a werewolf, but she'll be okay." When no one answered, I shot Elena another glance. "Right?"

"She's upstairs," was all Elena said. "With Adrien."

"Where are the others?" Sam demanded, his voice more wolf than human.

"Monique is downstairs..." Elena's voice wavered. "With Claire and Sophie. I didn't want them anywhere near this—" She broke off and drew in a shuddering breath. "Aimee is on her way here now."

I couldn't help myself. I threw my arms around Elena's shoulders and wrapped her in a hug. It was the only thing I could think to do.

Her arms slowly closed around me, as though she

couldn't allow herself any sympathy right now. "Adrien wants you two upstairs to help."

Sam was gone an instant later. I barely even saw him move.

"His wolf..." I whispered.

Elena nodded, then stepped back from me. "Help him keep control. Adrien doesn't need a wild animal running amok right now."

"I will," I promised. "Are you coming up?"

Fresh tears welled in Elena's eyes, but she nodded. "I just came down when I heard Sam's car pull up."

I clutched Elena's hand and gave another squeeze. "Let's go."

Together, we stepped farther into the house. But this time, it was quiet. As silent as the grave. No one chatting, no children running about, nothing but a room full of anxious werewolves, which didn't do much for my nerves. I felt my wolf respond to my emotions and start pawing at the barrier between us, demanding to be set free. Not here though. Not now. Sam needed me to remain calm, and that was exactly what I would do.

I hurried up the stairs alongside Elena. I didn't need to ask which room, not when I could follow the scent of Sam's rage to the end of the hall, last door on the left. The doctor stood in the hallway, her eyes full of sorrow. That could mean anything, though, so I refused to assume.

But when I stepped into that room, I stopped dead in the doorway, my hand flying to my mouth.

I'd never met Izzy, and yet my entire being seemed to shatter the instant I laid eyes on her. She looked so young and so pale, this little thing that had been utterly broken. Someone had placed her on the bed and tucked a pillow beneath her head, much like they had for Daniel and Brenda. But there was one stark difference between them and her.

Izzy had no heartbeat.

Heat welled in my eyes as I fought back tears. Anna had told me that my heart hadn't been beating when she'd first found me, so perhaps there was a chance Izzy would still survive. I had, after all. And right now, we needed all the hope we could get, even just a glimmer.

Sam staggered to his sister's side, then dropped to his knees next to the bed. He reached for her hand but paused when he caught sight of her crooked fingers. Each one laid at an awkward angle, some protruding with bone. A faint whimper escaped my throat, one I quickly tamped back. Brenda and Daniel had been mauled, but their wounds had almost seemed calculated. Izzy's seemed different somehow, as though her attacker had lost control and inflicted as much damage as possible.

"Someone purposely did this to her," Sam growled. "Broke her, tormented her."

Bile rose in my throat.

"It was him, wasn't it?" Sam demanded. "The bastard I let get away."

My eyes slipped closed as guilt slammed into me. Sam had only let that bastard escape because of me, because I'd been injured, and he'd refused to leave me. And now, Izzy...

I drew in a deep breath, sampling the scents covering Izzy, but I couldn't pinpoint just one. There were too many. Her pain, her despair, and something strangely bitter beneath it all... something I couldn't place.

"Wasn't it?" Sam shouted.

I jumped a mile in my own skin. I'd never heard Sam raise his voice like that.

"Yes," Adrien finally muttered. "At least, we think so. The scene was chaotic. And our team couldn't lock onto just one scent to track."

Sam shot to his feet, his chest heaving. He slowly turned his head until he met his father's gaze, and I gasped at the sight of his glowing eyes. "Where's Gabriel?"

"Dead," Adrien said.

Sam seemed just as startled as me.

"Dead? Gabriel is dead? He was supposed to protect her."

"And he did," Adrien said, "until his dying breath."

Oh my god.

Sam turned and stared out the window, his body practically shaking with rage. I crept around Adrien and slowly approached Izzy. There was hardly anything left of her. Her black hair shone against the pillow, but otherwise, she was little more than a litany of injuries. Far worse than anything we'd seen. No one had ever described the extent of my injuries to me, but I'd known from Anna's face that they'd been severe. Likely to the same extent as Izzy's. And I'd lived, so I had to believe Izzy could too. Heartbeat or not.

I knelt and reached for Izzy's fingers. One by one, I gently eased them back into place. With each snap, her father and brother flinched, but neither questioned my actions. I couldn't leave her like that. If she did wake, fixing her fingers was the least I could do for her.

"She's been like this since they found her," came Elena's soft voice. "I've been here with her the entire time, talking to her, begging her to wake, promising her that everything will be alright, like you did with the others, Lucy. But there hasn't been any change."

Hope vanished like a snuffed-out candle. An hour without a heartbeat. That didn't seem like a good sign. Before now, I hadn't been sure if talking to the victim truly helped them overcome their injuries and make the change. But now it seemed like it held no significance other than comfort. And for some reason, that broke a small part of me. Knowing we had absolutely no control over any of this.

"She's gone, isn't she?" Elena asked, her broken voice damn near destroying me. A mother should never have to grieve her child.

Sam's body tensed at his mother's question, but he didn't offer a response. Adrien also remained silent.

I rose to my feet and faced Elena. Her tear-streaked face was difficult to look at. "I'm no expert. The others had heartbeats, but I didn't, so Izzy could still—"

Elena's face paled, and she choked on a gasp. "Do you... do you smell that?"

I sniffed the air again and noticed that same bitter scent from before, that faint odor I couldn't place. Except, now I understood. It was the scent of death.

Izzy was gone.

Despair swept over me.

"Oh my god." Elena cupped her face and collapsed to her knees, sobbing into her palms. "Oh god. My baby. My sweet baby."

Adrien dropped to his wife's side and gathered her into his arms, tears rolling down his cheeks.

I couldn't fight back my own tears. Not while watching the two of them keen for their lost daughter together.

Instead, I grabbed Sam's hand and pulled it to my chest.

Sam, however, didn't utter a single word. Nor did he join in his parents' grief. He simply stood there and stared out Izzy's window, his hand gripped in mine.

EVERYTHING HAPPENED SO QUICKLY AFTERWARD. Preparations were made, such as moving Izzy's body until she could be buried. Next came the arrangements for Gabriel, who'd died protecting her. Then came the most terrifying part.

The hunt.

Led by Sam.

I stood surrounded by pissed off werewolves, all hungering for revenge. Sam stood off to the side of the room, his face still blank. I knew him well enough now to know it was a sign of his wolf fighting to take over. It made me ache inside to see him struggling like this. To know he was in pain and not be able to fix it.

"We start at her house," another wolf growled.

My gaze leapt from Sam to him—Lukas, if I remembered correctly. His stark red hair didn't match the terrifying expression carved into his face. Each of the other five wolves nodded in response. I scanned their faces, memorizing them and their names. Sam had only briefly introduced us, and there were so many people present I was finding it difficult to keep track. I had to try though. Had to make the effort. These people belonged to Sam's pack. They cared for him, for Izzy, and I would show that I did too, even though I was an outsider.

I needed to call Reggie, to fill him in and ask if he'd learned anything more since our last discussion. But right now, Sam was my main priority. The Mississippi Pack didn't need me like he did.

"And then what?" someone else asked. I racked my brain for a name and settled on Rory.

"We track him."

"Joseph hasn't been able to track him. What makes you think we can?" someone else asked.

My head started bouncing back and forth as they argued.

"We have to try! The bastard killed Izzy. I'm going to rip out his throat."

"Oh, please. You couldn't kill a rabbit, let alone—"

"Enough," came Sam's dangerously deep voice.

Everyone snapped to attention. Even me. He turned to face us, his expression bleak, but his hands fisted at his sides. I found myself walking to his side without even thinking about it. And when I approached, his startlingly bright amber gaze landed on me, as though staring through me. I offered a meek smile, then placed my hand on his arm if only to show him my support.

"I'm going to check out Izzy's place," Sam said without breaking eye contact with me. "See if I can pick up a fresh scent. Lukas, take Rory, Vincent, and Diego. I want you four in the French Quarter. Take the image composite my father and I put together and start asking around. Check the local haunts, the vampire dives, anything that caters to our kind. I want a name by the time you return."

"You think someone's seen this asshole?" Lukas demanded.

"I think he has to be hiding somewhere, and we're going to find him. When you get a name, you call Adrien, then me. Do not engage without permission."

Lukas dipped his head respectfully, then he snapped his fingers and pointed at the front door. The others marched after him, clearly as eager as I was to find this guy.

"I'm coming with you," I said. Sam immediately shook his head, but I squeezed his arm. "I wasn't asking for permission."

His mouth twisted, but after a few short breaths, Sam nodded. "Thank you. I'll let you know when we're ready to leave. I have a few more things to do first."

I wanted to tell him that I would do anything for him, anything to help his family bring Izzy's killer to justice, but there were others still present in the room, and I didn't feel like airing our relationship to the rest of the pack. Instead, I offered another smile, then left him to handle his other packmates while I slipped into the kitchen.

The house had a morose atmosphere to it, but it was the child standing in front of the kitchen counter that nearly broke me. Claire, Monique, and Sophie had come running upstairs the instant they'd heard their mother start crying. I would never forget the look on Claire's face when she'd spotted her sister. Like Sam, her eyes had started to glow, and a terrifying stillness filled her, one that screamed of rage and anguish.

Monique, on the other hand, had dropped next to her parents and wrapped her thin arms around them, comforting them as only another child could. Sophie had stood back, clearly at a loss and struggling with her own emotions.

The sight almost made me not want children. I never wanted to experience that level of pain.

"Hi, Claire," I murmured as I stepped up beside her.

Her head slowly turned, and she unleashed that burning gaze on me. I wondered if mine did the same thing. Or if her wolf rode closer to the surface than most people.

"Are you going to help Sammy find the guy who killed my sister?" she asked.

Her question stabbed me in the heart. "Yeah, sweetie. That's the plan."

Unspeakable emotions whisked across her face as she turned back toward the window. "Good."

The word sent a chill down my spine. Claire was only nine, for crying out loud, and already she was wishing for another person's death. In this case, I couldn't blame her, but the thought terrified me. She was so young to have already been exposed to the brutal violence of the world.

I couldn't find it in me to say anything. So, instead, I offered comfort. I slipped an arm around her frail shoulders and drew her close.

"You're Sammy's mate, aren't you?" When I didn't answer, she tipped her head up. "I heard my parents talking about you that first night you visited."

Ah. "Yeah, I am."

Her little head bobbed. "Good. I'm glad he has someone."

"Why's that?"

She shrugged. "Everyone deserves someone. Sammy's the best, you know. But you should also know"—those devastatingly bright eyes slammed into mine—"if you hurt him, I'll hurt you."

Such a comment from a pre-teen shouldn't have frightened me, but holy cow, did a shiver scream down my spine. I had a feeling little Miss Claire here was an alpha through and through. A future hellion. And likely another pack leader. Even I could feel the power flowing through her. So when she said she'd hurt me, I believed her.

"Don't worry, I have no intentions of hurting your brother."

She gave another slow nod, then sighed and rested her head against my waist. Alpha, yes, but still a child, and still a little girl mourning the death of her big sister.

"Are you hungry?" I asked.

"No."

Werewolves were always hungry, but grief had ways of tricking us into believing otherwise. "I could make you something. A sandwich?"

Her lithe body trembled before she spoke, "Izzy used to offer me sandwiches all the time. She said it was the only way to keep the beast fed." Claire sniffled and wiped her face. "She meant me. She always called me the Beast. Because I'm always hungry."

My arm tightened around her. "I don't have to make you a sandwich. I can make you anything you want."

"No. I want a sandwich." Her face turned up toward me. "Please."

I wanted to cry for this little girl, but I had to put on a brave face. So with another soft smile, I nodded, then headed toward the fridge. Hopefully I didn't anger Elena or Adrien by rifling through their supplies.

I held a loaf of bread in hand when I realized Claire likely wasn't the only one who needed food. I glanced at the clock and noted the time. Nine in the morning. Sam and I had arrived shortly before one. So it'd been eight hours since Izzy had passed. Eight hours in which no one in the family had eaten.

I set to work, making sandwiches for all of them, even Aimee, who'd arrived a few hours ago. Since the pack was slowly filtering out, I didn't make them anything. They could fend for themselves, and I didn't feel right emptying Sam's parents' fridge of food. Not right now. Later, I would order them groceries and keep them supplied as best I could. I didn't want them to have to think of anything beyond taking care of Izzy's and Gabriel's arrangements. The rest I could handle for them.

Two piles of sandwiches later, and I was done, along with their bread supply. I quickly used a grocery delivery app to order more, along with anything else they needed, then handed Claire a sandwich. She stared at it for a moment, tears rolling down her cheeks.

I didn't offer her any comforting words because what good would that do? Instead, I dropped to my knees and folded her into my arms, holding her as she cried over a sandwich. I'd never truly lost anyone I cared about, but I remembered how I'd felt when Anna transitioned into a vampire. I hadn't believed it possible until she'd first woken. Before that, I'd truly thought her dead. And it'd wrecked me.

Footsteps approached, but I didn't pull away from Claire.

I lifted my gaze and watched as Elena entered the kitchen. Her eyes widened at the sight of us, then darted to the plate of sandwiches I held in my hand. Her face crumpled, but she mouthed the words "thank you" before kneeling beside us.

"Claire, honey?" Elena whispered.

Her daughter pulled away from me and threw herself into her mother's arms, her body racked with sobs. Elena pressed her lips together to keep from crying herself and held my gaze. I pointed toward the sandwiches. When she nodded, I rose to my feet, touched her shoulder in silent sympathy, then placed one on the counter for her. Plate in hand, I left the kitchen and went in search of the other family members.

Sam was the easiest to find. I just let my heart guide the way. He'd left the living room and now stood in his father's office. When I entered, they paused their somber discussion, but both took a sandwich with a grateful nod. Sam even leaned down and pressed a kiss to my cheek before I sought out his other sisters.

Monique sat with Sophie in one of their bedrooms. I had to assume it was Monique's due to all the Harry Styles posters hanging on her walls. Sophie took two sandwiches from me, then gave them a sniff, no doubt ensuring the food was safe. A part of me wanted to feel a bit insulted, but deep down, I understood. Their sister had just been murdered, and Sophie didn't know the first thing about me, least of all if she could trust me. Probably didn't even know I was Sam's mate yet.

All that remained was the eldest sister, Aimee, who I found sitting on a swing in the backyard. When I opened the door and stepped outside, she glanced over her shoulder and nodded, before facing forward again, her hands gripped around the support ropes.

I climbed into the swing next to her and offered up the plate. "Hungry?"

"Thanks." She took the sandwich and held it between her hands on her lap. She stared down at it, as though eating required every bit of energy she possessed.

Everyone had already offered their apologies, which meant very little, so I tried a different tactic. "We're going to find him. And when we do..."

She lifted her head and brushed aside her brown hair. "Is it terrible that I want him dead?"

"No," I said. "I don't think that's terrible at all."

"I just..." She sighed and rested her head against the rope. "I hate him. And I don't even know who he is. I've never hated someone like that before. So completely. I don't even know his name. Or why Izzy. Why us?"

I had a theory about that. But I swore to keep it to myself. Sam didn't need to know that I suspected Izzy had been more about revenge than turning her into a werewolf. That this was payback for us killing the attacker's partner. That would only cause the family more pain.

"I don't know," I said. "But when Sam and I find him, he's dead."

Her gaze darted to mine. "You swear it?"

I nodded. "We won't let him get away with this, and we're going to stop him from hurting anyone else."

"Good. And Lucy?"

I started at the sound of my name. I didn't even realize she'd known about me. "Yeah?"

"Make it hurt."

Another nod, another promise. But this one would be easy to keep.

SAM STOOD at the edge of Izzy's driveway and stared up at the two-story house. It was smaller than her parents' but clearly well-cared for. Azalea shrubs lined the front of her porch, adding a splash of color to an otherwise blandly painted home.

"My parents own this place," Sam said, offering his first words since we'd left the house. "They keep it for us. When we go to school, they let us live here instead of staying on campus." A half smile graced his lips. "Izzy wanted to live in the dorms with all the other college students, but my father was adamant that she have her own space."

I nodded, encouraging him to continue.

"Most of us have stayed here. I was first, then

Aimee, then Sophie, and now Izzy." He brushed a hand through his hair. "I suppose they'll sell it now. I can't imagine Monique or Claire wanting to stay in the home where their sister was…" His voice broke.

I stepped close to Sam and wound an arm around his waist, tucking my head against his chest. His arms closed around me, so tight it was hard to breathe, but I didn't complain. For Sam, I could handle a little lung-bruising.

When Sam didn't budge an inch, I faced the house. I couldn't imagine how difficult this was for him. Investigating Daniel's scene had sucked, seeing as how they were best friends. But that was different. Daniel had survived. This was a whole new level of misery and torment.

"Why don't you stay out here," I said, running my hand down his chest. "I know what we're looking for, so I can go in and have a look."

Sam's eyes narrowed. "I need the bastard's scent."

"You already know it," I told him. "You know his face too. You don't need to go inside. All we need is a fresh trail. Let me do this for you." Before Sam could argue, I slipped out of his embrace and rose on my tiptoes, placing a gentle kiss on his jaw. "I won't be long."

I barely took a step before Sam's hand grasped mine. I glanced over my shoulder to find his unwavering stare latched onto me.

"Be careful," he said.

"Absolutely. If I think there's anything remotely dangerous inside, I'll shout."

He nodded, clearly appeased by that. I could only imagine his werewolf instincts were going haywire right now, urging him to be protective of his mate. The last thing I wanted was to make life more difficult for him.

I turned back to the house, drew a steadying breath, then stepped inside. The second I entered the foyer, I nearly gagged. It'd been hours since Izzy's attack, and the coppery scent of blood seemed to permeate the entire place.

"Lucy?" Sam called.

"I'm fine," I choked out, waving a hand at him.

It'd be a miracle if I could even pick up the attacker's scent. But I'd promised Sam I would try, and I refused to let him down.

I stepped inside the hallway and progressed toward the stairs, where the scent of blood grew stronger. My nerves seemed to jump with every step, as though they expected someone to jump out of the shadows.

Grasping the railing, I started to climb the stairs. By the time I reached the top, my cheeks were soaked with tears. Unlike Daniel's place, Izzy's was an absolute wreck. Smashed pictures, tattered wallpaper, torn carpet, broken doors, shredded blankets and pillows—the place looked like a war zone. Gabriel must have put up one hell of a fight. I made a mental note to pass that information along to his family. I could only imagine they would want to know that he'd fought for Izzy's and his life with everything he'd possessed.

I followed a blood trail into the main bedroom and choked on the cloying air. The combined scent was almost too much. I could barely differentiate between everything. My eyes scanned the room, from the demolished canopy bed to the massive crack in the wall next to the dresser. Someone had been thrown into it, the force of which had nearly shot them outside.

I first reached for the bedcovers and lifted them to my nose. I gave an unstained corner a sniff and winced. My stomach rebelled, but I caught a whiff of something. A hint of azalea and vanilla. Izzy. I recognized that fragrance from Sam's parents' place. A perfume, possibly?

Dropping the blanket, I moved for a random

scrap of material sitting in the middle of the floor. Whatever it was, it carried the stench of something sweet. I couldn't place it, but when I opened the cloth and saw a ruddy handprint embedded on it, I cursed.

A rag doused in chloroform.

Was that how they were incapacitating their victims? And if that were the case, why didn't it work this time? Had Gabriel startled the attacker, resulting in a fight that had left Izzy broken and dead? Now that I was a werewolf, I understood how utterly fragile humans were. Izzy wouldn't have stood a chance against two werewolves. Maybe she hadn't been tortured. Maybe she'd simply been caught between two savage creatures hellbent on ripping each other to shreds. Or maybe the attacker had knocked her out and restrained her. Perhaps he'd started torturing her afterward. Gabriel might have already been out of the picture by then. Truly, there was no way of knowing, not unless I found some evidence.

I continued studying the room, looking for anything that might stand out. I needed something that possibly belonged to the werewolf or something he'd touched.

When my gaze landed on bits of broken wood, I

dropped to a knee and started sorting through the debris. These bits of wood differed from the canopy frame. Lighter-colored and cheaply made. A chair perhaps? That would confirm my restraint theory. Except there weren't enough pieces to make up an entire chair.

I gave up and moved on. I took a few steps toward the closet when something small caught my eye. Something that certainly didn't belong. I paused and peered through the strewn wreckage only to see something light-colored and adorned with something shiny.

What the hell?

I kneeled in a pile of torn curtain fabric and rifled through the folds. The second I made contact, I gasped and snatched my hand back.

A finger.

The ring finger, to be precise. Complete with a fancy—albeit bloodstained—emerald ring. I pressed a fist to my mouth and fought back a gag. Last I'd heard, Gabriel had died with all his pieces, and seeing as how this was a man's finger, it certainly hadn't belonged to Izzy.

Which meant it belonged to our attacker.

Fighting to keep my stomach in check, I ripped

off a piece of curtain and wrapped it around the dismembered digit.

"I'm holding an amputated finger," I told myself, "in my hand." I couldn't believe this was my life now.

With the finger in hand, I completed the rest of my sweep. But when nothing else turned up, I hurried back downstairs and into the kitchen. It took a few tries, but I eventually found the cupboard stocked with Ziplock bags. In the finger went. Then I zipped up the baggie and stuffed it in my pocket. Out of sight, out of mind. At least for now.

I quickly hurried outside to find Sam standing exactly where I'd left him. Once he spotted me, his shoulders rounded, and he released a long breath. Without a word, he dragged me into his chest and held me close, his fingers combing through my hair, as though reassuring himself that I was fine.

"Did you find anything?" he finally asked.

I nodded, my cheek brushing against his shirt. "It's gross."

"What is?"

"The thing I found."

"Gross?" he repeated.

I stepped back, then plunged my hand into my pocket and liberated the bag. Out here, in the sunlight, the finger seemed even more repugnant. The torn flesh and jagged bone twisted my stomach. I nearly spewed my guts right then and there, but I tamped it back, then handed the bag over and forced my gaze in another direction. Any other direction. I watched the children two houses down play hopscotch, all the while giggling and teasing each other. It drove a knife through my heart to see them here amid the violence. Thankfully, they remained blissfully unaware. But it sickened me to think that late last night, while they'd been safely tucked into bed, Izzy had been dying.

"This is great," Sam said.

"I might argue that."

His hand found the small of my back, and he applied the smallest amount of comforting pressure. "This will help us identify him. We can easily heal these sorts of wounds, but we can't regenerate parts. So the man we're looking for is down by one finger."

"And one expensive-looking ring that he might be wanting back," I added.

Sam lifted the bag to the sunlight, and I choked on my breath. "Put that away before someone sees!" I jerked my chin toward the children. They were too far away to see what Sam held, but the last thing we needed were two innocent kids running home to mom because the neighbor's brother was holding a finger.

"Were you able to find a fresh scent to track?" he asked as he slipped the finger back into my pocket. Guess that made me the delivery girl. Yay me.

"No. I'm sorry. There was too much going on in there, I could only pick up your sister's."

Sam's face fell, but he nodded. "Let's do a perimeter check first before we leave. See if we can pick up anything out here. If not, we'll head home and get this finger to Adrien. He might be able to ID the ring and see who it belongs to."

Anything to get out of here and get rid of the damn finger just chilling in my pocket. I shivered, then followed Sam in a wide circle around the property. Neither of us picked up on a fresh trail, so we called it a day and headed back to the car.

"Wonder if Lukas found anything."

"Here's hoping. I'm not sure how many more dead leads I can take."

We slid into our prospective seats, and Sam fired up the engine. But instead of sliding into drive, he leaned his head back. Exhaustion had bruised the undersides of his eyes. I had to imagine mine were similarly dark. Neither of us had slept last night.

And what should have been the happiest night of our life had quickly become one of Sam's worst.

"Do you want me to drive?" I asked. I hadn't just lost a family member, nor was I as emotionally drained as him, so it felt like I would be the safer driver.

"No, I'm fine. I just need a moment to collect my thoughts."

Fair enough. I silently sat next to him, giving him all the time he needed. After a short interlude, he put the car in drive, and off we went, back to his parents' house.

"We're going to catch him," I told Sam. "We know what he looks like, and we have his finger and his ring. It won't be much longer before we have his identity. And then we'll track him down and handle it."

"Handle it how?" Sam asked.

"I don't know. That's not up to me to decide. That's up to Adrien."

Sam shot me a quick smile, though it didn't quite reach his eyes. "You're starting to sound like an heir."

"Guess I learned from the best," I told him. "When we get back to your place, I'd like to call Reggie. Maybe he's heard something."

"Or maybe he'll force you to come back," Sam muttered.

"He can't force me to do anything," I announced. "And if he tries, I'll just have to add his balls to my little baggie here." I patted my jacket pocket. "Maybe I'll start a body parts collection for people who piss me off."

Sam's eyes widened. "Damn. That's cold."

I chuckled. "I'm just kidding."

"I sure hope so because I'd hate to be included in that *Texas Chainsaw Massacre* bag of yours."

"You? Why would I ever add one of your body parts in here?"

"We're mates, but we're not perfect," he said. "I'm sure the day will come where I piss you off, and vice versa."

I shrugged. "That may be, but I promise never to castrate you."

"Phew," he teased, pausing to throw me a casual wink and a smile.

I didn't hide the smile that pulled at my lips. It made me happy to see that I could still make Sam smile after everything he'd been through today. It gave me hope that everything would work itself out in the end.

We'd just pulled up in front of Adrien's and

Elena's when my phone rang. Seeing as how it was early afternoon, I knew it wasn't Anna. My mom, maybe? I hadn't seen her since the wedding and could only imagine she was growing impatient.

At the sight of Reggie's name on my screen in bold letters, I grimaced. I so wasn't in the mood to deal with him, even though I'd already intended on calling him. Maybe the man was psychic. Except, that couldn't be true. If he were, he'd know all the unpleasant things I thought about him.

I showed Sam the screen, then connected the call as I slid out of the car. "Yeah?"

"Yeah? That's how you answer the phone?" he asked.

"When it's you." Recalling what Elena told me about him and my mom and how he'd played and lied to her didn't endear him to me in the slightest bit.

"And here I was calling to offer you some help."

"Some help," I repeated. "From you?"

"Careful," he growled. "You might be my heir, but that won't stop me from kicking your ass if you keep mouthing off."

Sam's head snapped toward me, his lips curling up. Without another word, he snatched the phone from my hand and put the call on speaker.

"If you ever lay a fucking finger on her, I'll make sure to feed them to you for breakfast," Sam threatened.

My eyes widened. "Sam!"

"Sam?" Reggie repeated. "As in the heir of the New Orleans Pack?"

"Give me my phone back."

Sam ignored me and instead turned his back to me and held my phone closer to his mouth. "I've heard a lot about you too. Like the fact that you've barely helped Lucy adjust to being a werewolf. Two shifts in a year? Are you fucking kidding me? Are you trying to get her killed?"

"Sam!" I shouted. I ran behind him, reaching for my phone. But considering Sam was a freaking lumberjack, I couldn't reach it when he lifted my phone into the air above his head.

I ducked and weaved around him and jumped in the air, snatching at my phone. My fingers grazed his biceps and latched on. Much like the proverbial tree he was, I climbed him as quickly as I could and ripped my phone out of his grasp.

This time, I gave him my back as I took the call off speakerphone and lifted it to my ear. I felt Sam's presence behind me, so I turned and unleashed the most Anna-worthy glare I could muster. It must have worked because Sam jerked to a stop with a deep frown, as though surprised at his own actions.

"Reggie," I said.

"What the fuck was that all about?"

"Don't ask. It's been a very difficult day."

Reggie's growl vibrated across the phone. "Who the fuck does that kid think he is? What's he to you?"

I sighed and forced my hand through my hair. This wasn't how I'd envisioned telling Reggie about my mate, but it seemed there was no hiding it now. Not after Sam's antics. So, I filled Reggie in on everything. About Sam's and my relationship, about the attacks, the finger and ring, Izzy's death. Everything.

Mercifully, Reggie kept quiet the entire time. It wasn't until I took a breath and told him I was finished that he finally spoke.

"Come home. Now."

"Yeah, no, that won't be happening."

"Lucy!" he snapped.

"Reggie, I just told you I have a mate whose sister has been murdered. His pack is in danger, and it's all connected to me. So no, I'm not going anywhere. Honestly, I don't give a shit what you think about it. Just because I came from your sperm doesn't mean you have any control over what I do. And while I don't approve of Sam's methods, I will admit he's right. You didn't give a shit about me or my training. All you cared about was acknowledging that you had an heir. Therefore, I'm going to stay here until I deem I'm ready to return to Jackson. In the meantime, you can either accept my decision and, for once, be helpful, or you can suck on a rotten egg and leave me the hell alone."

I listened to the sound of Reggie having what sounded like an aneurysm in the background. I couldn't imagine anyone had ever spoken to him like that before. I was happy to be the first.

"What if I order you to come home?" he asked.

"Unless you're planning on driving here, I don't see how you can force me to do anything."

"Don't test me, girl."

"Don't test me," I snapped. "You may be an alpha, but in my world, that doesn't mean shit. I've faced vampires far scarier than you and survived."

Reggie unleashed a series of curses that would have made my mother blush, but I didn't back down. Once he was finished, I said, "Well?"

"Well what?"

"Are you going to help us?"

He unleashed a growl that might have terrified

me if he were here in person. Over the phone, it just sounded kind of... tinny. And so not scary.

"Fine," he snapped. "Send me the photos. Adrien knows how to contact me. I'll see what I can find out."

I grinned saccharinely. "Thank you."

"Don't thank me. This isn't over."

Oh, it was over all right. So much so that instead of retorting, I simply ended the phone call and slid the phone in my back pocket. Now, I had the other werewolf to deal with. I took a moment to gather my thoughts. This wasn't the time to berate Sam for his behavior. Even I knew his wolf was riding incredibly close to the surface, and he was fighting its protective nature.

"I'm sorry," came his gruff response behind me.

When I turned, I found him sitting on the porch steps, his head bowed over his knees.

Sympathy softened my mood. I crossed the distance between us, then sat on the steps next to him and rested my head on his shoulder. Scolding him seemed pointless, especially knowing that were the roles reversed, I would have done the same thing for him.

"I love you too," I whispered. He hadn't said it. But actions spoke far louder than words.

Sam tensed. "What did you just say?"

A small smile curved my lips. "I said I love you too."

"But I never said I love you."

"That's okay."

A moment of silence passed. Usually, this was the part where I ran away with my tail tucked between my legs. But I was done with all that. This was the only place I wanted to be.

"I do, though," Sam said. When I didn't speak, he continued with, "Love you."

I brushed a kiss against his cheek. "I know."

20

TOGETHER, Sam and I entered his parents' house, but there was no warm welcome to greet us. I suspected it would be a while for things to return to normal. If they ever did. Aimee and Sophie sat at the kitchen table, their hands wrapped around a pair of steaming mugs. From the smell of it, they were drinking hot lemon water, though it didn't look like either had taken a sip yet. Comfort from the heat, perhaps.

They both glanced our way, sadness dimming their eyes. Sam strode to Aimee and half-heartedly ruffled her hair. Her faint smile seemed to lift the depression a little.

"Did you find him?" Sophie asked.

"Not yet. But we're getting closer," Sam said.

I bit my tongue to keep from saying something disheartening because I sure didn't think we were getting closer. A finger didn't really give us much. Maybe we could have it printed and learn his identity, but I wasn't sure that would help us find him.

"Where's Dad?"

"In his office," Aimee said, "with mom. They haven't come out for a few hours."

I couldn't blame them. They probably wanted some time alone to gather their thoughts and sort out their emotions. If it were me, I wouldn't want my children to see me grieving. I'd want to put on a brave face.

Sam's head bobbed. He cupped the back of Sophie's head, then left the kitchen, likely heading for the office. Since I was the one carrying the finger, I followed him toward the back of the house. Once we reached the office, he lifted his hand to knock, but the door swung open, and there stood Elena. Her eyes were rimmed red and her skin sallow and pale, but she offered us a shadow of a smile before letting us enter.

"Did you find anything?" Adrien asked.

He sat in his chair, his hands folded on his chest and his head resting against the seat back. His eyes were closed, but I could feel his focus narrowing on us.

"A finger," Sam answered.

Adrien's eyes slowly opened, just as red as Elena's. "A finger?"

I fished in my pocket and drew out the baggie. "I don't know how he lost it. Gabriel, maybe? But I found it hidden beneath some debris. Maybe we can get it fingerprinted somehow? Or identify the ring? It's a pretty unique piece."

Elena cupped the bag and lifted the torn digit up to the light. We'd have to get it on ice pretty quickly here if we intended to fingerprint it.

"I have a contact with the local police," Adrien commented. "I can send it in. But I suggest we keep the ring to ID ourselves."

Dibs out of that. I wasn't touching that thing again. I'd had my fill of dismembered parts for the day. Thankfully, no one asked me to. Instead, Adrien rose to his feet and slowly approached. He snatched a few tissues, then took the bag from me. The second he opened it, I pressed my hand under my nose and stepped back, reminded of the stench from Izzy's house.

Using the tissues, Adrien removed the ring, then resealed the bag with only the finger left inside.

"I can clean it," Elena offered.

Adrien handed it over without argument, and Elena left. This time there was no smile or kind words. The whole house and everyone inside were nothing more than shells of their former selves, and it hurt to see it.

"No trackable scent?" Adrien asked.

"Unfortunately not. Has Lukas arrived yet? Any word?"

"Not yet. But they checked in about half an hour ago. They're still canvasing the French Quarter. It'll take a while longer yet still, I should think."

"Reggie has agreed to help," I said. "He just needs to see the sketch of the wolf. He also said you would know how to send it to him."

Adrien nodded. "That's kind of him. Make sure to send him my thanks."

I almost laughed at the thought of offering Reggie any form of a thanks. Dude didn't deserve it. But I simply nodded.

"You two should get some sleep," Adrien

commented. He rounded his desk and returned to his chair, resuming his previous position. I wondered if he'd been trying to sleep when we entered.

"Do you want us to stay here? We can bunk in one of the rooms upstairs."

"That's up to you. If you want to stay here, you can. Aimee and Sophie have decided to stay, and they've taken the last guest room. Daniel and Brenda are in the other two. So you two would be camping on the couches downstairs."

A full house. Which sounded pretty damn miserable, but I wouldn't complain if that was what Sam wanted. I couldn't imagine he wanted to be far from his family right now.

"Thanks. But I think we'll go back to my place."

Adrien cracked open his eyes. "You sure? He may know where you live too. We can't assume otherwise."

Sam seemed torn by this. So I offered a suggestion, one I wasn't sure he would accept. "We could stay at Vlad's and Anna's. Doubtful this wolf knows about them. I have a room there where we can stay, and Anna and Vlad are on their honeymoon. So we'd have the place to ourselves."

Adrien looked to Sam, who nodded. "It's not a bad idea. At least we'd be able to get some sleep."

I pulled out my phone and fired off a quick text to Anna, explaining the situation and telling them we'd be crashing at their place for a few nights. I honestly didn't think either Anna or Vlad would have a problem with it, considering the circumstances.

"Then it's settled. But stay in contact."

Sam nodded. "I'd like to know when Lukas and his team get back. Will you let me know what they've found?"

"Of course. But promise me you won't go off on your own in search of this asshole," Adrien insisted. "We do this as a pack. It's safer that way."

Sam's gaze shifted to me right before he nodded. I didn't need to be a mind reader to know where his thoughts had strayed. I could practically read them on his face. "I have my mate to protect, so trust me, I wouldn't be that stupid."

A genuine smile graced Adrien's face. "Then you two have figured that out? Your relationship is official?"

I took Sam's hand and nodded, my stomach a bit anxious. What if Adrien rejected me?

"Have you come up with a solution regarding your living arrangements?" he asked.

"I had a thought about that..." I hesitated, my gaze darting to Sam.

"You have?" Sam asked.

My teeth raked across my bottom lip as I nodded. "I'd like to transfer to your pack."

Shocked silence spread through the room.

"You... do? But what about the Mississippi Pack?" Sam blinked at me as though never in a million years had he thought I'd make that suggestion, which seemed silly considering he knew how much I disliked Reggie.

"I figure they can suck it," I said with a light laugh. "They've gone this long without a proper heir. I'm sure Reggie can find someone to replace me. It's not like he's always had an heir to depend on."

"You do know he can deny your request," Adrien chimed in.

"So I won't let him."

Adrien chuckled. "As strong-willed as Reginald, I see."

"Don't worry, I get it from my mother too."

His chuckle grew into a full-blown laugh. One that startled both me and Sam. Though it warmed my heart to hear it.

"Lucy, you are always welcome in my pack,"

Adrien said. "I would be a fool to turn you away. Not only because my son clearly loves you—"

I winked at Sam. "See, I wasn't the only one who knew."

Sam rolled his eyes.

"But also because of everything you've done for us. You've helped us during this dark time. I think you'd be a great fit for our pack."

I beamed at both Adrien and Sam. For the first time since I'd been turned into a werewolf, I felt like I'd found my home. The Mississippi Pack had never felt like this. I'd made acquaintances out of a few of the pack members but no relationships that drew me back to them. Louisiana was my home. Anna and Sam were here. My mom and dad were here. This was where I wanted to be.

"Lucy." Sam's hand tightened on mine. "Are you sure about this? You'd be giving up a prestigious position within your pack—"

"And gaining an even better one with yours, as your mate. Sam, I love you. I want to be with you. I don't want a long-distance relationship or worry about pack politics between us. I just want you."

My proclamation brightened the shadows on his face. He leaned down and kissed me, though we kept it chaste in front of his father.

"Well, at least something wonderful came of today," Adrien said. "Your request to join our pack is, of course, approved. But it's up to you to convince your alpha to release you from the Mississippi Pack. And I dare say, you may find that task more challenging than anything you've faced thus far. Reginald has wanted an heir for quite a long time. He may not willingly give you up."

Determination swept through me. "Then I guess I'll just have to piss him off enough to fire me."

Even Sam laughed this time. "If anyone can accomplish that, it's you."

"Damn straight." I tugged on his hand and gestured to the door. "Let's go. We both could do with some sleep."

"Be careful," Adrien said. "And Lucy?"

I glanced over my shoulder.

Adrien winked at me. "Welcome to our family."

THE SECOND we stepped foot inside Vlad and Anna's home, Sam pulled me into his arms. He rested his head on top of mine and simply breathed me in. I closed my eyes and sank into the embrace.

"I needed this," Sam mumbled into my hair.

Understandable. We'd been alone this afternoon, but considering we'd been standing outside his recently deceased sister's house, it hadn't been the same. Even I felt it, this need to take comfort from Sam and to offer him the same in return. I stroked his back, my fingers finding the edges of his tousled hair and combing through it.

The past twenty-four hours had been quite emotional and had put both of us through the wringer. Sam more than me.

"My room is on the second floor, third door on the left. Why don't you head on up and get comfy, and I'll make us something to eat."

"Does Vlad keep the place stocked with real food?"

I chuckled. "Don't worry. His kitchen is always well-stocked."

"He's a vampire."

"With a human blood bank at his beck and call."

Sam's arms briefly tightened around me before he let go and started up the stairs. I waited for the sound of my door opening, then made my way into the kitchen. Usually his staff milled about, but I didn't hear a single soul beyond Sam upstairs. Vlad must have reduced the staff. I only hoped that meant there was food. If not, I'd order us a pizza.

Thankfully, there was enough in the kitchen to sustain us for a day or two. Not much had been left, which made sense, considering the Draculas were off on a two-week adventure somewhere very south of us. I wasn't sure where the Falkland Islands were, but any islands had to be better than New Orleans in the winter.

With a pile of peanut butter and jam sandwiches and a couple glasses of water, I headed upstairs. My stomach cramped with anticipation, eager to fill it with something yummy. I eased open my bedroom door and paused on the threshold.

Sam lay sprawled on the bed, his legs half-dangling over the edge and his head buried in the pillows. The double-sized bed wasn't large enough for his lumberjack frame. All six-foot-five of him. His gentle snores told me he'd long since passed out while I was downstairs preparing food.

I couldn't blame him. Even I felt the pull to crash. We hadn't slept since the night before, thanks to our adventures between the sheets last night.

Setting down the plate, I lifted Sam's legs and placed them fully on the bed. Then I set to work, gently undressing him. The bed was pristine likely due to Vlad's cleaning staff. Even though I didn't live here anymore, they'd taken great care of everything. I'd have to thank him when he returned.

Once I had Sam stripped, I grabbed a spare blanket from the closet and draped it over him. Unfortunately, there wasn't a lot of room for me. The man was massive, after all. Sometimes I forgot just how massive. Like ducking his head beneath doorframes and taking up an entire double bed massive. Anna loved to call him the Lumberjack Wolfman, which had always made me laugh. Put him in plaid—which was the majority of his wardrobe—and he fit the description to a T.

I rubbed my face with my hands and studied my room while eating the sandwiches. There really wasn't anywhere for me to sleep. So, I considered my options. I could slink away to Vlad and Anna's room and tuck myself into their bed. The idea didn't quite sit well with me. Sleeping in a vampire's bed... I shuddered. That might be a bit too far for me.

There was the new couch downstairs, which was comfortable enough, but really, I didn't love the idea of sleeping on a couch. Who did?

All that left was trying to find a way to sneak into bed with Sam. Truthfully, that was the only decision worth considering. My heart tugged in one direction and one direction only. I pondered the options and finally decided to first strip, then crawl over Sam's legs and tuck myself between him and the wall. The second my head touched the pillow, his beefy arm came around my waist, and he hauled me up against his chest. I settled into the crook of his other arm and sighed contentedly. This was where I belonged. With luck, I'd never have to leave.

21

An annoying chirp kept invading my dreams. It sounded like a strange tweety bird circling my head while I shared a plate of mini shrimp lettuce wraps with Michelle Obama. In my dream, she started laughing at me while I swatted at the offensive creature while it divebombed my head. I wasn't a huge fan of birds, so I found myself growing angrier and angrier with every failed swat.

"Lucy..." a deep voice rumbled in the distance.

I turned away from Michelle Obama's laughing face and stared behind me, but now I stood alone in a field of green, surrounded by blood-red calla lilies. What the hell? Where was I?

The knee-high grass rustled in the breeze, and

through the blades, I spotted movement. It wasn't until the massive bunny came to a stop in front of me that I blinked. "Uh... hello?"

"Lucy," it growled, its lips curling back to expose sharp teeth.

I gasped and stumbled back a step.

That was no Bugs Bunny. More like the Easter Bunny crossed with Frankenstein.

Its pink button nose twitched twice before it spoke again. "Lucy, wake up!"

Oh yeah, this was definitely a dream. But I couldn't seem to find my way out. I hated lucid dreams. Sighing, I reached down and grasped a bit of arm between my index finger and thumb. One hard pinch, and I shot awake, gasping for breath.

"Don't hurt me, bunny!" I cried out.

Amused laughter echoed through the room. "Leave the bunnies alone and answer your phone."

My phone. Right. The chirping.

The cell gave one last ring, then quieted. With an annoyed groan, I scrambled over Sam's impossibly long legs and scooted out of bed. I'd tossed everything in a pile before falling asleep, so I had to fish through my clothes to find the damn thing. When I did, I noted three missed calls, all from Reggie.

Great. This so wasn't how I wanted to start the day. Or finish it? Honestly, I had no idea what time it was or how long Sam and I had been asleep. I glanced at the window only to find it pitch black outside, meaning it was either super late or super early. Another quick glance at my phone revealed it to be ten p.m. We'd arrived here at Vlad and Anna's sometime before dinner, so we'd only been asleep for a few hours. No wonder I didn't feel refreshed.

Sam had already drifted back off, evidenced by his soft snores, so I slipped on a robe then tiptoed out of our room and into Vlad and Anna's. Once upon a time, they'd slept in coffins up in the attic, but thanks to new technology and vampire-friendly businesses, they could now snooze together happily in what looked like a California king bed. Anna had mentioned their new UV ray-proof windows. Guess they worked, seeing as how neither Anna nor Vlad were a steaming pile of ash.

I sat on the edge of their bed and redialed Reggie's number.

"'Bout freaking time," he snapped.

"Nice to hear from you too."

"I have been trying to get a hold of you for hours."

I rubbed the bridge of my nose. "Look, it's been a

damn hard day, okay? Excuse me if I needed to get a little rest."

"Rest, huh? Or were you just too busy screwing the alpha's son?"

Every muscle in my body tensed. My eyes slammed open, and I stared at a single spot on the nearest wall, willing myself to keep calm. I couldn't reach through the phone line and rip off Reggie's head, so getting angry wouldn't do anything other than piss me off. And I wasn't in the mood to be pissed off. I couldn't let everything he said irk me. If I did, we'd never get through a single conversation without killing each other.

"Listen, you need to come home, right now. I don't care where you are, and I don't care how hard it'll be. You aren't safe there."

Anger bled into terror. "What? What do you mean I'm not safe? I'm with Sam. Of course I'm safe."

"Like hell," Reggie snapped, his frustration clearly carrying through the call. "Need I remind you someone is hunting the human-born in New Orleans? You'll be safer here with me."

"Need I remind you that I'm not a human-born anymore. So I'm not in any danger."

"Lucy!" he snapped.

"Oh, save it. How about you first tell me why you think I'm in danger, and we'll go from there. We both know ordering me around won't get you anywhere."

I listened as Reggie softly counted to himself and grinned. For some reason, it pleased me to know I could piss him off so easily.

"Fine. You know that picture you asked Adrien to send me? The composite image?"

"Of course." It was the only task I'd given him after all.

"Well, I know this wolf."

My body jerked straight, and my breathing quickened. "What? You do? How?"

"You need to listen to me carefully, okay? Forget for one moment that I'm your father, and you're pissed at me or whatever. Put all that aside and just listen. Because this is fucking serious, Lucy."

A chill skated down my spine. "Okay."

"About eight months ago, I received a call from one of the outer pack members who reported an unknown wolf in our territory. When we tracked this wolf down, the situation nearly came to blows. His name was Corbin, and not only did he not have permission to encroach on my territory, but he also was a rogue wolf who'd abandoned his pack, so I gave him strict instructions to leave. If he failed to comply,

I would be forced to retaliate. As far as I knew, he complied, so I considered the matter dropped."

"Okay..." I still wasn't sure how any of this related to me.

"I want you to know, though, that I did take the appropriate steps," Reggie said. "I reported Corbin to his alpha, which was how I learned that he'd gone rogue."

"The other wolf, Damon, was rogue too. He used to belong to the South Arkansas Pack."

"Lucy." Reggie drew a deep breath. "Corbin belonged to the England Pack."

My heart stuttered to a dead stop. "What?"

"This is why I want you to come home right now. I'm not saying Corbin is the wolf who attacked you, but what are the chances of a wolf from that particular pack going rogue, then ending up in Mississippi, where you are?"

Fear rooted me to the spot. Almost as though my whole body had gone numb. My breath lodged in my throat until I had to force it out and remind myself to keep breathing. Everything within me had locked up, to the point where my head was starting to pound.

"Do you understand now?" Reggie demanded. "If this is the same wolf who attacked you, you could be in danger."

If, could, maybe. But if it was, then wasn't I safer here? With my mate and his family? My sperm donor hardly gave a shit about me other than finally landing the legacy he'd always dreamed of. Maybe that alone would force him to protect me, but would he do as good a job as Sam? Sam loved me. Sam's parents had welcomed me. Reggie tolerated me only because I could give him something he wanted.

"You don't know for sure though, right?"

"No, of course not."

"Then I'm staying. You might think I'll be safer in Mississippi, but I wholeheartedly disagree."

"Lucy!" he snapped.

I flinched at the sound of his raised voice. I knew Reggie would never harm me. We might not like one another, but we'd never resorted to physical violence. Yet. Besides, I was four hours away. Yelling at me on the phone was truly about the only thing he could do to me.

Slowly, I started to regain control of my body. The fear lingered, but I could control it. I had to. I wouldn't let Reggie terrify me into running back to him. I had to trust that Sam and his family would help protect me. But beyond that, I had to trust in myself as well. I couldn't always rely on someone else to handle my problems.

"I'm not leaving," I said, steeling my voice so Reggie would know he couldn't force the issue. "This is where I belong. In fact, I'm not planning on ever coming back."

A rasped breath hissed through the line. "What did you just say?"

"My mate is here in New Orleans. So is my family. Anna, my mom, my real dad."

"Your real—" His voice cut off when he unleashed a series of creative curses. "Lucy, you cannot do this. You're my heir."

"Yeah, but you never asked me about that. You just made me the heir without even considering me and my wants. So why shouldn't I give you the same courtesy? I never wanted to be your heir, and I certainly never intended to move permanently to Mississippi. I came to you for help, and you barely even provided that. All you care about is your legacy. You don't give a shit about me. So I'm not returning to Jackson. I've found my pack here. With Sam."

A strangled curse echoed in my ears.

"If you think I'm going to let you pull this shit—"

"Reggie, enough." I sighed and rubbed my face. "Aren't you tired of this? Always fighting with me? Constantly bickering about something. It's exhausting. Just... appoint your second as the heir. Seriously, no one is going to give a damn."

"Everyone will give a damn!" he shouted. "This is not how things are done. Packs have heirs—"

"Then name someone else. It's as simple as that. Or, I don't know, hunt down all your other illegitimate children and see if any are interested in being turned."

He choked on a breath. "What? Are you insane?"

"Why not? You were so desperate to make a werewolf that you have, like, what, a dozen abandoned children throughout the country?" I was guesstimating, of course, but it didn't seem too wild of an assumption. "I bet one of them would be interested."

"Request denied," Reggie growled. "If you think I'm going to let you—"

"I think you don't have a choice in the matter. Unless you plan on going to war with Adrien's pack."

His next muffled curse told me Reggie wasn't willing to push things that far. And I didn't blame him. I'd seen both packs. I knew Adrien's had far greater numbers. New Orleans attracted the paranormal about as much as it attracted the humans. Here, we fit in.

"Thank you for telling me about Corbin. I truly appreciate it. I'll pass that information along to Adrien but consider this our last conversation. I'm done with you and your pack."

"Lucy—"

I hung up the call, which seemed to be how all of Reggie's and my calls ended. I dropped my phone onto the mattress next to me and forced myself to breathe. On the one hand, it felt like a weight had been lifted from my shoulders. I'd taken care of the Reggie issue, and now I could stay with Sam and build our life together. On the other hand, there was a new weight pressing on my chest. If this Corbin was the wolf who attacked me, what did that even mean?

I rose on shaky legs and left Anna and Vlad's room. When I entered mine, I found Sam sitting up in bed, concern darkening his expression.

"I assume you heard everything?"

He nodded. "I need to call my father and tell him. We have people who can help us track this Corbin down."

"Okay."

Sam rose from the bed and gathered me in his arms. I tucked my head against his chest and focused on my breathing. Slow and steady would trick my body into believing it could be calm right now. No matter what, I couldn't let myself panic, no matter how badly I might want to. Panicking wouldn't accomplish anything.

"Are you okay?" Sam asked.

"I don't even know. I think I'm too shaken right now to understand what I'm feeling."

His arms tightened. "You know I won't let anything happen to you."

I nodded.

"And we'll protect you."

"That's not what I want," I told him. "I don't think I could handle everyone treating me with kid gloves. I'm not completely helpless. I'm not as skilled as you all are, and I know I have a lot to learn about fighting. But I handled myself in the last fight. So I don't want to be treated as useless."

"No one thinks you're helpless, Luce. Or useless. We just want to keep you safe."

"And that's perfectly fine," I told him. "But let's handle this like a team, okay? A partnership. Not like an overprotective wolf who expects me to do everything he says without question." I'd had enough of that from Reggie.

"No, of course not. We are a team. We're mates."

I smiled and sank into his embrace. I already

knew I'd made the right choice in choosing to stay, but this only emphasized that matter. Had I returned to Mississippi, I didn't doubt that Reggie would lock me up somewhere he considered safe and keep me there until the matter was resolved. No thank you. Obviously, I wouldn't stupidly risk my own life, but I did want to help and be included in decisions.

"Let me call Adrien," Sam said. "Find out if they've learned anything, and then have him look into Corbin. I didn't catch a last name. Did Reggie give you one?"

"No, but I'm sure Adrien could get it just by contacting the England Pack. Luckily for us, it's late enough that they'll be awake over there."

Sam grunted his response, then released me and went in search of his phone. While he did that, I tidied the room and dressed. I knew we would be going back to bed, but I couldn't, not without eating something first.

Down in the kitchen, I opened the fridge to find it full of food. My eyes widened, then I caught a note on the counter informing me that Anna had arranged for a few staff members to return and care for the house and keep it stocked so long as Sam and I were here. I smiled and touched the note, reminding myself to thank her when she returned.

The staff must have come in while Sam and I were sleeping, and we'd been so clearly exhausted, they hadn't woken us. Yikes. Probably not a good thing considering the current situation. Still, I was grateful for more food options beyond sandwiches.

As quickly as I could, I whipped up the easiest meal I could find for me and Sam. It wasn't anything great, but considering I couldn't cook for the life of me, I'd chosen to err on the side of caution and just heat up a pizza in the oven. Luckily, and likely for the first time ever, I hadn't burned the crust.

I carried the two plates upstairs, only to catch the tail end of Adrien and Sam's conversation. From the sounds of it, Adrien didn't have any new information, but he intended to contact the England Pack immediately and learn all he could about Corbin.

Once they hung up, I presented my proud display with a massive grin.

Sam chuckled and took one of the plates. "I don't know. After everything you told me, I'm a bit leery." He lifted the plate to his nose and sniffed. "But I don't smell anything poisonous."

I scoffed and slapped at his bulging arm. "I didn't make the pizza. Just heated it up in the oven. Anna must have gotten our message because she's arranged for a few of the staff to return and help take care of the place for us. Including food."

Sam lifted the slice and took a bite. "It's good."

"Well, it came pre-made, so I'm sure it is."

Once we'd had our fill of pizza, which shamefully consisted of the whole pie, we climbed back into bed.

I tucked myself into Sam's side. "How are you doing?"

His mouth flattened, but he nodded. "As good as can be expected, I suppose."

"With luck, this will all come to an end soon."

Sam pulled me tighter, then dropped a kiss on the top of my head. "Hopefully. Let's get some more rest. Adrien called a pack meeting for eight a.m. So we have the night to sleep."

Good. Because I was still so bagged. Emotions really did cause a lot of wear and tear on a person.

I snuggled deeper into Sam's side and fell asleep with a small smile on my lips. Regardless of the circumstances, I was happy here with him. And I never wanted that to change.

22

How was it possible to sleep a solid eight hours and feel more exhausted than before?

I stared in the bathroom mirror at the purple bruising beneath my eyes and sighed. This had been a long week. So much had happened, and Sam and I were wearing those marks on our bodies.

After a quick shower, Sam and I dressed, grabbed a quick breakfast, then set off for his parents' place. Again. This time, it was for a pack meeting, one I would be included in. I wasn't an official member yet, but hopefully soon. I hadn't passed the news along to Adrien that I'd left the Mississippi Pack. It didn't seem as important as everything else right now. There'd be plenty of time to discuss my affiliations after we dealt with Corbin and put this matter to rest.

Sam inched the car into his parents' cramped driveway, then killed the engine. We shared a bracing glance, then gave each other an encouraging nod and climbed out. The front door stood open, but the smell of freshly baked cookies wafted out from within. It brought a smile to my lips.

Hand in hand, we entered the house. Sam led us on a small detour into the kitchen, where he placed a chaste kiss against his mother's cheek, ruffled Claire's and Monique's hair, then tugged me into the massive dining room.

Every chair at the table was taken, but Sam and I stood near the back, among the others.

Adrien stood at the head of the table, a stack of papers placed before him. I caught the image of Corbin's face and really studied it. But I didn't recognize it. Not that I would. If he was the same guy who'd attacked me, I'd only ever seen him in wolf form. And thanks to my human senses back then, I wouldn't have known his scent. I had to trust that Reggie's information was correct because nothing about Corbin sparked any recognition in me.

"Welcome," Adrien said. "I think the majority of us are here, and I'd like to honor your time, so we'll get started. Those who come late can be filled in later."

A few murmured their agreements.

Adrien lifted his head and squared his shoulders, his gaze sweeping through the room. "I'm sure most of you are aware, but just in case, you should know that our daughter, Izzy"—Adrien's voice broke, and he cleared his throat—"passed early yesterday morning. She was the third victim and succumbed to her wounds."

The murmuring lessened as everyone absorbed that news, whether they'd already known or not.

"During the investigation, we turned up a dismembered finger that we believe belongs to the wolf responsible for these attacks."

Mercifully, Adrien did not present the evidence. My stomach was off enough without adding yet another day of rot into the mix.

"Then last night, we had a bit of a break in the case when Lucy's father, the Mississippi Pack alpha, handed us the wolf's name. It seems he has a bit of a history with him. The name, composite image, and finger were sent to our contact with the local PD. And we've thankfully been given confirmation of identity. Our target's name is Corbin Brown. He's a rogue wolf from the England Pack."

More than one person glanced my way, but I held my ground and refused to buckle under the pressure of their stares. I knew how it looked, like I'd brought this mess to New Orleans with me. I refused to accept the blame though. If there was one thing I'd learned from seeing Brenda and Daniel go through the same mess as me, it was that we were not responsible for the actions of Corbin.

Instead, I stared at the composite photo and recommitted every bit of him to my memory once again. I wanted to make sure I could recognize him among a crowd of people. Because the next time I saw him... my memory flashed to Damon, the wolf I'd killed outside Daniel's house. Yeah, I wouldn't mind getting my jaws on Corbin's throat. Doubt I'd feel any regret this time either. Bastard deserved everything that was coming to him and more.

"We've learned that Corbin has been staying in local motels, moving every couple nights. We expect him to change locale tonight, so it'll be up to us to track him down. Elena and I have broken the pack into teams of four, and each team will be given a quadrant to search. We've made photocopies of his image for you to use at the establishments. Find out where he's staying. But that's your only job. Once he has been found, report his location to Elena since she'll remain here at home base. She will then notify all the teams, and we will reconvene. We handle this as a pack. Do not take him on yourself, do you understand me?"

"Yes, alpha," rang through the room.

"Good. Check with Elena to learn your assignments, and then you're dismissed. Meet with your team and begin the search. Most motels don't allow check-ins until around three p.m., so there's no need to start before then. Our PD contact has Corbin's credit card flagged, and he'll report to me the instant a new charge is placed, but I want us out there searching anyway. I will not allow him to escape. There's no room for error here, people."

When no one argued his plan, Adrien rapped his knuckles against the table and dismissed everyone. Sam and I hung back, allowing the others to receive their team assignments. We could find ours after.

"Lucy." Adrien waved me over. "Have a seat."

Oh boy. Here we go. If I had to wager a guess, I would bet Reggie called Adrien last night and screamed his ear off about my "leaving the pack" plan. I couldn't imagine Reggie would accept my decision gracefully.

I sank into the nearest chair and braced myself.

Adrien took the seat next to me, then fished

through his stack of papers and withdrew a smaller sheaf. Once organized, he tapped them on the table, then lifted his gaze to mine. "There's something you should know."

Bad news commencing in three... two... one... "Okay."

"I had my contact look into Corbin Brown."

I pursed my mouth. He'd mentioned that already.

"We think..." Adrien's gaze flicked to Sam, and he sighed. "There's really no easy way to say this, so I'm just going to come out and say it."

I lifted a questioning brow. That was never a good thing to hear.

"We think Corbin has been following you."

The hairs on my arms stood on end. "What?"

"First, this must stay between us, alright? This information wasn't obtained legally."

I gave a slow nod.

Adrien nudged the stack toward me. "These are Corbin's credit card and phone records. My contact has a few connections of his own, and he was able to pull these this morning." He tapped the top page. "See here? You took the bus from Mississippi, right? Jackson, to be exact?"

"Yeah."

"Well, the same day you left, Corbin also purchased a bus ticket. Right here." He ran his thumb along a single line, one that showed a familiar purchase. "My contact reached out to the bus company and was able to pull the invoice." Adrien flipped the page. "A one-way ticket from Jackson, Mississippi, to New Orleans. Same as yours."

My lungs contracted, and I struggled to draw breath. "The same bus as mine?"

Adrien's silence told me everything I needed to know. Sweet Lord, I'd sat on the same bus as this lunatic and not known it. How could I not have known? Wouldn't I have sensed him? Smelled him? Not that I'd known his scent then. Nor what to look for. I'd been so distracted by the idea of seeing Sam and Anna again that I'd barely paused to glance around the bus. I remembered boarding, then forcing myself to doze to pass the time.

"There was another charge on his credit card after his arrival for a rental car," Adrien continued. "We contacted the rental company and acquired the license plate number. Further investigation showed a recently issued parking ticket for the night after your arrival." Adrien's gaze flicked to Sam again. "Two blocks away from your place."

This time my lungs compressed, and every air molecule whooshed out. Two. Blocks.

"Lastly..." Adrien slid yet another sheet across the table. "These are his phone records, showing him in New Orleans. He's been making calls from here to all over Louisiana, Mississippi, and South Arkansas."

I stared at the papers spread before me, utterly stunned by these revelations. How—*how*—could this man have been following me and neither Sam nor I noticed? Had he followed me to the wedding? Watched me and Sam with our friends? Followed us here? Then back to Sam's? What about last night?

"How?" I choked out. "How have we not picked up a scent or anything?"

"He likely always kept himself downwind from you. A simple but effective tactic."

I shook my head. "Then why reveal himself to us the night we were at Daniel's?"

"He may not have intended to," Sam commented, his voice a bit raspy from shock. "I remember the wind shifted that night. And rather fast too. Most likely, he hadn't had enough time to react, so we caught his scent."

"There's more." Adrien leaned back in his seat and tousled his hair. Somehow, the action made him seem almost younger. "After we spoke last night, I contacted the England alpha, and he confirmed that Corbin is the wolf who attacked you in England."

My heart stuttered to a stop.

"According to the alpha, since they were under the queen's orders, the alpha chose to overlook it when he regained control of the pack after the queen's death. But apparently, Corbin has always been a cause for concern. Not only does Corbin desire to start his own pack, but he also takes great joy in causing pain—the alpha's words, not mine."

My eyes slipped shut, and I focused on slow, deep breaths to help calm my heart. Right now, it was racing out of control, ruled by the fear coursing through my veins.

Corbin was him then.

The wolf who'd hunted me in Camilla's house before taking great pleasure in trying to kill me. It was only because of a freak accident—me being born half-werewolf—that I'd survived. And that miracle had now resulted in all of this. These people were being attacked—killed—because of me.

"Stop," Sam growled. "Stop blaming yourself for this."

My wide eyes darted to him. "What? How did you—?"

"Because I know you. And I know what it means when you get that tiny wrinkle between your eyes."

I might have smiled, touched that he knew me so well, if it weren't for the circumstances. "It's not easy to just shut out those thoughts. I might not have been the one to hurt Daniel and Brenda and"—my voice cracked—"Izzy, but this does all stem from me."

"No, it stems from the batshit crazy queen, who ordered a bunch of werewolves to attack you in a home full of vampires. It's not your fault that you survived, Lucy, no matter how much you tell yourself otherwise. I know survivor guilt is a real thing, but the fault lies on Corbin for this. He's the one who chose to pack up his life and head to America. He's the one hurting people. Not you."

"Sam's right," Adrien said. "It's unfortunate that you're involved in this, but that hardly means you're responsible."

Deep down, I knew they were right, but that didn't make it any easier to accept. I couldn't shake the knowledge that if I just hadn't survived, hadn't turned into a werewolf, none of this would be happening, and Izzy would still be alive.

"Let's stop worrying about blame and focus on what we can do to fix this situation," Adrien pressed. "With luck, we'll put an end to all this tonight."

Luck being the operative word.

"What happens when this is over?" I asked.

"We resume our normal everyday lives," Adrien said. "As best as we can."

"But what about other werewolves? Eventually, word is going to spread about Corbin's actions. People talk. Other packs will learn about his intentions. Then what? Do we just let them walk around attacking human-borns?"

"That's not for me to say." Adrien pressed his thumbs against his brows. "I can't worry about other packs. I have my hands full as it is worrying about my own. I would be surprised if this all came to an end though. There are far too many human-born out there longing to become werewolves. Preferably, they will be the ones to make the choice, rather than having the choice forced upon them. But I can't keep them from trying."

Yeah, Corbin had certainly opened a can of worms here, and there'd be no closing it. Once word spread, packs from all over the country would be looking at their human-borns with renewed interest. It made my skin crawl just thinking about it. If I'd learned anything in my nearly thirty years of life, it was that humans—and non-humans—loved to make things worse. Containment was never an option. I could only imagine some packs "forcing" their human-born to undergo the change, just to bolster their numbers. It wouldn't be by force per se, but it wouldn't be voluntary either. Nor could I expect Adrien to rein in the developing situation. He was only one alpha, and he had his own people to worry about.

"Why don't you two get some rest?" Adrien said. He rose to his feet and gazed down on us. "I expect tonight will be a rather difficult one, so we'll need you at your best. I've paired you with Joseph and Lukas and assigned you four plus another team to the French Quarter."

Nodding, Sam rose, and I quickly followed, my head still reeling with everything we'd learned.

At the door, Adrien laid a hand on both Sam's and my shoulders, stopping us. "Be careful tonight. Both of you. I don't want to hear about any heroics or risks you took in capturing Corbin. Follow the rules, hunt as a pack, and we'll all be here to see the sun rise."

Sam offered his father a comforting smile. "Of course."

Adrien and I shared our own little look, one that told me to keep an eye out for Sam. I nodded, silently promising to keep him safe. The family had already lost one child, and they certainly didn't need to lose another.

Together, Sam and I stepped out on the porch. The sun had long since risen, but an ominous winter chill wrapped itself around me. I shivered and tucked myself deeper into my jacket. Winter chills were to be expected this late in January. It didn't mean anything.

But I couldn't shake this feeling, this dire sense that we were doing everything wrong, and tonight was a mistake just waiting to happen.

23

Since this afternoon, the temperature had dropped to an unpleasant thirty degrees. It wasn't the first time we'd experienced such low temps, and it wouldn't be the last, but that didn't change that the weather sucked tonight. The meteorologist had even called for snow, which I doubted, but now that we were outside, breathing in the crisp air, I had to wonder.

"You okay?" Sam asked.

He must have noticed my shiver as I pulled my jacket tighter around me. I wasn't used to these sorts of lows. Once a year, at most. And those nights were often spent tucked inside my house with a mug of hot cocoa. Not patrolling the streets in search of a crazed werewolf hellbent on attacking innocent people—oh, and stalking me too. Mustn't forget that lovely little detail.

"Yeah," I murmured. My teeth, however, had the audacity to chatter, giving away my lie.

"Hopefully this won't take too long," Sam said. He pulled me into his side and ran a hand up and down my arms. "Lukas and Joseph should be here any minute, and then we can start searching."

I nodded. The second team had arrived only moments ago, but Sam had sent them on their way, not wanting us to stand out by gathering in a large group. He'd assigned them Rampart to Royal Street, while we would handle Royal Street to the waterfront. We currently stood on Decatur Street, near Artillery Park. I could see Jackson Square, where the shops were flooded with people. A quick glance at my phone revealed the time to be four-thirty. Another hour and a half, and the shops would close. The square wouldn't be completely empty though. People liked to linger and hang out.

"Sam," a gruff voice sounded to our right.

We turned and greeted Joseph and Lukas with brief nods.

"Anything yet?" Lukas asked.

"We were waiting on you guys to start looking.

My father is adamant that we stick together all night."

Gah, all night. The thought of being out here while the temperature kept dropping made my shoulders hunch for warmth. But I wasn't about to let a little cold stop me from putting an end to all this.

Determination warmed my blood. After a few small hops to get that blood pumping, I gestured toward the waterfront. "Shall we?"

Together, the four of us tramped through the streets, stopping at the many different inns, motels, hotels, and hostels. After the tenth or so fail, my determination waned and frustration surged.

We stepped out of the French Market Inn, and I released a long breath. "This is ridiculous. There has to be a better way than this. Should we call your father? Maybe see if Corbin's made a new reservation yet?"

Sam checked his phone. "I don't see any messages from him. But gimme a sec, I'll call."

I blew warm air into my palms and stomped my feet. The streets were still crowded with tourists. They didn't seem to mind the cold like I did. Of course, they weren't ducking in and out of hotels.

Sam's baritone voice rose to my ears, and I

listened as he and his father discussed the situation. My heart dropped when I heard his father confirm we had no new leads. Corbin hadn't made any new charges tonight, nor did the team spot him near the motel he'd last registered at. From the sounds of it, his room had been cleared out. He had to have found new lodgings by now. This didn't make sense. Why the change in pattern?

Fear grabbed hold of me. What if Corbin hadn't found new accommodations yet because he was out hunting another human-born? I couldn't stand the thought of us finding yet another victim. Or what if Corbin was too busy tracking us while we tracked him? Ugh, this was giving me a headache. Why couldn't it be simpler than this? Why couldn't we just stumble across each other in the middle of the street?

"No, that's okay. Thanks," Sam said before ending the call.

He didn't repeat anything his father had said. He didn't need to. We'd all heard. No new leads. None of the teams had caught even the slightest whiff of Corbin.

I drew in a deep breath, counted to ten, then released it, watching as it fogged in the air.

"Back to pounding the streets?" Lukas asked.

"Unless anyone has a better idea," Sam grunted.

No one spoke.

I growled when we resumed our previous task, heading for the next hostel down the road.

"I know," Sam said. "I'm frustrated too."

"I just need to find this guy." I pushed my chilly hands through my long hair. "I need to know why he's been following me. Why any of this? I mean, I get it. He wants his own pack. But that's not a good enough reason to hurt all these innocent people!"

Sam slid an arm around my shoulder and drew me into his side, but he didn't offer any comforting words, because honestly, what could he even say?

"Let's finish our task. We have one more street, and then we'll reconvene with the pack. Hopefully someone will have found him."

It took us until just before seven. Two and a half hours of beating the pavement and harassing local establishments, all for naught. Corbin was nowhere to be found. I stood on Bourbon Street and tucked my hands in my jacket pockets. New Orleans wasn't huge geographically, so it shouldn't be this hard to find him.

"Unless he knows we're looking for him," I murmured.

Sam stopped and tilted his head toward me. "Why do you say that?"

"He checked out of his hotel at ten this morning. The team assigned to his room said his scent had begun fading. No clothes, no food, no toiletries remained. But there's been no movement on his credit card, meaning he hasn't checked in anywhere new. Not to mention our entire pack has failed to locate him. Doesn't that seem unlikely to you? Either he knows we're hunting him, or he's left town. Those are the only two explanations I can come up with."

"If he was watching us, we'd know," Lukas said.

"Sadly, he's proven us wrong in that regard."

Joseph raised a questioning brow. "How so?"

"This morning, we just learned that he's been following me since I left Mississippi, and I had absolutely no idea."

"Yeah, but you're a new werewolf. We're—" Lukas broke off.

"More experienced?" I said, winking.

Relief colored his cheeks. "That works for me."

"Well, you more experienced werewolves didn't notice either. Considering he'd been camped outside Sam's house a few nights ago without anyone knowing."

Joseph cursed under his breath. "This wolf... he's..."

"Tricky," I said. "Smart too. Unfortunately."

"Not too smart. He's attacking innocent people, and he killed my sister," Sam growled.

I reached for Sam's hand and gave it a squeeze. "I only meant that he's smart enough to stay one step ahead of us."

One step ahead of us... I rolled that thought around my head. If he knew we were tracking him, what would he do? Would he leave town? I would if it were me. The second I knew the local pack was onto me, I'd tuck tail and run. But maybe he wasn't the sort to take cover. Maybe he was the sort to wait for an opening.

"Maybe it's time for us to think like him," I suggested. "He's been following us for days." I shook my head. "No, not us. Me. He followed me here from Mississippi. He followed me to Sam's. He attacked Izzy after I killed his partner."

"What are you suggesting?" Lukas asked.

"We need to stop thinking like the good guys and start thinking like this bastard." I slowly turned and took in all the surrounding shops. "What if he's following us while we're tracking him? The French Quarter could mask his smell."

I lifted my nose and sniffed, wincing when the stench of primordial swamp oozed into my senses. With the unique smell of seafood, booze, smoke, and stale river water surrounding us, it was near impossible to track him that way. Meaning he could be following us right this second, and we'd never know.

"We need bait," I said aloud, though I immediately regretted my words.

"Bait?" Sam shook his head. "I'm not putting another human-born in his path. That's too dangerous."

"Well..." I bit my bottom lip and prepared myself for the impending storm of fury. "What about a former human-born?"

"Former...?" Sam's face went slack the instant he understood my suggestion. "No, Lucy. Absolutely not. No fucking way."

"What?" Lukas asked, still a few steps behind.

Joseph winced and shook his head. "I'm with Sam on this one."

"It's not up to you," I told Joseph. My gaze rose to Sam's. "Or you. This is my choice."

"I disagree," Sam snarled. "I'm not letting you put yourself in danger like that."

"Oh," Lukas mumbled when the lightbulb finally

lit. "Damn, girl. You trying to give your mate a heart attack?"

"Listen. There's a chance he's out here watching us." I lowered my voice just in case, even though I doubted he could hear us over all the music. "Which means our teams aren't going to randomly stumble across him."

"You don't even know he's here," Sam countered.

No, I didn't. But my instincts told me I was onto something. I had this otherworldly tug in my gut that told me he was watching us. Me.

"So, let's find out," I suggested.

Sam was seething. I could see it in his narrowed eyes and in the grim line of his mouth. I had a feeling he had some choice words for me but was valiantly trying to restrain himself.

"There's a coffee shop on the corner. Sam and I can go in. Lukas and Joseph, you two need to look like you're leaving. We did just fail our task, after all. Maybe you're planning to report back to the pack. Once inside, Sam leaves. Maybe he takes a call, or maybe he needs to go back to the car for something, leaving me alone in the coffee shop. Hopefully Corbin will approach me."

A threatening growl rumbled deep in Sam's

chest. I lifted my hand and placed it over his heart. This was a lot to ask, and I knew that.

"You don't even know if this will work. If he'll show."

"So, let's find out," I said. "I haven't been alone once since returning. From Anna's wedding, until now, we've been together. The one time I wasn't with you, I was with Vlad and Anna. Maybe he just needs the opening."

"And you don't think he'll sense the trap?"

"I'm hoping that the bait is too enticing for him to pass up."

"The bait," Sam repeated. "You, Lucy. You are the bait."

"I'm the one he's been following. Let's find out why. And hopefully, you, Lukas, and Joseph can take him out when he does show up."

"And if he doesn't?" Sam asked.

I shrugged. "Then no harm, no foul. We return to the pack with our disappointing news."

A shiver coursed through Sam. I stepped closer to him, pressing our bodies flush against one another. "You'll be here the whole time. He just won't be able to see you. I won't be in any danger."

"I don't like this. What if he hurts you?"

I considered the question but quickly shook my

head. "I think if he wanted to hurt me, he would have by now."

"And you're basing that on what, exactly?"

I didn't quite have an answer to that. "Let me try, okay? It's a public spot, and you three will be nearby, so I won't be in any danger."

Sam groaned, then tipped his head forward and rested his brow against mine. "What happened to no heroics? We promised my father."

"Please," I said, laughing. "There's nothing heroic about me pretending to get a coffee. Heck, I'm cold enough as is. I could actually use one."

Sam's burning amber eyes peered into mine. "Five minutes. That's all I'm giving you. If he doesn't show, you get the hell out of there."

"Deal."

Sam leaned in and kissed me, his lips lingering against mine even as he said to the others, "Go. Pretend you're leaving to report back to Adrien."

When we broke from the kiss, we stood alone in the French Quarter with soft jazz music rising all around us.

"You know, if we weren't hunting down a rogue, murderous werewolf, this might be a nice spot for a date," I said.

Sam chuckled. "When this is all done, I'm taking you on a real date. One you won't forget."

Oh, that sounded promising. I smiled up at him, then stepped back and hiked a thumb over my shoulder. When I spoke, I lifted my voice just in case. "There's a coffee shop just around the corner. I'm cold. Wanna get a drink?"

Unease flickered in Sam's eyes, but he nodded. "Sure. That sounds great."

Hand in hand, we strolled toward the shop while trying to look inconspicuous. It took more effort than I expected to keep my attention on Sam and the path before us, and not on our surroundings. But I did strain my hearing just in case, picking up on all the familiar sounds of the French Quarter. We approached Royal Street, where the music changed to a more traditional sound, then slipped inside the nearest coffee shop.

Careful to stay in sight of the windows, I pointed toward a booth in the back corner, right next to the bathrooms, then left Sam at the counter to place our orders. Once he had our coffees in hand, he approached. But right before he could sit, his phone rang. Sliding my coffee toward me, he reached for his phone. I saw Joseph's name on the screen and nodded.

"Why don't you take that outside?" I said, covertly gesturing to all the people surrounding us.

"Yeah, that's probably for the best." Sam's gaze shot to me once more. I could read the warning within. He mouthed the words "five minutes," then lifted the phone to his ear and exited the shop.

And just like that, I was alone.

For the first time in days. Almost a week. Gosh, I couldn't even remember how long it had been since I'd arrived. So much had happened. My whole life had changed.

I reined in those thoughts before they started to spiral and gripped my to-go cup. Heat blasted my palms, but I relished in it, letting it warm my poor, miserable hands. The temperature had dropped to twenty-eight while we'd been canvassing the establishments. Compared to up north, twenty-eight was nothing. But for us southerners, it froze my thin blood. I shivered, then lifted the cup to my nose and inhaled the pleasant aroma.

Time passed faster than I expected. I thought the five minutes would drag, but that wasn't the case. I glanced at the clock and noted I only had a minute or two left before Sam returned.

Maybe I'd been wrong in assuming Corbin would approach me. Maybe he'd gotten everything he needed while watching me the last few nights. Hell, maybe he had left New Orleans. Maybe he'd bailed after killing Izzy. I certainly wouldn't stick around if I'd killed an alpha's daughter.

I continued nursing my coffee, all while watching the clock tick down. Then I pretended to glance at my phone. Sam had texted me a one-minute warning, but beyond that, nothing. Still, I frowned at my cell, continuing the act just in case Corbin really was watching.

When my five minutes came to an end, I rose from the booth. Guess I had been wrong. At least now we knew. It didn't bother me too much. Corbin was the last person I wanted to see or speak to. But I did worry about what he might be doing. If he wasn't here watching me, was he out there somewhere, hurting someone else? I hated the thought of that.

I stepped away from the booth, about to head for the front door, when a pair of unbelievably strong hands gripped my arm and yanked me around the corner, into the back of the shop. Something pushed me, and I stumbled, hitting the wall. Before I could cry out, a hand clapped over my mouth while the other grabbed my wrist and twisted until I gave a muffled moan.

Sucking in a sharp breath through my nose, my

eyes darted upward, and I found myself staring at a familiar face. The same one I'd seen from Sam's sketch. The one who'd escaped after I'd killed his partner.

Corbin Brown.

Dark eyes blazed down at me, his face half-obscured by his equally dark hair. "You have two options. One, you come with me. Two, you die. Make your choice."

My eyes flicked around the area, but found it abandoned. Apparently no one needed to use the bathroom right now. And the only other door was the back exit.

"You have three seconds to decide, Lucy," Corbin rasped in my ear. "Oh, and if you choose death, know I'll kill your Sam too. Small little bonus there."

When I didn't respond, he growled and pressed me tighter against the wall, drilling his arm into my throat and cutting off my air supply. "I'm not kidding around here, Lucy. Three, two, one—"

Eyes wide, I nodded frantically.

"Good choice," Corbin grumbled. "Out the door, now. There's a car. Get in. Don't make a sound. Don't draw any attention to yourself. You do, and both you and your mate are dead. Believe me when I say I have someone tailing him right this second. Understand?"

I gave another jerky nod.

"Good girl."

He released me and stepped back. I sucked in a choking breath and reached for my aching throat.

"Hurry up," Corbin barked. "Get moving."

My legs almost didn't work when I pushed off the wall. They threatened to give out on me. But with a small growl, I forced them to move, to lead me outside.

Guess my bait plan worked a little too well.

THE INSTANT WE STEPPED OUTSIDE, I scanned the street for any sign of Sam. He'd given me five minutes, which had run out at least a few minutes ago. He had to be somewhere nearby. Right? I only hoped this other wolf hadn't attacked him.

I wrung my hands together as I walked, my nerves absolutely shot. Somehow my plan had completely backfired on us.

Biting my lip, I stole a glance back at Corbin. I could barely see his face through all the hair, but I could feel those soulless eyes of his tracking my every move. I needed to be smart about this. I couldn't outwardly attack him—I'd lose. I hadn't learned to fight properly yet, and Corbin had a good fifty pounds on me. Probably more. I couldn't scream for help because then he'd order the other wolf to kill Sam.

"So..." I hedged, hoping maybe to stall enough for help to arrive. In the movies, villains always monologued. Maybe, with a little luck, I could get him talking and delay the inevitable. "What's your plan here, Corbin?"

He jerked, likely shocked I knew his name. But instead of answering my question, he simply shoved me toward a dark sedan sitting on the side of the road. As a woman, I knew better than to get into the car. Those who went in rarely came back out again. And Sam was here somewhere. My odds of survival were better here in the French Quarter, surrounded by tourists, than alone in the car with this psychopath.

Think, Lucy, think.

I couldn't shift. Not only did that eat up precious time, but it gave Corbin another chance to order Sam's death. I couldn't run. I couldn't hide. I couldn't fight.

"Get in," Corbin commanded.

He grasped the door handle and wrenched open the back door. Heat blasted out from inside, along with loud music.

Digging my heels into the pavement, I asked, "Where are you taking me?"

A threatening growl rose from his throat. "Get. In."

"No, thank you."

Corbin dug in his pocket and fished out his cell phone. At the sight of him punching in a message, I freaked out. I couldn't let him kill Sam.

I didn't think—I just let my instincts react.

And I slapped the phone out of his hand.

Corbin blinked, stunned by my response. I had to admit, it stunned me too. I watched his device sail over the hood of the car, then listened as it clattered to the ground. My eyes widened as I stared at Corbin, waiting for his reaction.

I expected him to manhandle me into the car or hit me or something. I didn't expect him to start shifting in the middle of the street. My mouth gaped as I watched him struggle to control himself. I'd never seen anything like this before. Like he and his wolf were fighting for dominance. One moment, his eyes were burnt umber, the next brown. The next second, he had fangs, then none. Fur sprouted in patches across his face, rolling down his arms, only to vanish with his next breath. He couldn't shift in public—we both knew that. But apparently, I'd pissed him off to the point where his wolf was taking over.

And why the hell was I still standing here?

Run, Lucy! A voice screamed in my head.

Right. Run! Without his phone, he couldn't order Sam's death, meaning I could run.

Shoving Corbin backward, I rounded the car. The sight of his cell phone spurred me into action, and I came down on it as hard as I could. The screen shattered beneath my heel, and I kept running. I needed to get him away from the tourists and out of sight before he did something stupid like fully shift. But I also needed to escape.

Unfortunately, I'd barely made it a block when clawed hands gripped my arms and threw me into a nearby alleyway. I went crashing down on my hands and knees, the cement tearing up my palms. Wincing, I scrambled back to my feet and turned, only to find myself trapped between the brick wall at my back and the pissed off werewolf in front of me.

Corbin rolled out his shoulders as he approached, but it was the sight of him half-shifted that struck me speechless. I'd never seen anyone caught between forms like this. Hell, I didn't even know that was possible.

He lifted a clawed hand and pointed a garish finger at me. "You're dead."

Well, not just yet. And I needed to keep it that way. I wanted to scream for help but couldn't. Corbin would kill anyone who came to investigate. Humans wouldn't stand a chance against him. Not to mention, it would expose us as werewolves.

"Then your boyfriend's dead," he snarled, his voice more animal than human.

"My mate," I snapped back, though I had no idea why. It truly didn't matter.

Even Corbin laughed.

Yeah. Those were the best last words I could come up with.

He stalked toward me, his steps a bit unbalanced. My gaze swept up his legs, and I noted their malformation. How in the world was he still standing and walking? His thighs looked more like a satyr's in this position.

"I was curious about you, you know," he muttered.

Oh great, here came the monologue. When it so wasn't helpful to me.

"The first human-born turned. I hadn't intended for you to live."

As Anna would say, duh.

"Yet here you stand. I have you to thank though. If you hadn't survived"—he threw open his misshaped arms—"none of this would have been possible."

Bile churned in my gut.

"Now I can turn any human-born I want."

"Lucky you," I mumbled.

I studied every inch of the alleyway, searching for anything that could help me. But unless I could smother him beneath mounds of garbage bags, I was pretty much SOL.

"I intended to offer you a place in my new pack," he continued, much to my dismay. "But then you killed Damon."

"How unfortunate."

Corbin's eye twitched, and his lip curled back to reveal a set of very sharp fangs. Fear slammed into me as memories rose. This scene was all too familiar to me. Him stalking me into Anna and Vlad's bedroom, effectively trapping me, then tearing into me with those teeth and claws. My heart hammered a panicked rhythm in my chest, all while I silently screamed for help.

"Now, I'm going to enjoy killing you, like you did him."

"Close friends, were you?"

Corbin blinked. Honestly, I had no idea where this sassiness was coming from. Maybe I was channeling Anna, hiding behind false bravado to keep me from falling apart. Because that was what I really wanted to do. I wanted to curl up in a ball and cry. Except, I couldn't. I needed to be strong. Needed to show his asshole I wasn't the same scared human he'd attacked back in England. I was faster now. Stronger. And hopefully, smarter than a killer.

As I inched backward, something snagged my attention out of the corner of my eye. I flicked it a quick glance and caught sight of metal hiding among the bags of garbage. I had no idea what it was or if it would even help me. But metal tended to suggest something strong. I just needed to time everything right.

Like right now!

Corbin dashed forward, his movements far too quick for my liking. I sprinted to the side, narrowly ducking under his arms. Scooping up what looked like a crowbar, I turned and swung it like a bat, putting all my strength behind the blow. The crowbar connected with Corbin's head with a loud crack and sent him sprawling to the ground.

With no time to waste, I turned and dashed for the street. Unfortunately, I barely made it to the sidewalk before Corbin's grotesque hands grabbed my jacket and wrenched me backward. I barely had time to suck in a breath before I was airborne, the wind whistling through my ears as I flew through the alley. I slammed into the farthest wall, my head ricocheting off the bricks.

Darkness crept in on my vision, and I moaned, lifting a hand to my head. It felt like I'd been creamed by a truck. My god. Who the hell threw someone into a wall? I guess the same person who just took a crowbar to the head.

Unable to see, I flinched when the feel of hot, rancid breath hit my cheek.

"I'm going to enjoy this," Corbin snarled.

"Not as much as I am," came a deeper, angrier voice.

I blinked away the darkness, only to find myself staring up at a shadow hovering behind Corbin. I couldn't make out his features, but I knew that voice to the depth of my very soul. Relief loosened my muscles, and I sagged against the ground just as Corbin whirled around.

Claws flashed, but not quickly enough to escape the fist that came crashing down on the side of his face. Corbin dropped to the ground with an enraged snarl, one that sent a shiver down my spine.

"Sam," I called out in a trembling voice.

His burning gaze quickly scanned me for injuries. Seeing none, his expression gentled until his attention once again fell to the wolf at my feet. For a moment, I thought he had everything well under control. But I should have known better. Corbin was wild and unpredictable.

With a sharp yell, Corbin launched to his feet and tackled Sam around the waist. The two tumbled to the ground and started pummeling each other. The sound of fists meeting flesh had me scrambling to my feet and screaming Sam's name.

I could barely follow their movements. The alleyway wasn't exactly well-lit, and they were moving too quickly. But I could tell they were moving closer and closer to the street.

"Oh god," I whispered.

This was bad. So very bad. If anyone spotted Corbin in this form, we were screwed. Not to mention, humans tended to call the police when things like this happened. And they were the last thing we needed right now.

Slipping a hand in my back pocket, I fumbled for my phone. I didn't have many numbers, but I had the ones that mattered. Like Joseph and Lukas. Where the hell were they? I punched the first name, not even glancing to see which one, and held the phone to my ear, all while clutching my head with my other hand.

"Lucy!" came a shout from the other end.

"We need help. Right now. They're fighting. And someone is going to see!"

"Where are you?"

"I-I don't know!" It wasn't like I'd noted the street signs.

"Think, Lucy."

"Um, Corbin dragged me out of the back exit of the coffee shop. There was a car there. He tried to force me in. I ran. I don't know which direction! The car was pointed in the direction I ran," I yammered. "He followed. I didn't make it far. We're in an alleyway nearby. Just... You'll hear them, okay! Hurry up!"

"We're coming. Calm down. Are you hurt?"

I shook my head, then winced. My damn head throbbed. But I guess that was to be expected after Corbin introduced it to the hard brick wall. "I'm fine. But Sam and Corbin—"

"Sam can handle himself. Just don't get involved. Let him take care of this."

Don't get involved? Like I even could! The two were like vicious attack dogs, lashing at every weakness they could find. Hardly pausing for breath. I watched as the two tumbled into a sliver of street light. Sam hopped to his feet and lashed out with an impressive roundhouse kick that struck Corbin in the jaw. If he were human, he'd be dead right now, the way his head snapped back. Instead, he retaliated with a throat punch that sent Sam stumbling back a few steps.

"Are you almost here?" I shouted. "They're going to kill each other!"

"Just calm down, Lucy," one of them said. I think I was on speakerphone. "We're almost at the coffee shop."

"Hurry!"

Corbin leapt to his feet, but instead of snapping out another attack, he reached behind his back and grabbed something. I couldn't make it out. But it glinted under the faint light. For a moment, I wondered if it was a gun. Until he turned and brandished it in the air. The way he stood, the way he held it, I knew immediately what he had.

"He has a knife of some sort, guys," I wheezed, fear clutching my throat. "That's bad, right?"

"A knife won't kill us."

"Unless it's silver," I whispered. "Oh my god. What if it's silver?"

The line fell silent.

"Where the hell are you?"

Sam danced backward, his gaze on the knife. His expression darkened, and fury radiated from his massive form.

"Oh shit," I breathed. "I think it's silver."

"Lucy, we're almost there! Do whatever you can to keep them apart."

Cursing under my breath, I threw my phone down on the ground. The conversation wasn't important anymore, not now that the stakes were so high. If that was a silver blade, Corbin could kill Sam. And I refused to let that happen.

My gaze dropped to the ground, and I searched the pile of garbage for something—anything—that could help me. I didn't even hesitate, I just ripped into the first bag and started chucking everything I could grab at Corbin. A half-eaten apple, a pair of moldy old shoes, a busted coffee maker, I didn't care.

Corbin cursed and fell back a step, his hands raised to defend himself from my attack.

And that was when Sam made his move. He kicked the knife out of Corbin's hand, then took him out at the knees. The two fell with a hard thump, their hands struggling as they both reached for the blade. I shot to my feet and bolted toward them. If I could get to the knife first, then Sam could hold Corbin down, and backup would be here any second.

But just as I reached the blade, Corbin twisted free of Sam's grip and lunged.

My eyes widened when I realized he was going to reach it first.

The logical part of my brain told me to stop, to turn away, to keep that knife as far away from me as possible. But my heart saw Sam within striking distance. All Corbin had to do was turn and drive that blade home.

I couldn't let that happen.

I *refused* to let that happen.

With a scream worthy of a banshee, I snatched at Corbin's hand. But he was too quick. Instead of turning toward Sam, he turned toward me.

It was like time stopped, like the world paused for just a moment, long enough for me to watch Corbin thrust his arm forward, to watch as the blade sank hilt deep into my gut. Then time resumed, and I was hit with a pain unlike anything I'd ever experienced. Like someone had pressed searing hot coals against my flesh.

"Lucy!" Sam shouted, his voice reverberating through the alley.

I stared down at the blade lodged in my gut and released a long, slow breath. Huh. So... that just happened. I'd been stabbed. Corbin had actually *stabbed* me. I lifted my gaze and stared dumbly at him, stunned to find him so close.

With an evil grin, Corbin yanked the knife free and stumbled out of reach. My hands leapt to my stomach and cupped the wound. Blood seeped through my fingers and trickled down my middle.

I slowly turned my head and met Sam's grief-stricken gaze. He scrambled to his feet, his steps clumsy in his hurry to reach me. The second his hands touched me, my knees gave out, and I dropped like a stone.

"You're okay," Sam mumbled, his hands pressing down on mine. "You're okay. You're okay."

Except, I wasn't. I couldn't feel my legs. And even though I had no medical experience, I knew that was bad.

"Stay with me, Luce. Okay. We'll get help—"

A shadow rose behind Sam. One with a bloodstained blade clutched in its grasp. I rasped out a warning, one Sam didn't seem to hear. He was too distracted by me to notice Corbin's presence. I saw the blade rise, saw it glint in the dim street light. A half-strangled cry rushed past my lips.

Sam whirled around, but before Corbin could strike, two other shadows appeared in the alleyway.

"Hey!" one shouted. I thought it might be Joseph, but things were starting to grow hazy, and I wasn't sure.

My eyes started to droop, and I felt one hand fall away from my stomach, too weak to keep it in place. Sam's hand replaced it, his palm pressing against the wound to staunch the blood flow.

"Lukas!" he shouted, his eyes locked on mine. "Stay with me, Luce. Look at me. Breathe. Stay with me. Lukas!"

Footsteps thundered toward us.

"Shit," someone cursed. "Was it silver?"

Sam's devastated cry answered that question. "Get the car. Now! And Joseph, you follow that son-of-a-bitch. Do not let him get away. I'll rip his fucking head off myself."

My slowing heart dropped at those words. Corbin must have escaped.

Lukas and Joseph vanished from sight—I didn't know to where. I couldn't think. Couldn't breathe. My eyes drooped again, and this time, they didn't reopen.

"Luce, open your eyes, baby."

Except that required strength I didn't have. I just

wanted to sleep. Sleep was good. Sleep was comforting.

I drifted in a sea of darkness, drowning. In the distance, I could hear Sam's voice, but I couldn't call out to him, no matter how badly I wanted to. I was lost, and somehow, I knew I wasn't going to be able to find my way back.

25

AWARENESS TRICKLED INTO ME, drop by drop. It began with a touch—just a simple touch. More like a caress across my cheek. Then a small squeeze of my hand. Soon, I could hear, but the words didn't quite make sense. Something about internal damage and bleeding. Next came my sense of smell, and with it, the scent of weakness and despair. One by one, the drops filled my cup until finally, I could open my eyes.

I was lying on a bed in an all too familiar room. One I'd stood in not a few days ago while clutching Brenda's hand and promising her everything would be all right. Guess it was my turn now. Except the hand holding mine belonged to someone else.

My gaze lingered on a mop of ruffled black hair, his head hanging down as he stared blindly at the floor.

Sam.

Memories came in sharp flashes. Corbin chasing me into the alleyway, our fight, his and Sam's fight, until finally culminating in my stabbing. My attention slowly turned to my abdomen, but I couldn't see anything beneath the swaths of blankets tucked around me. I could feel it though. This tightness in my gut that was entirely unpleasant. It felt like I'd been sewn back together and the slightest movement might rip me apart again.

Bright side? I was alive.

I think.

No, I knew. I was alive. If I were dead, I wouldn't be lying in a bed with Sam sitting next to it. Heaven wouldn't deny me my greatest desires. Like Sam in bed with me.

I dragged my tongue across my lips, dampening the chapped flesh. Definitely needed some water. Any drink, really. Anything to wet my parched mouth and throat. They felt as dry and scratchy as a desert.

When I spotted a glass of water sitting on the table next to the bed, my body instinctively reached for it. I didn't get far. Agony ripped through my middle, and I gasped, my eyes slamming shut as a wave of pain tore through me.

Sam's head shot up, and his eyes widened when they landed on my face. "You're awake!"

I gave a slow nod, then gestured at the water.

Sam dropped my hand and grabbed the glass, holding it to my lips. I managed just a few small sips, but even that felt amazing, soothing the blazing heat in my throat. Once he pulled the glass away, I laid my head back and watched him. I didn't ask what happened because I remembered everything. Instead, I rested my hands on my stomach, careful not to press too hard.

"You scared me," Sam whispered. He leaned his arms against the side of the bed, then placed his chin on the back of his hands, his focus never wavering from my face.

"Scared myself," I rasped, wincing at the sound of my voice. Why did my throat hurt so much anyway?

"Uncomfortable?"

"A little."

He slid one hand out from under his chin and stroked my face, brushing my hair back from my cheek. "We had to intubate you. We almost lost you."

Ah.

I forced another swallow, but this time didn't wince. I'd never been intubated before, and from the feel of it, I never wanted to be again. Time to avoid all sharp, pointy knives. Not that I hadn't avoided them before, but I'd try even harder now.

"You nearly died," Sam repeated, as though I hadn't heard him the first time. "And I've never been so terrified in my life. We barely got you here in time. But thankfully, our pack doctor is a miracle worker. She stitched you up really well."

Stitches, ugh.

"Silver blade?" Which I already knew.

"I'm so sorry," Sam whispered. "I should have expected Corbin would pull something like that. I shouldn't have let that fight get so out of hand. But when I saw him standing over you like that, all I could think of was Izzy, and—"

"It's okay." I raised my arm and plunged my fingers into his hair, careful not to jar my torso. "It wasn't your fault. I was the one who literally ran into his knife."

Sam gave a dark chuckle. "How about you never do that again?"

"Deal."

He extracted my hand from his hair and brought

it to his mouth, pressing a gentle kiss against my palm. "Good. Because I can't go through this again."

I didn't blame him. Were our situations reversed, I probably would have lost my mind with worry. "I'm sorry."

"Don't apologize," Sam growled.

After a few moments of comfortable silence, I gripped Sam's hand and asked, "He escaped, didn't he?"

Darkness shuttered across Sam's face. "Bastard left Louisiana. Joseph followed him all the way to the state border. The second he crossed into Mississippi, we had to pull back. But we were able to get a message to the Mississippi Pack. Hopefully, they resumed the search."

I groaned and stared at the ceiling. "Does Reggie know I was injured?"

"No. Considering the circumstances, my dad and I felt it would be best to keep that information from him. The way we see it, you're joining our pack, so you're our responsibility, not his."

"Gee, thanks."

Sam chuckled, then brushed a kiss against my cheek. "I mean that in the best way possible. We're thrilled you're joining us. I couldn't be happier about it."

I nodded, relieved they hadn't informed Reggie of my little accident. He probably would have been breaking down the door to retrieve me. And not because he cares, but because he saw me as little more than a possession. Something to help grow his legacy.

"I'll call him in a few days when I'm feeling better, see if he has any information on Corbin or if they've found him."

"That'll help. The packs have firm rules about crossing into each other's territories. We can't enter Mississippi without Reginald's permission, just like he can't cross into ours. If we sent people into his territory, he could call it an act of war."

"Werewolves," I mumbled. "Always so dramatic."

Soft laughter spilled past Sam's lips. "What can I say? We like our rules."

My mouth curled into a smile. "That you do."

After a few more minutes of quiet, Sam ran a hand through my hair. "You look exhausted. I should leave you to rest."

"No." I snatched his hand before he could pull it away. "I've rested enough. I don't want to be alone."

Sympathy softened his eyes. "You're never going to be alone."

"Is everyone else okay?" I asked. "No other attacks? And how long have I been out?"

"A few days," Sam said, answering my last question first. "Your body needed time to recuperate. While you were out, we buried Izzy and Gabriel, which I know my parents are grateful for."

I squeezed his hand. I wished I'd been there, but I understood their needs outweighed my wants.

"And thankfully, there haven't been any more attacks that we know of. Corbin seems to be in hiding right now."

"Or he's gotten smarter," I groused.

"What do you mean?"

"He knows we're onto him. He knows we know his plan. Attacking people outright would draw more attention to him."

"You think he's gone underground?"

"No, I think he's just going to be more careful now. He won't leave bodies lying around, especially now that he understands the process. He's successfully changed two people. It's just a matter of time before he strikes again."

"We'll find him before then," Sam vowed.

"Yeah, we've thought that before. Now look at me."

Sam tightened his grip on my hand and cupped

my face with his other. "We've got this, Luce. I know things look grim right now, but once you're back on your feet, you'll feel better."

"Once I'm back on my feet, you're going to teach me to fight," I said. We'd discussed this before, and he'd agreed, but we hadn't made it past the first step of building cardio. I needed more than that. I needed a crash course.

He pursed his lips. "You're injured."

"After I'm healed," I countered. "I don't want this to happen again. And I hate feeling useless. When you two were brawling, I had no idea what to do."

"You called for help. That was the smartest thing you could have done."

"And then I ran into a knife. I'm not a strength out there, I'm a weakness. Make me into a strength."

Seconds passed while Sam considered my request. Then he nodded. "Okay. If that's what you want, we'll get you big and strong and in fighting condition in no time."

"Thank you," I whispered.

"Hey, I'd do anything for you," he said. "Even turn you into an ass-kicking machine."

I couldn't help but grin at the sound of that. When Anna was first changed, Vlad had given her to

Camilla for training, and Camilla had honed her into a weapon. I wanted that. I wanted to know I could help and protect myself. I refused to be a liability any longer.

"It's going to take time," Sam said.

"I know." I also knew it was going to hurt. I'd seen how Camilla trained, had watched her break nearly every bone in Anna's body. It made me sick to think about, but Anna knew how to fight now. So it seemed worth it in the end.

A knock on the door interrupted our conversation. Before I could call out, it swung open, and Adrien and the pack doctor entered. Both offered me gentle, albeit sympathetic, smiles.

"How are you feeling?" Adrien inquired.

"Oh, like I got stabbed," I teased, hoping to lighten the mood.

Adrien released a stunned laugh, then shook his head. "Glad to see you still have your sense of humor."

"Sure, it's just not a good one."

"I can attest to that," Sam grumbled, but at least he was smiling.

The doctor stopped at my bedside and shooed Sam out of the way. Then she pressed her hands down on my abdomen. I sucked in a startled breath and flinched back.

"Sorry," she murmured. "I just need to make sure there's no unusual swelling or signs of infection." Then she lifted the blanket and my shirt. White bandages encircled me, ones she unwrapped with great care. At the sight of my bruised and slightly swelled flesh, I winced. The stab wound wasn't particularly large, but it sure did look nasty.

A low growl slipped past Sam's mouth, but he cleared his throat and turned to stare out the window. I caught Adrien's gaze, but he just winked, silently assuring me Sam's reaction was normal.

"You're progressing nicely," the doctor finally said. "Do you feel up to a walk?"

I stared at her. "Can I?"

"Sure. You'll experience some discomfort but moving around is good for you."

She taped me back up, pulled my shirt down, then offered me a hand. Before I could reach for it, Sam was there, his fingers sliding between mine.

"I got it, Doc," he said. "I'll help her get around the house in case you have others to check on."

"Nope, everyone else has been cleared," she said. "Daniel and Brenda are both all healed up and back on their feet. Ms. Lucy is my only patient now."

"Lucky me," I deadpanned.

Sam's other hand slid under my back, and with a little nudge, he had me rising from the bed. I sucked in a sharp breath when I started to move, my eyes welling with tears. Discomfort my ass, this downright hurt.

"Easy now," Doc said. Her hands curled around my shoulders, and together, she and Sam helped me to my feet. Once upright, I took a deep breath and waited for the gray spots in my vision to fade.

"Good job, Lucy," she said. With a pat on the shoulder, she turned and headed for the door. "Let me know if you experience anything that doesn't feel right. If the pain worsens, if you have trouble breathing, chest pains, anything like that."

I nodded.

"And take it easy. No fighting bad guys for a least a few weeks, okay?"

I chuckled. "Okay."

"Good." She nodded at Adrien then stepped out into the hall.

"Come on," Sam said. "Are you hungry? We can go to the kitchen and get you some food."

The thought of eating turned my stomach. I wasn't quite ready for that. But maybe a drink would suffice for now. Something rich and chocolatey. "Hot chocolate?"

"Hot chocolate it is," Sam said. I had a feeling he would have given me the moon right now if I asked.

I hobbled out of the room and started the long trek to the kitchen. Which, of course, meant stairs. At the sight of them, I inwardly groaned. Surely, this had to be classified as torture.

"I could carry you down," Sam teased.

"Don't you dare." I curled my hand around the banister and took the first step. Relief swamped me when I managed the next and the next. Going down didn't seem so difficult now. But I imagined the same couldn't be said for going up. That might take a bit more time.

Once the three of us finally made it to the bottom, Adrien strode off into the kitchen. By the time we entered, he'd already boiled some water and filled a mug. I appreciated his efforts and his willingness to help.

Adrien handed me the mug, then perched his hip against the counter and stared at me. "I know you two decided to call Reginald in a few days, but Lucy, I'd like you to call him now, if you don't mind. We need an update on Corbin's location. I admit, I'm growing concerned. I haven't been able to reach any of Reginald's inner circle in the last two days. In fact, we haven't heard from anyone since Joseph spoke with someone named Dirge the day of your attack."

My brows knotted. "Really?"

"I'm sure it's nothing serious. But I would feel better if we had an update from your father."

Nodding, I glanced around for my phone. Honestly, I had no idea where it was.

"I'll get it," Sam said, then left to retrieve it.

"Maybe he's ignoring us out of spite," I said. "Since I told him I wasn't going back to Jackson."

"I wouldn't put such immature behavior past Reginald. But I would like to know for sure what's going on."

Understandable. Heck, so did I.

When Sam returned, he had my phone in hand. I reached for it, then winced. I'd need to be more careful with my movements.

For being out for three days, I didn't have too many missed notifications. Of course, those who cared about me had either been at my bedside or on their honeymoon. The only missed call I had from my mom, along with a worried voice mail asking me to check in with her. I made a mental note to give her a call, then pulled up Reggie's contact info. A quick tap, and the call started ringing.

And ringing.

And ringing.

When his voice mail kicked in, I scowled at the device and disconnected the call. That wasn't like Reggie. A horrible parental figure, yes, but he'd never ignored my calls before. And I couldn't see him shunning me. If anything, it'd be the opposite. I expected him to answer if only to beg me to come back.

On a whim, I tried again.

Voice mail.

Sighing, I picked through my phone and found Reggie's second's info. I didn't know Cole well, but we'd met a few times. He seemed the stoic type. Perhaps even unkind. But he'd never done anything to harm me.

I dialed his number.

On the second ring, he picked up. "Lucy."

Relief blasted through me. "Hey, Cole. I've been trying to get ahold of Reggie, but he isn't answering. Do you know where he is?" Silence carried over the line. Long enough that I frowned and stared at Sam. "Cole?"

"Lucy, open the New Orleans's alpha's front door."

Huh? The front door?

Even Adrien appeared alarmed by that statement. He pushed off the counter and stormed toward his entryway. Sam and I trailed behind him. Had someone left me a package or something? Why else would they need me to open the door?

But when we did, both Adrien and Sam cursed. Except Adrien's was far louder.

There on the porch stood Cole and five other Mississippi Pack inner circle members.

26

"WHAT. The. Fuck are you doing in my territory?"
Adrien snarled.

Oh shit.

This was bad.

My hand immediately went to my stomach,
cupping my wound. I knew I wasn't in danger.
Neither of my packs would ever harm me, but my
anxiety still spiked, and I instantly wanted to protect
my weakness.

Cole lifted his nose and sniffed, before his
narrowed eyes darted to me. "You're injured."

"I..." My gaze flicked back and forth between
Cole and Adrien. The way he'd outwardly ignored

the alpha—that wasn't a good sign. "I'm fine. But you should answer Adrien's question."

Cole's stare returned to Adrien, and boy, it was cold. "We aren't here to cause trouble, Alpha Adrien."

"The hell you aren't. You storm into my territory without permission, come to my house, and you expect me to believe you aren't here to cause trouble? This is incredibly inappropriate, not to mention illegal, behavior. We have our laws in place for a reason—"

"Reginald is dead," Cole stated.

Adrien, Sam, and I all froze. My pulse leapt, and I stumbled forward, placing myself between Adrien and Cole. I hated the feel of two angry werewolves surrounding me, but I couldn't let this descend into a fight. Not after everything. And not after what Cole had just proclaimed.

"What?" I demanded. "What did you just say?"

"Reginald, our alpha—"

"I know who Reggie is!" I shouted.

Something flickered in Cole's eyes. "He's dead."

"He's dead," I repeated. "Reggie is dead?"

A sharp nod was all Cole gave.

My breath rushed past my lips, and I reached out for the doorframe. I didn't love my sperm donor—

hell, I didn't even like him—but that didn't mean I didn't feel this loss inside.

"What happened?" I hissed, even though I already suspected the answer.

"I believe you called him Corbin," Cole said. "That rogue wolf. He killed our alpha."

"Oh god..." I slumped against the wall and covered my face with my palms. This was my fault. He killed Reggie because of me, because I'd escaped. "The pack..." My eyes flashed open. "Tell me the pack isn't his now."

"No," Cole grunted. "It wasn't a sanctioned fight. The bastard waited until your father was alone, then murdered him."

I tipped my head back and unleashed a string of silent curses in my head. I hated Corbin more than I'd ever hated anyone. For what he'd done to me, to Brenda and Daniel, Izzy, and now Reggie. The list kept growing because we continuously failed to take him out.

"Lucy," Sam murmured. "Are you okay?"

"No, I'm not."

"We thank you for passing along this information," Adrien said. "But I must insist you leave now."

"We're not going anywhere," Cole said.

Adrien's hackles rose, and Sam's eyes ignited with a preternatural glow.

"Not without her." Cole pointed a meaty finger my way.

"Me?" I squeaked. "What about me?"

A deep frown swept over his face. "You're our heir. Reginald is dead. That means—"

"No!" I shouted, making the connection before he could say the words. "Absolutely not."

"You are our alpha," Cole said. "By our laws, you are the next to lead."

I stared at my sperm donor's second, my mouth pitifully gaping open. This could not be happening. I refused to accept this. "I told Reggie I didn't want to be the heir, that I was joining Sam's pack. I'm part of the New Orleans Pack now—"

"Not exactly," Adrien muttered, cursing quietly under his breath. "Lucy, you haven't been formally inducted into my pack yet. There are procedures and ceremonies. It takes time. And if Reginald never formally renounced your position with his pack..."

Despair slammed into me. I knew it wasn't as simple as simply proclaiming my allegiance to another pack, but I hadn't expected this.

"It's just paperwork," I whispered. "And

formalities. You agreed I could join this pack. And Reggie knew—"

Adrien turned, his face a grim mask. His hands cupped my shoulders, his eyes heavy with disappointment. "I truly am sorry, Lucy. With everything that's been going on, we haven't had the time to take the appropriate measures. You are not a member of my pack yet, regardless of how much I wanted you to be. You are still a member of the Mississippi Pack. And if Reggie never renounced you, then there's nothing that can be done."

"Absolutely not," Sam snapped. His hand slipped into mine, and he gently pulled me away from his father. "For crying out loud, has everyone lost their minds? She's injured. Corbin nearly killed her. And you want to haul her back to Mississippi?"

"Sam—" Adrien sighed.

"I don't want to be alpha," I whispered, my gaze springing between the many different expectant faces.

"Right now, you don't have a choice," Adrien said.

"To hell with that. She's the only one who can choose," Sam argued.

"It's not that simple."

"She isn't going!"

"Sam." I squeezed his hand. I understood his frustration. Hell, I felt it. I didn't want to go either. But if he kept this up, he'd likely start a fight between the two packs.

"There are steps you can take to name a new alpha," Adrien continued. "But it has to be done right."

Fear flickered through me, and I cupped my stomach. "But in the meantime…"

"You have to return to Jackson." Adrien glanced over his shoulder at Cole and his lackeys. "A moment, please."

Sam closed the door in their faces, then stomped after us into the living room. The farthest we could go for a little privacy.

"Lucy, the Mississippi Pack is currently without any leadership. They need an alpha."

"That's not her problem!" Sam shouted. "You can't expect me to just let my mate be dragged across state lines against her wishes!"

"She isn't *only* your mate," Adrien cautioned him in a steady, firm voice. Almost like he could sense how close his son was to breaking. Even I could see it. His eyes were frantic, and his hands were slowly closing into fists, as though he intended to fight his father on this.

412

I needed to calm him down before this escalated further. "What about Cole?"

"Cole is a second. And while he likely could lead, as I said, there are steps to take. But right now, you have no choice. You need to return to Mississippi and take up the mantle of alpha. Only then can you begin making changes, including choosing a new alpha. But I caution you to make the right choice. This is one of our neighboring packs. If you choose unwisely, it could cause a lot of trouble for us. Which in turn can cause trouble for you."

Trapped. There was no ideal choice here.

"I can't leave Sam." I pressed myself against him. "I won't. Not again."

Sam's hands gripped my shoulders, his fingers kneading deep into my flesh.

"Then he'll just have to go with you," Adrien finally said.

The vice on my chest loosened. "Really?"

"Yes," Adrien said. "It may even be for the best. Sam will be of great assistance to you. He'll teach you how to run a pack, how to manage your people, and he'll help you choose the right successor."

My shoulders slumped as I exhaled. "Thank you."

The thought of being parted from my mate hurt

more than the damn stab wound. I couldn't bear being separated from him, not again. Not ever.

I felt Sam's body relax, along with the tension in the room. "Thank you."

Adrien smiled, then shot me a glance. "And Lucy?"

I lifted my eyes and met his.

"I truly am sorry for your loss. I know you and Reginald weren't close, but—"

"But he was still my father. Sort of," I whispered. "I honestly don't know how I feel about this yet."

"It's also perfectly fine if you don't feel anything," Adrien said. "It isn't as though you two were close. However you feel is up to you."

With a small smile, I stepped toward Adrien and slipped my arms around his waist. He stiffened in surprise, then returned my embrace with a gentle pat on my back.

"Thank you," I said. "You've been so amazing to me. After everything—"

"None of that now," Adrien said. "We can't focus on the past. But we can focus on the future and ensure we secure the best one possible."

Once we parted, he gestured for us to return to the front door, where Cole and the others waited. They'd fanned out along the porch, each domineering in their own way. I'd almost forgotten how massive some of the inner circle members were. Cole, himself, was an enormous brute with icy blue eyes and lips that never smiled.

"Well?" he grunted upon our return.

"When do we leave?" I asked.

Cole's gaze swept over me once more, and I could read the disappointment in him. As though he hated the thought of me taking over the pack. A feeling I understood completely. There they stood, each over six feet tall, their presences screaming alphas, and here I stood, a little over five-foot-four. This little sprite of a thing was to become their alpha. But according to everyone, rules were rules, and I couldn't just hand the pack over, not without taking the proper precautions.

"As soon as possible," Cole said.

I sighed, then nodded. I considered my belongings. But really, the only stuff I owned in New Orleans was all at Anna's. While Mississippi had everything I needed. Sam, however, would need to pack first.

"We leave tonight," I stated, lifting my chin. Steeling my spine with confidence I didn't really feel and ignoring the pain from my still healing wound, I continued, "Sam will be accompanying us, and I would like to give him time to pack his stuff first."

Cole's eyes narrowed. "We don't need a New Orleans wolf involving himself—"

"I'm the alpha now, correct?"

Cole's jaw snapped shut.

"That's what I thought. I will dictate who can and cannot come with. And seeing as how Sam is my mate, I assure you I will not be leaving without him."

Surprise widened Cole's eyes, which flicked to Sam. Guess Reggie hadn't told them that either. The man loved to keep his secrets, that was for sure.

"Very well, alpha," Cole said. "With your permission, we'll accompany you to your mate's house and wait while he packs."

I nodded. I had a feeling they weren't going to be willing to head back to Mississippi without me. Not with Corbin on the loose. And speaking of... "Do we have a lead on Corbin?"

"No," Cole bit out. "But that is my first priority once we're home. The bastard won't get away with this." His gaze dropped to my stomach. "I assume that is also courtesy of this asshole?"

"Language," I chided. "And yes. Unfortunately."

"Then he has a great deal to answer for." I saw the promise of death enter Cole's eyes. I knew it wasn't about me either. Cole didn't give two craps about me. It was about avenging his alpha. And honestly, I was A-OK with that, provided Corbin died. There were no other options in my mind. He would die as punishment for his crimes.

We just had to find him first.

Turning, I reached for Sam's hand and wound our fingers together. "Ready?"

He shot his father another glance, then nodded. "Tell Mom I'll call her, please?"

Adrien dragged his son in for a hug and patted his back. "Don't be gone for long." A comment he directed at me with a telling glance. Translation: hurry the eff up and get back home, where we belonged.

I acknowledge his comment with a slight head tilt.

I hated the thought of going to Mississippi now that I'd found my true family. So I decided to make myself a promise that we would be back. The New Orleans Pack was my home. And I refused to let Corbin take that from me.

In the meantime, we had work to do, and a killer to track down.

Good times.

EPILOGUE

You KNOW, this whole werewolf business is exhausting.

I mean, in the span of a week, I reconnected with my best friend and my mate, saved a few people's lives, lost a few others, and got stabbed. And you know what? Being stabbed isn't as fun or cool as it sounds. It just hurts. Plain and simple.

And now, I have to return to Mississippi, which in my opinion, is a huge step down from New Orleans. But at least Sam is coming with me. I don't know what I do if we couldn't be together. Maybe go on my own murderous rampage...

Maybe not. Too much effort.

Anna and Vlad returned home a few days after

Sam and I settled into my sperm donor's house in Mississippi. From the sounds of it, they had a blast on their honeymoon. Glad *someone* had fun these last few weeks. They deserved it, though. I just hope my own happily ever after is somewhere in the cards, because right now, it doesn't feel like it.

I was finally able to talk to my mom, and she's sad I'm leaving, but understands. I love her. She's always so understanding and caring. She did ask to meet Sam's parents, though. Cue my heart attack. The future in-laws meeting? Gulp. Thankfully, Sam's parents are amazing, and I think my mom is pretty damn awesome too, so hopefully, they won't kill each other.

As for the Mississippi Pack... well, they're struggling. Reggie had been their alpha for years, and many were deeply loyal to him. They understand I'm his heir, but they don't appreciate an outsider taking over. And I don't blame them. In their shoes, I might have felt the same way. Hopefully, I can prove to them I'm worthy. And find someone equally worthy to take over for me, because this whole alpha business is not for me. No thank you. I just want a quiet life with my mate. No drama.

Is that too much to ask?

Guess we'll find out soon enough.

MATING THE WOLFMAN SNEAK PEEK

SAM SAT me on the edge of the tub before returning to the sink and turning on the taps. The sound of running water soothed me, and I found my eyes drifting closed as I took a moment to breathe. Moments like these didn't come too often.

I jumped, my eyes flying open, when a warm washcloth touched my face.

Sam crouched before me. "Sorry," he murmured. "Didn't mean to startle you."

I chuckled. "Guess I'm a bit on edge."

"Understandably."

With careful strokes, Sam continued wiping my face, pausing every few moments to rinse the cloth. I didn't need to look at the sink to know the water had turned a murky brown. Dirt and blood didn't make a pretty color.

"You really scared me," Sam admitted, his voice gruff.

My gaze shifted to his, but I didn't utter a word.

"When that car pulled up, and I saw you slumped in the back seat..." He shuddered. "I thought I knew fear when Corbin stabbed you. But today..." He blew out a breath and rested his forehead against mine. "You really need to stop frightening me like this."

A breathless chuckle slipped past my lips. "If it helps, I definitely don't intend for these things to happen."

"Yeah, that scares me more."

My smile faded as I reached up and cupped Sam's cheeks. "I love you. More than anything."

His face softened and the fear eased from his expression. "Lucy, you are everything to me. I don't know what I would do if I lost you. It's like I can't breathe without you."

"I'm not going anywhere," I promised, my thumbs caressing his face.

He nodded and released a deep sigh. When he leaned back, I lowered my hands into my lap drew my own breath, centering myself.

Sam lifted his hand and returned to cleaning my face. "How are you feeling?"

"Tired. Frustrated. Angry. Sad. It's all a jumble up here," I said, tapping my head. I winced, immediately regretting all my life's decisions. My entire body throbbed with pain, so I hadn't really noticed the headache until now. Distantly, I remembered Corbin landing a few good swats that had likely jumbled my poor little brain.

"We'll find him," Sam assured me. "I don't doubt that in the slightest."

Oh, but I did. If Corbin could outmaneuver Sam's father, he could undoubtedly outsmart me. Adrien was the epitome of an alpha. If he'd failed to take out Corbin, what made me think I would succeed?

Sam gently brushed a strand of hair off my face and tsked under his breath. "Stop questioning yourself."

Heat flamed my cheeks. "How did you know what I was thinking?"

"Please. I can always tell what you're thinking just from the look on your face. You wear your emotions on your sleeve."

"Great. Something else I'll need to change."

"Change?" He lifted a brow. "Why would you need to change anything?"

"Alphas can't show their emotions. That would be considered a weakness."

Sam chuckled under his breath, then rinsed the cloth once more before getting to work on my neck. I could feel the grime abrading my skin as he washed me. "It's only a weakness if you let it be one. Every alpha leads in their own way, and only you can choose your method. Don't let Cole make you into something you aren't. You saw how compassionate and caring my father is. Our pack doesn't consider that a weakness. In fact, we consider it a strength."

I considered Sam's words with a slow nod.

"Listen." He placed the cloth on the bathroom counter, then handed me a brush to comb out my rat's nest. "Being an alpha isn't just about being the most powerful or ruthless. Alphas need to be equal parts strong and sympathetic. They lead by example. By molding themselves into what they believe is the best version of themselves, and hope that the pack does the same. A pack is only as strong as its weakest member."

"Yes, Yoda," I teased.

Sam snickered. "I'm serious. I know it sounds a little out there, but you have to keep in mind we aren't human, nor do we function like one. We're a seamless blend of man and animal. And animals don't play by human rules. You do whatever it takes to be the best alpha you can be."

I took a moment to absorb Sam's words, all while tonguing a small cut on the inside of my cheek. I'd been so concerned about becoming a strong leader that I hadn't given much thought as to the leader I wanted to be. I didn't want to be a totalitarian. Nor did I want to lead through brute strength. No, I wanted my pack to respect and admire me, like the New Orleans pack did Adrien. He'd earned it, busting his ass off to be worthy of their trust.

That was the kind of leader I wanted to be.

ACKNOWLEDGMENTS

Thank you so much to everyone who helped make Wooing the Wolfman the story that it is.

This book certainly had its challenging moments —and not because of the story, but because I was quite sick for a few months during the process. My poor head was loopy and fuzzy. It's only because of my critique groups and my editor, Missy, that we were able to whip this book into shape!

So, on that note, I'd like to thank my critique groups for all their help on this project. A few chapters required substantial rewrites, but the book came out stronger because of it. I'd also like to thank my editor, Missy Borucki, for her wonderful edits and suggestions.

Thank you again, everyone!

ABOUT THE AUTHOR

 Kinsley Adams is a thirty-something-year-old author who stopped counting when she turned twenty-five. When she isn't writing uproariously hilarious romantic comedies, she's raising her womb-gremlin with the hopes that he might one day become the world's first Supreme Leader (and yes, *Debbie*, that's a Star Wars joke). You can find her and her books online at kinsleyadams.com.

If you enjoyed this book, please leave a review! Your support and feedback are greatly appreciated. And be sure to sign up for Kinsley's newsletter at kinsleyadams.com/newsletter for updates on new releases, sales, and more!

ALSO BY KINSLEY ADAMS

DATING MONSTER MAIN SERIES

DATING DRACULA

LOVING DRACULA

MARRYING DRACULA

WOOING THE WOLFMAN

MATING THE WOLFMAN

WEDDING THE WOLFMAN

SMITTEN WITH THE VAMPIRE KING

HOOKED ON THE VAMPIRE KING

HITCHED ON THE VAMPIRE KING

DATING MONSTERS SIDE STORIES

WHEN VLAD MET ANNA

MR. & MRS. DRACULA

MONSTERS & CHOCOLATE